DEADMAN ON THE TRACKS

A Matt Deadman novel

IAN FLETCHER

ISBN: 9781794563858

Also in the Matt Deadman series:

DEADMAN AND THE TWELVE DAYS

USA Today Best-Selling author,
Sue-Ellen Welfonder, has this to say about
Deadman and the Twelve Days:

'I LOVED *Deadman and the Twelve Days*!!! The book is incredible. Grabs you from the first line and takes you on a nonstop and exhilarating whirlwind of a ride. Great characters, each one so real. Loved the twists and turns and surprises, and your powerful sense of place. I was right there, everywhere Matt went. Saw the sites, ate the food, felt/experienced the adventure. CANNOT WAIT for the book. *Deadman on Tracks*. Counting the hours and minutes for another wonderful read. The book is brilliant.'

1

SEARS CROSSING, NEAR AYLESBURY, THURSDAY, 8 AUGUST 1963

'This is it! This is it! This is it!'

A voice crackled over the walkie-talkie being grasped tightly in the hand of a large, burly man dressed in a boiler suit and wearing a balaclava. His heart skipped a beat as he heard the message but otherwise he remained calm. He turned towards two men crouched beside him.

'Right. Any minute now.'

His breath caught upon the early morning air as repeated the words quietly to himself.

'Any minute now.'

A quick glance at his watch told him it was just before three o'clock in the morning.

'Any minute now.'

It was pitch black but there was a touch of warmth in the air on this early August morning. The two men waiting behind the man with the walkie-talkie were also wearing boiler suits and balaclavas. All three were lying low at the top of a railway embankment at Bridego Bridge which carried the main line to London.

Jimmy Damon was one of the men crouching beside the railway line. His pulse seemed to be running faster than it had ever done before, whilst his heart was pounding away so much he thought it was going to burst through his chest. Small beads of sweat were running down his forehead. Still, he was not alone. Two of his best mates were with a second group of men waiting on the other side of the track. Danny Higgins and Lenny Bragg had gone to school with Jimmy just after the war when, at the age of seven, the three boys first trundled into Cobourg Road School, off the Old Kent Road in Peckham, South London, entering beneath the old arch bearing the word 'BOYS' upon it. Little did they know that some sixteen years later they would find themselves part of the gang that was about to carry out one of the most audacious robberies in British history.

Suddenly, the feint light of a locomotive could be seen approaching in the distance.

The man with the walkie-talkie glanced over his shoulder again. 'You two okay?'

There was no reply, just a nod from the two of them.

The rumbling of the train could now clearly be heard whilst the light on the front of the train grew more discernable as it approached. Suddenly, there was the squealing of brakes and a hissing sound as the train gradually began to slow, eventually grinding to a halt at Sears Crossing, a few hundred yards from where Jimmy Damon and the rest of the gang were waiting. It was still dark but the feint light from the engine's cabin was enough to allow Jimmy to see one of the men in the cabin get out and climb down onto the track. A few seconds later another man emerged from the darkness at the side of the track, followed shortly afterwards by several more men who scrambled up to cabin and began pushing their way into it. It was clear to Jimmy that some kind of struggle was going on but the train was too far away for him to make out exactly what it was. About a minute or two of anxious silence followed, broken suddenly by a long, drawn out hissing sound, and a few moments later the train began to lumber slowly forwards once more before finally coming slowly to a halt right in front of Jimmy at a point where a white sheet had been stretched across the line between two posts. The enormous bulk of the train loomed large against the early morning sky. It seemed massive to Jimmy who was still crouched by the railway line.

'Let's go!' The man slid the walkie-talkie inside his boiler suit and barked out the order and with that Jimmy snapped out of his trance and scrambled to his feet. It was fifteen minutes past three.

The nightly mail train had been running back and forth between London and Scotland for almost one hundred and twenty-five years without a problem. Security was minimal. The train had left Glasgow at just after six o'clock the previous evening and consisted of the locomotive, a parcels carriage and eleven further carriages in which almost seventy post office employees were diligently sorting Her Majesty's mail. But what interested the gang that waited patiently by the side of the track was not the mail itself. No, it was the scores of sacks full of used bank notes that had been collected at Glasgow after a Scottish Bank Holiday that had yielded up more than its usual stash of cash, the notes being collected in bundles known as High Value Packages. More sacks had been collected en route, so that by the time the train was brought to a halt at Bridego Bridge no fewer than one hundred and twenty-eight sacks, full to the brim with bank notes, were stacked up in the High Value Package carriage.

There were five men working inside the carriage, none of whom took much notice of the sudden halt. After all, it was not unusual for the train to stop for some reason or another during the run south. It was probably just another irritating delay. What they didn't know was that, when the train had shunted forward again after the initial halt, the rear ten carriages had been uncoupled and left standing on the line while the locomotive, the parcels carriage and the High Value Package carriage were moved slowly forward to the place where Jimmy and the gang were waiting.

The five post office workers continued sorting the mail when the glass windows of the door suddenly exploded sending shards of glass everywhere. An axe smashed against the door whilst other heavy metal objects hammered away as the robbers tried to force their way in. The post office workers were stunned by what was happening. It seemed surreal. After hours of tedious sorting throughout the late night and early morning this sudden and violent attack seemed like a dream. One of the workers suddenly snapped out of it and quickly began piling mail sacks against the door, shouting at his colleagues to do the same, but they were fighting a losing battle. The mail sacks were thrown against the door but it was no use and they tumbled down as the door finally gave way, the wood splintering and shattering before the gang's axes and crow bars as the attackers hacked and smashed their way inside. One by one the robbers fought their way into the carriage like soldiers storming the breach in a fortress. But this time there was no opposition, just a handful of hapless workers who put up a brief fight before their resistance ended in a flurry of punches and blows delivered by the robbers who had no intention of letting this brave show of defiance get in their way.

'Get down and stay down!' yelled one of the gang, threatening the postal workers by brandishing an axe above his head. The five workers did exactly what they were told. This was no time for futile heroics.

Jimmy Damon never got the chance to enter the High Value Carriage himself. Instead, he joined some of the others in forming a human chain down the side of the railway embankment leading to their getaway vehicles, being two Land Rovers and an old army lorry that waited in the darkness by the roadside close to the bridge. Then, one by one, the sacks containing the used bank notes began to appear from the blitzed carriage. They were passed quickly down the line and stacked in the back of the lorry. The work went on for a further fifteen minutes until one hundred and twenty sacks were crammed into the lorry. It was hard work. The sacks weighed a total of one and a half tons.

'Okay, that's it! Let's go!'

One of the gang lingered inside the carriage where seven more sacks remained.

'There are seven more sacks here!'

'Leave them! Let's go!'

The man reluctantly turned, leaving them, Along with one other sack that had been dropped.

It was just past three-thirty in the morning. The raid, carried out with military precision, had taken barely half an hour to complete. Then, as quickly as they had burst on to the scene the robbers were gone, fleeing into the darkness of the balmy early morning, having carried out one of the greatest and most audacious raids in British history.

Barely a soul noticed the convoy as it wound its way along the narrow Buckinghamshire lanes, nor did they hear the gang singing along to Tony Bennett's *The Good Life* as they celebrated on the way back to their hideout. Few of the gang, Jimmy Damon included, dared to believe what had happened. It had all gone like clockwork and just over one hour after they had fled the scene of the crime the gang were tumbling from their vehicles into the courtyard of their hideaway, a dilapidated old farmhouse that one of the gang had bought a few weeks before. It was then time for the reckoning.

One by one the sacks were emptied and the parcels of carefully bound banknotes counted and stacked in a corner. When the last of the packs had been stacked up the gang stood back in silence to take stock of their morning's work. Jimmy Damon had been tasked to count the money as it was emptied from the sacks. His mates called him 'Posh Jimmy' partly because he had always been top of the class at school and partly because his grandmother lived in a house that not only had a back garden but a front one too. Of course, being clever didn't make you posh but in the working class backstreets of South London having better than average intelligence certainly put you in the frame for such a sobriquet.

'Well?' asked one of the gang impatiently. 'What's the score?'

Jimmy stood back, took a deep breath, and with an extravagant wave of his arm said in his best fake upper-crust accent, 'Well, gentlemen, give or take a few quid, you see before you just over two and half million quid.'

He turned round and repeated the figure to the rest of the gang who stood in silent awe.

'Two and a half million quid…'

A huge grin then came across his face as he switched back to his natural Cockney accent. 'Not bad for thirty minutes graft eh?'

And with that the place erupted in a frenzy of cheers, screams and backslapping. Some of the gang did an impromptu knees-up, others hugged each other and sang, some jumped up and down whilst two of the gang lit cigars with five pound notes. One or two of the older members of the gang ruffled Jimmy's hair. It was complete, joyful mayhem. Suddenly, one of the gang entered the room.

'Hold on a minute, lads! Shut it! I've just picked up the Old Bill on the radio!' They listened for a few seconds more before bursting out laughing. 'They say we've nicked the train!'

There were more cheers. More bottles of beer and whisky were opened. The dancing continued. The celebrations were just beginning to die down when the sun rose. Exhausted by their night's work, by the sheer elation at their haul, and by the large quantity of downed alcohol, each of the fifteen men slowly began to crash out in the sleeping bags that lay scattered in and around the farmhouse. It had been a tiring but very profitable morning.

It was just before noon when Jimmy woke after a couple of hours' sleep. One or two of the other gang members were already up. The kettle was whistling away in the kitchen and the first round of tea was being drunk. The elation of the morning's work and the subsequent celebrations had left a few of them with sore heads, not that this troubled them. Indeed, hard drinking in the bars, pubs and clubs of South London and the West End was a way of life for most of them. It was also where most of them had met.

The fifteen men now slumped in corners of the farmhouse, in sleeping bags, or sitting in the kitchen, making or eating breakfast, came from similar backgrounds. Brought up in pre- and post-war London where petty crime was considered a way of life for those who had nothing, most of them had been detained at His or Her Majesty's pleasure at one time or another usually for some minor misdemeanour such as theft, handling stolen goods, or forgery, but nothing particularly serious. For example, despite having a reputation for major crimes the gang's leader, thirty-one-year-old Bruce Reynolds, had found himself in prison on no fewer than eleven occasions for nothing more serious than petty theft, including poaching. Others had done time for stealing pencils, sports equipment and clothing, for shoplifting, embezzlement, and other small crimes. This changed in late 1962 when five of the gang, including Reynolds, Gordon Goody, Buster Edwards, Charlie Wilson and racing driver Roy James, came away with sixty-two thousand pounds following a raid on an office building at Heathrow Airport. This gave them the funds to buy the farm in which they were now hiding out. But none of the other fifteen-strong gang could be called master criminals. The morning's events had changed all of that.

The morning turned to afternoon by which time all fifteen members of the gang were wide awake. It was then time for the spoils to be divided. Few of the gang members could be said to have been close friends. Indeed, Jimmy and his two mates had only met most of the gang when they had arrived at the farmhouse. Others, however, knew each other well and had been on jobs together. One of the gang members, John Daly, was Reynolds' brother-in-law. Otherwise, it had really been only the train robbery that had pulled them all together. It was only natural, therefore, that when the money was divided each of the gang kept a close eye on the process. There was no such thing as honour amongst thieves.

The two and a half million pounds haul was divided into seventeen equal shares or 'whacks' of around one hundred and fifty thousand pounds each. These were distributed amongst the fifteen men who had carried out the robbery, plus a share to Brian Field, a solicitor who had acted as the contact between the gang and the real mastermind behind the whole operation, an insider known only as 'The Ulsterman,' a mystery man who worked for the Post Office and had tipped off the gang. He also received a full share. Two smaller amounts or 'drinks' as the gang called them, were left for a retired train driver who had been brought along to move the train forward after the initial hold up but who, ironically, had found the train too difficult to handle, and to another man whose job it was to burn down the farm and destroy any evidence left behind after the gang had left.

Whilst the packets of money were counted out in one of the rooms the gang continued to monitor the airwaves with their short-wave radio set. By now the police – and the world generally – were waking up to the news of the robbery and a flurry of messages flew between the local police force and Scotland Yard.

Two of the men monitoring the radio suddenly began laughing. Reynolds, wondering what the fuss was all about, turned from the business of dividing the money.

'Oi! What's all the noise about then?'

'They reckon we've nicked a million! Blimey, they hadn't got a clue have they?' The man continued laughing.

Reynolds allowed himself a smile. 'Jesus. He's right. They haven't got a clue how much we've got here. Not a clue.'

According to the reports on the radio early estimates put the haul at just over a million pounds, although this continued to rise throughout the day. It was also reported that roadblocks had been set up across all major roads in the area, something that was irritating to the gang but was not unexpected. After all, they planned to lie low at the farmhouse until the heat was off. Only then would they venture out and go their separate ways. But, as they say, the best laid plans.....

On the afternoon of 8 August a high level conference was held in London which was attended by leading Scotland Yard detectives, the local police and officials from the Post Office. There was little to go on, however. No evidence was found at the crime scene apart from a couple of iron bars used during the attack on the High Value Package carriage. Other than that the police had nothing. Then, completely out of the blue, one of the local police inspectors just happened to mention that one of the gang had warned the Post Office workers in the carriage not to move for thirty minutes, claiming that a man with a gun would remain behind to watch over them. It was assumed, therefore, that the gang needed thirty minutes to reach their hideout, if indeed they hadn't already made off for London. A quick calculation was made and, based on the thirty minute clue, the police reckoned the gang was probably holed up within thirty miles of Bridego Bridge. It was with some alarm, therefore, that the two men listening to the radio suddenly heard a report on the radio that the police were conducting a sweep of every farm and isolated building within a thirty mile radius of the crime scene.

'Bruce, Gordon, you'd better come and hear this.'

Reynolds and Gordon Goody, one of the other main players in the act, listened with dismay as the report continued.

'Well,' said Goody, 'I hadn't planned on sticking around here much longer anyway. I'm getting out now.'

'Yeah,' replied Reynolds, 'I reckon we're for it if we stick around much longer. Let's split.'

Some of the gang were already making plans to leave the farmhouse earlier than planned and the report, along with others which claimed locals had spotted a convoy of military style vehicles heading west, decided the issue. It was time to move.

Throughout the late afternoon and evening of 8 August, and with the dust having barely settled over the crime scene, itself now awash with policemen, there was a flurry of comings and goings at the farm as friends and associates arrived to collect the gang members and spirit them away from the area. There were no cheerful goodbyes, no farewells. It was every man for himself.

Jimmy Damon was busy stuffing his share of the loot, amounting to almost one hundred and fifty thousand pounds, into a couple of holdalls when one of the other men tapped him on the shoulder. It was John Daly, Bruce Reynolds' brother-in-law, a stocky man with a rounded face, and a gentle, amiable smile. He stood there with a holdall in each of his powerful hands.

'Jimmy, mate, I need a favour. I need you to look after these. It's my share of the cash.'

Jimmy looked stunned and surprised. 'Why can't you take it yourself?'

'Look, my wife's pregnant. If I turn up at our flat with these in tow she'll go nuts. I can't risk her having a bad turn or anything like that. If I'm fingered for this job the cops will be down on us in a flash. I don't want to be caught with this lot in the kitchen cupboard now do I?'

Jimmy looked round at the others who were hastily getting ready to leave. 'But why me? I mean, we hardly know each other?'

Daly looked around at the others and nodded towards them. 'Look, if I leave the bags with any of this lot I'll never see them again. Look at them. Would you trust any of them?' He shook his head. 'I can't risk it, not even Bruce. You're the youngest and, maybe I'm wrong, but you seem like a decent sort of bloke. Get this lot hidden somewhere and I'll pick it up when the heat's off. You know what I mean.'

Jimmy was still taken aback but agreed to look after Daly's share of the loot. 'Okay, alright then. But I'm not having it lying around for too long. You get it? If the cops find me with a double share of the cash they'll stick me in the bleedin' Tower and chuck the keys away.'

Daly put the holdalls down and shook Jimmy's hand. 'Look, I've got to leg it now. I'll be in touch when things die down. Don't worry about it. I'll see you right when all of this is over. Cheers Jimmy.'

And with that Daly jumped into a car with Reynolds. Then, with a screech the car disappeared in a cloud of dust.

Jimmy Damon had already given some thought to how he was to make good his escape in the event of the raid coming off and on Friday morning, the day after the raid, he was cycling to a nearby telephone box.

'Hello. Terry? Is that you? Listen. I need a favour.'

Just after four o'clock on the Friday afternoon, and with the radio reporting increased police activity in the area around the crime scene, a blue Austin Cambridge Mark II pulled up outside the farmhouse.

'Hello Terry. Nice to see you.'

Jimmy Damon stepped forward and shook Terry Newell's hand as he emerged from behind the wheel of the car.

'Fuck me. The place is crawling with coppers. They're everywhere.' It was Terry's way of saying hello.

Terry Newell was Jimmy's uncle. Tall, dark haired, argumentative and a man who always had to have the last word in any argument, he was only seven years older than Jimmy. At the age of seventeen he was called up for National Service and had served his eighteen months in the RAF, six months of which was spent in prison after being found guilty of stealing the silver from the officer's mess where he was based. No stranger to the darker recesses of life in South London he guessed what the fuss was all about the minute Jimmy told him where he was.

'You've done the train job, haven't you? Your mum's going to go mental when she finds out.'

Jimmy pulled him aside. 'Look, never mind that. I need to get out of here, and I need to do it now.' He gestured to a couple of other cars that stood in the farmyard, their engines ticking over. 'It's only a matter of time before the cops find this place. We're shifting out. Danny and Lenny are here too.'

'What? The three of you are in it together? Oh, that's really fucking nice isn't it? You pull this one off and never ask me. I'm your bleedin' uncle for Christ's sake.'

'Look, Terry, it wasn't my idea. It's nothing to do with me. Danny and Lenny always work with me. They saw us as a team.'

'And who are *they*, might I ask?'

'Now you know I can't tell you that can I, even if you are family.'

Terry sighed and looked around. One of the other robbers nodded as he got into the back of an Austin Healey.

'See ya Jimmy. Good luck mate!'

Jimmy waved as the car sped off. 'Look, we can't stand around here all day talking. I've got my stash loaded into a couple of holdalls. Danny and Lenny have got theirs stuffed in bags as well.'

'Well if I'd had known I would have nicked a security van and brought that with me.' Terry sighed. 'Anyway, you'd better hurry up. I don't want to get nicked on the way back with you three and all that cash in the back. You know they'll throw away the key if they nick you?'

'Don't worry about that,' said Jimmy, throwing his loot into the boot of the car. 'And thanks. We'll see you right over this.'

'I should think so too. A few grand will do nicely.'

Terry fired up the motor. 'From what I've been hearing on the radio you lot can afford it.' He put the Austin Cambridge into gear and screeched off down the drive.

'You don't know that half of it,' said Jimmy. 'They haven't got a clue how much we've nicked.'

Danny and Lenny laughed. Terry looked in the rear view mirror. 'In that case, I'll have a donation from all three of you!'

'Fucking hell, that was a close one. I never thought we'd get out of Buckinghamshire.' Terry Newell switched off the engine outside Jimmy Damon's house.

'Yeah. Blimey, I've seen more police cars today than I have in all of my life put together. Thanks Terry.'

'Well, that's what family are for, isn't it? Oh, and a few grand chucked in as well!' Terry laughed as he got out of the car. He stretched out after the long drive back to South London. He had already dropped off Danny and Lenny at Danny's house. He could relax for a while now and have a cup of tea in Jimmy's kitchen.

Home for Jimmy Damon was the middle floor of a three-storey house in Silcote Road, just off Albany Road, Camberwell. Built in the 1880s by a Christian mission it had survived the Blitz, as had all the other houses in the street. It was one of those houses where the door remained open all day long, only closing its front door after dark. A certain Mrs Summers lived downstairs with her two black cats, her budgerigar and her eccentricities. She also owned an old upright piano with which she used to torture the other residents each Sunday and on special occasions. Her son Pat and his wife occupied the flat on the top floor. Jimmy lived on the middle floor with his mum and dad, the family sleeping in one large bedroom, the other rooms being a kitchen, a living room and a large front room which only seemed to be used on a Sunday. There was no bathroom, with the toilet being situated on the balcony outside. The balconies were so close to each other, in fact, that when the water froze in the pipes in winter neighbours whose pipes were still okay would hand over buckets of water to the less fortunate. Community spirit was alive and well back in 1963.

Jimmy's dad worked in a small factory in Queen's Road, Peckham, specialising in chrome plating. He was fond of telling everyone that the kettles in most people's homes were probably plated in his factory. Jimmy used to watch his dad cycle to work each morning, in all weathers, and cycle home again in the evening, again in all weathers, and decided the routine of mundane nine-to-five working was not going to be his destiny when he grew up, not that he had much choice. There wasn't much future for a boy educated in a basic London County Council school in Cobourg Road. Nevertheless, Jimmy was considered by his teachers to be a bright lad, of above average intelligence and much was expected of him when he grew up. Being constantly at the top of the class and able to read books intended for much older boys earned him the nickname 'Posh Jimmy'. But it was on the shell-pitted bombsites that lay liberally sprinkled around Silcote Road that he was most at home, living out his fantasies with his friends as a pirate or a Viking, fighting with rival gangs over barren wastelands that became their battlefields.

Somewhere along the line Jimmy's fantasies began to become real. Perhaps it started with the regular visits to the local ABC cinema. Like so many other kids in the 1950s Jimmy had gone along to the pictures with his mates each Saturday morning, belting out the ABC Minors' song to the tune of *Blaze Away*. It was all great fun, cheering and booing all morning at the heroes and villains. Jimmy just happened to find the villains more interesting. The gangsters that Jimmy watched each Saturday morning always seemed to have guns, and although there was never a shortage of ex-army handguns kicking around in post-war London Jimmy was hardly likely to ever get his hands on one. Still, he could dream. And in any case being a local big shot seemed to have more appeal than being a cowboy on the Lonesome Pine Ranch.

At the tender age of seven he was already being chased around the streets close to his home by hapless flat-footed coppers after nicking fruit from the stalls set out in front of the greengrocers or for chucking wood, nicked from the workmen's huts along the numerous canals, into the water. One of his favourite dodges was to walk into a shop and claim the chocolate bar machines outside had not worked when he had put his money in. This would force the shopkeeper to hand over a bar free of charge. Jimmy and his mates would also go round the houses and dumps collecting empty bottles before taking them back to the shop and claiming the deposit. It hardly made Jimmy a master criminal but it was exciting, it brought him a modest profit and, as long as he kept out of reach of the law, was great fun.

When Jimmy and his two mates, Danny Higgins and Lenny Bragg, left school they were all aged fifteen and all three faced an uncertain future. There was no work, at least not of the sort that appealed to any of them, and prospects were not good. It seemed easier to continue to use the skills that had given them a reputation for being petty crooks, operating on the periphery of South London's criminal world. They were the youngest members of the gang that had just robbed the mail train and the limit of their criminal activities previous to the raid had extended to burglary and shoplifting or the traditional pastime of stealing the lead from church roofs. By the time they reached the age of twenty all three had criminal records. In a world dominated by two rival gangs, the Krays to the north of the Thames and the Richardsons to the south, the three friends had remained on the outside, preferring to 'go it alone', not that they were unknown to other criminals. Indeed, their misdemeanours had not gone unnoticed. One night in June 1963 the three young men were drinking in the Thomas A Beckett pub in the Old Kent Road. They had gone along to watch some of the local boxers training in the gym on the first floor. Danny went downstairs to get some drinks but returned in the company of Buster Edwards, a well-known but small time crook, who asked them whether they might be interested in 'upping the ante' and coming along on what might be a very profitable job. To three young men whose criminal activities to date had not exactly been profitable the carrot that Edwards dangled before them was too tempting to resist.

Jimmy and his two mates had swallowed the bait but never in their wildest dreams could they have imagined just how spectacularly the gamble would pay off. The problem now was how to get their loot safely stashed away and how they were going to evade the long arm of the law, for it was almost inevitable that, as night follows day, Scotland Yard's finest would be on the trail of known criminals following a raid of the magnitude that had just been pulled off at Bridego Bridge.

But first things first. Jimmy needed to smuggle to holdalls inside his home. He was lucky. Hid dad was out drinking in the Trafalgar Arms, in the Old Kent Road, which he preferred to the much noisier Thomas A Beckett. His mum was out visiting her best friend, Eva, in nearby Calmington Road. Jimmy managed to stuff the two holdalls into the back of an old but very large Victorian wardrobe in which he kept all of his clothes. It was huge, dark and untidy and was a place where even his mum feared to look. *Perfect.*

The trouble was there was no room for the holdalls belonging to John Daly. Where on earth was he going to hide these?

'Terry? I need another favour.'

Jimmy's Uncle Terry was enjoying the last drops of tea from a large mug, one of those commemorative mugs marking the coronation of Queen Elizabeth the Second. Her Majesty's portrait was neatly picked out in gilt and enamel on the side of the mug which Terry placed on the table. He looked up.

'What now?'

Jimmy explained how one of the other members of the gang had asked him to look after his share of the loot for a week or two until things died down.

'Oh, for gawd's sake. You must want your head seeing to. I mean, it's bad enough that you've nicked all this money yourself without having some other geezer's stash. For Christ's sake.'

'Come on Terry. It's the only thing I can think of at the moment.' A grin spread slowly across his face. 'And don't forget, you're my favourite uncle.'

'Bollocks. Don't give me all that flannel.' Terry sighed again and stood up. 'Oh, come on then. But only for a week or so. I don't want those bags hanging round any longer than they have to.' He walked down the stairs muttering to himself. 'Fucking hell. This is all I need, having Captain Kidd's treasure in my own back yard.'

Jimmy followed him down the stairs, laughing.

Terry Newell's home in Kelvington Road, Peckham, was as neat and tidy as Silcote Road was old and claustrophobic. A nice wide road with 1930s semi-detached houses on either side, it was a picture of suburban bliss.

There had been no bomb damage during the war and as barely thirty years had passed since they had been built the houses still had a new feel about them, each semi looking identical to its neighbour. The wooden fences still looked relatively new, hedges had grown to a good height whilst already a line of trees were maturing nicely all the way along the road. It was all very neat and quiet, and all very respectable, and it was here that Jimmy Damon was about to hide John Daly's two holdalls containing almost one hundred and fifty thousand pounds.

Terry's Austin Cambridge pulled up outside his house in Kelvington Road.

'You'd better check and make sure Gran isn't home.'

Terry was still living with his mum at the time, his mum being Jimmy's grandmother. As long as she had a fag and a cup of tea she was happy. But she wasn't the sort to stand any nonsense or lawbreaking, not under her own room at least.

'Yeah. She'd go fucking mad if she knew what we were up to.'

Terry and Jimmy may well have been tough nuts but they still preferred to stay on the right side of the matriarch. It wouldn't do to get caught with a shed load of cash nicked a couple of days before from Her Majesty's Post Office. Terry went inside whilst Jimmy stayed in the car. A few moments later he emerged and gave the thumbs up. It was all clear. Jimmy got out of the car and took out the two holdalls containing Daly's share of the loot. He hurried inside, trying not to look too suspicious in case any nosey neighbours were watching.

'Right then. Have you got a shovel?'

'A shovel? What, are you going to bury it then?' asked Terry.

'Well I'm not here to do the fucking gardening am

I?'

'And what happens if one of the neighbours looks out of the window?'

Terry had a point. If one of the neighbours chose to look out of their back upstairs window they'd see Jimmy digging a hole in the garden. Knowing Jimmy's reputation it was bound to raise suspicions.

'It's a chance I've got to take. Anyway, who's going to be upstairs at this time of day? They'll all be stuffing themselves having their tea. And if we don't hurry up Gran will be back. We'll dig the hole and you can tell her you did a spot of gardening or something. She'll never twig.' Jimmy turned to Terry who was standing holding a shovel. 'Oh, and it would be better if you did the digging. You know, it'll be less suspicious.'

Terry sighed. 'Oh, thanks very much.'

He shook his head but knew Jimmy was right. He took the shovel, went out into the garden and rolled up his sleeves. He looked around and chose a spot beneath a pear tree that stood towards the back of the garden. There were no neighbours behind the garden, only a tall, grassy bank beyond which was a golf course. A few old balls lay half buried in the grass. Recent rainfall had at least made the ground a bit softer, and Terry's shovel went in quickly and easily. After a few minutes of hasty digging a reasonably deep hole had been dug. Terry wiped his brow and turned towards the back door of the house. He looked around. There were no twitching curtains anywhere so he gave the signal, whereupon Jimmy came hurrying out with the two holdalls. A couple of minutes later and the two bags were being covered up by the earth. The plot was smoothed over and some leaves scattered on it. Terry and Jimmy stood back to admire their handiwork.

'There. No one will ever know. Perfect. Capability

Brown would have been proud of us,' said Jimmy, grinning.

'Oh, fuck him, whoever he is,' said Terry. 'Just make sure it doesn't stay there longer than it has to. Okay?'

'Okay. Got it. Trust me, Terry. I'll be back in a week or two.....'

2

THE INNS OF TEMPLE, LONDON 2013

Misty mornings in spring had always been one of Matt Deadman's favourite times of the year and The Temple one of his favourite places in London. True, he always found the famous arch on Horse Guards Parade to be a very evocative place, steeped in history, particularly military history, but since leaving the army his professional work had taken him more often than not to The Temple, that labyrinth of wonderful old buildings, many of which dated back to the seventeenth century, that were occupied by the men and women of the legal profession.

It was still rather chilly on the Monday morning when Deadman entered the place via the gate in The Strand before walking down the cobbled Middle Temple Lane, a narrow lane barely wide enough to allow a cart through, let alone modern vehicles. The watery sun had no chance of penetrating the lane, flanked as it was on either side by tall buildings, a mixture of the old and the new, with the newer buildings being sympathetically built in the style of the early nineteenth century. It never ceased to amaze Deadman how the place had managed to avoid the clutches of modern architects who seemed to regard the City of London as their playground, pulling down fine old buildings and replacing them with hideous, freakish constructions of smoked glass and steel, interesting and functional but hardly pleasing on the eye. He also marvelled at the fact that the Temple had been spared the unwanted attentions of the Luftwaffe during the Second World War. It was an oasis of calm, of order, of tradition and good taste, things that were so often lacking in modern London.

The Temple was blessed with wonderful addresses such as Paper Buildings, Pump Court, Hare Court, Brick Court and Cloisters, but it was to King's Bench Walk that Deadman was heading. Half way along Middle Temple Lane Deadman turned left into Crown Office Row, with the Inner Temple Gardens resplendent on the right, before turning left again into King's Bench Walk, yet another fine, cobbled lane, liberally sprinkled with trees and ornate Victorian street lamps. Deadman stood for a while and drew up the collar of his overcoat against the cold. He looked around at the buildings. Not for nothing had the place featured in so many films. There were no yellow lines, no signs of any sort and nothing to indicate it was anything but the home of a few firms of solicitors. Indeed, it was like stepping back a couple of centuries in time.

Deadman glanced around and soon spotted number 4 King's Bench Walk with its graceful arched entrance framed by a Victorian street lamp, held aloft by a simple black iron arch. Dating back to the late seventeenth century, it was reputed to be the oldest of the Chambers in the Temple. It was also the home of Trubshaw and Goat, a firm of solicitors, who had written to Deadman, requesting that he visit them that Monday morning to discuss a case which he may or may not decide to accept. Taking a deep breath he walked up the two stone steps and pushed his way through the door. Before him was an old wooden staircase which creaked as a couple of clerks carrying a pile of cardboard folders came down from one of the floors above.

Deadman stopped one of them. 'Hello lads. Am I in the right building for Trubshaw and Goat?'

'Go straight up. You'll find them on the first floor, first door on the right.'

Deadman gave them a nod of thanks before starting to

climb the stairs which once again creaked beneath his feet.

Deadman knocked at the door and entered without waiting for a reply. A rather elegantly dressed lady sat at a desk and smiled as he entered. Deadman guessed she was in her early thirties and was evidently no a professional herself but merely a secretary, albeit a very efficient one.

'Mr Deadman, I presume?'

'That's me.'

'Here, let me take your coat.' The secretary got up from behind her desk and placed Deadman's coat on a stand and turned to her desk. She pressed a buzzer and announced his arrival. A voice crackled back over the intercom. 'Send him in please, Miss Reckless.'

Deadman grinned but said nothing. Miss Reckless smiled back, rolled her eyes and turned, cursing whoever saddled her with her surname. She opened the door into a second office. 'This way please. Mr Trubshaw will see you now.'

Deadman thanked her before entering the office. He was immediately struck by the musky smell of old paper, which was not surprising given the number of brown cardboard files, tied with pink ribbon, that lay everywhere in piles around the small office. Reference books were crammed onto the wooden shelves and on top of old wooden filing cabinets with their small brass handles. An old threadbare rug covered the bare wooden floorboards, whilst particles of dust were caught in the feint shafts of light from outside. It was like stepping back into Dickensian London. There was certainly no sign of any modern appliance, not even a computer.

'Ah, Mr Deadman. Please come in. Do take a seat.'

A thin, slightly balding man stood up from behind his desk and peered over his thin-rimmed glasses. Dressed in a black pin-striped suit with a bow-tie, the man also looked very much the relic of a bygone age. He sat down again.

'My name is Cornelius Trubshaw. I am, or rather was, one half of this establishment. I am now in sole charge, my partner, Mr Goat, having sadly passed away some years ago. I assume you received my letter?'

'Yes, I've got it here,' replied Deadman, still taking in the antiquated surroundings. He unfolded the letter and scanned it but said nothing.

'Good. Well, I won't waste time, Mr Deadman. Tell me, what do you know about the Great Train Robbery?'

Deadman was taken completely by surprise. There was no preamble, no small talk. It was straight down to business, although what that business was he wasn't sure. He certainly hadn't been expecting to be tested on his knowledge of recent British history.

'I'm sorry. The what?'

Trubshaw looked straight back at him. 'The Great Train Robbery of 1963. You must have heard of it, surely?'

'Well, yes, of course. You just took me a bit by surprise. The Great Train Robbery? Of course, doesn't everyone know about it? Bruce Reynolds, Ronnie Biggs, Jack Mills the driver.'

'Yes,' replied Trubshaw, smiling, 'that's exactly the same response I'd expect from almost everyone who has heard of the event. But, please, go on. Tell me what else you know.'

'Well, it was a few years before my time, but here goes anyway. If I've got it right, Reynolds put a gang of criminals together in order to rob the train carrying the mail from Glasgow to London. It was also carrying a load of sacks filled with used bank notes.' Deadman looked up at Trubshaw.

'Yes, yes, go on.'

'Er, well, having stopped the train the gang broke into the coach carrying the money and managed to take the lot before making off into the night. If my memory serves me right the haul was over two million pounds. Christ knows what it would be worth today.'

He looked up again. Trubshaw extended his hands in front of him. 'Yes, and then what?'

'Well, I think the gang were holed up in a farmhouse for a few days before they split up and went their different ways. The place was discovered soon afterwards and within a few days most of the gang were arrested with just a couple of them going on the run for the next few years until they too were arrested. I guess it was a case of so near and yet so far. What sticks in my mind was the public's reaction. I think most of them got thirty years in jail, which everyone thought was far too harsh. You could get less for armed robbery. But then there was the coshing of the driver, Mills. I think he died a few years later, his family claiming the attack had brought on an early death.'

Trubshaw took off his glasses and placed them on the desk. He sat back in his chair. 'Well, I suppose if I were a school master I'd give you seven out of ten for trying. Would you like some tea Mr Deadman?'

'Tea? Yes please. Milk, no sugar.'

Trubshaw leant forward to his intercom and buzzed through his request to Miss Reckless. He sat back again in his high backed leather chair.

'You are, of course, right, up to a point at least. The haul was indeed well over two million pounds, just over two and a half, in fact. In today's money it would equate to somewhere between forty and fifty million.' He waited for Deadman to react.

'Forty to fifty million eh? Blimey, that's quite a haul.'

Trubshaw seemed pleased with Deadman's

response and leant forward with a smile on his face.

'Quite a haul indeed. You were also correct as regards the farmhouse and the subsequent arrests.'

Deadman looked at Trubshaw and could sense something else was coming. The punch line. He said nothing, however, and let Trubshaw have his moment.

'But what if I told you that three of the gang got clean away with it, were never brought to justice and enjoyed a good life thereafter?' He sat forward with a serious but inquisitive look on his face. 'What do you think of that?'

Deadman shifted in his chair and shook his head. 'No, the police got the lot of them. We know them by name. Some of them have become almost household names. Let's face it, if any of them had got away with it surely we'd have known about it?'

'Not so, Mr Deadman, not so. Ask yourself this; if you were Scotland Yard would you come out and admit that some of the robbers had got away with it? And if you were one of the robbers who had been arrested would you have informed on those that got away? No, I don't think so. And if I were one of the lucky ones that got away with it I'd hardly go around bragging about it would I?' Trubshaw let out a long drawn sigh and shook his head. 'No, it was a bad time for the establishment. Criminals had to be dealt with harshly. Punishments had to be meted out for the sake of example. If the public knew some of the gang had got away with it you may well imagine how damaging it would have been to the reputation of our law and enforcement agencies.'

The door opened slowly and in walked the secretary with a silver tray, on which was a teapot, two cups, a silver milk jug and a sugar bowl. She placed them on a small table by the window.

'Ah, thank you Miss Reckless.' Trubshaw got to his

feet as the secretary left the room. 'You did say milk but no sugar?' He poured the tea into a cup, tipped some milk into it and passed the cup and saucer to Deadman. He did the same a second time before easing himself back into his chair.

'The reason you have been summoned here, Mr Deadman, is to investigate the possibility, nay, probability, that at least three of the criminals did indeed escape the long arm of the law and enjoyed their ill-gotten gains for the remainder of their miserable lives. The police were certain they knew who the culprits were and, indeed, brought two of them in for questioning. But in the absence of any evidence they were forced, rather painfully I might add, to let them go. It was a great blow to them, a great blow indeed.'

He reached into a draw and took out an old, dog-eared file.

'Many years ago Mr Goat and I were engaged by our client to investigate any rumours or stories that were remotely connected with the so-called Great Train Robbery in the hope that one day the culprits who had escaped prosecution might be brought to justice. Two other investigators tried but failed in this respect. You, on the other hand, were brought to my attention by someone who commands the utmost respect and said you were a man who might succeed where others had failed. We need not disclose the identity of this person; suffice to say that he recommended you without hesitation.'

Deadman rolled his eyes and took a sip of tea from his cup.

Here we go again. I'd like to know who these people were who kept on putting me up for these jobs.

'Well, that's very nice of them, I'm sure.'

'Yes, indeed,' replied Trubshaw.

Deadman shifted once more in his chair. 'But what's

brought this about? I mean, why the sudden interest again?'

'Ah, yes.' Trubshaw sighed and untied the pink ribbon which fastened the old file.

'One week ago this newspaper report arrived at our office.' He took the report from the file and slid it across the desk towards Deadman. 'As you can see, it's from a local newspaper, the Kentish Times. You will see it concerns the recent death in a nursing home of a man named Lenny Bragg who, upon his death bed, claimed to be one of the men who took part in the robbery but escaped justice. Now, every once and a while these sort of claims come to our attention and as wild as they may appear we are obliged to investigate them. This particular report was of great interest owing to other details which the man imparted. They have given us reason to believe that the deceased may indeed have been one of the gang.'

'In other words, his confession was a final two-fingered salute to the establishment.'

'Precisely, Mr Deadman, precisely, assuming the man was telling the truth. He had been living in Spain since the 1960s but had returned to England having fallen ill. The illness was terminal and he returned simply to pass his final days in the country of his birth, and to be buried here. This folder contains information that the previous investigators gleaned. You may find it of use. Otherwise, I'm afraid you will need to start from square one, as they say.'

Deadman looked around the office and sighed. 'Look, it's not that I'm ungrateful or anything like that, but why are *you* investigating this? Shouldn't the police be looking into this? I mean, it's not like I can bring these people to justice, even if they existed in the first place?'

'Oh, but I think they did exist, Mr Deadman. Our client was convinced of it. But as far as the police are concerned the case is closed. They've long since stopped looking, largely because they're too embarrassed to admit that the birds had flown.'

'But it's been nearly fifty years now. Surely nobody cares? Nobody is interested in something that happened half a century ago are they?'

'On the contrary, Mr Deadman, Nazi war criminals are still being sought and, indeed, are being arrested and brought to justice. And even you will not have failed to notice the clutch of so-called celebrities being arrested over claims of sexual misdemeanours dating back to the 1960s. Why should robbers be considered any different?'

Deadman conceded the point. 'Well, I guess so.' He finished off his tea and placed the empty cup and saucer on Trubshaw's desk. 'Well, I suppose I'd better start by speaking to your client. At least he ought to be able to give me some idea of where to start looking.'

Trubshaw sank back in his chair. 'I'm afraid that would be rather difficult.' He leaned forward again. 'Our client died some years ago.'

'He died? So why are you still acting for him?'

'Our client left us instructions in his will. There is a legacy and, if I may say so, a rather handsome one, for the man who solves the case and brings any of the escaped robbers to justice.'

'And may I ask who your client was?' Deadman leaned forward in his chair.

'Yes, of course.' Trubshaw opened the file again. 'Our client was a former police officer who was one of the main investigators at the time. His name was Chief Inspector Thomas Grappler. You'll find more information on him in the file. I'm afraid he has no relatives other than a daughter who lives in…' Trubshaw flicked through the papers in the file, '…in Staplehurst, Kent.'

'Then I guess I ought to start by paying her a visit.'

Deadman stood up.

'On the contrary, Mr Deadman, you might begin by attending a funeral.'

'A funeral?'

'Yes. The gentleman who died recently in Kent is being buried tomorrow. You might find it useful to be in attendance. Discreetly, of course. You'll find the details in the file.'

Trubshaw slipped the papers back into the file and tied the pink ribbon once more before sliding the file across the desk to Deadman.

'You've thought of everything haven't you?'

'I like to think so,' replied Trubshaw getting to his feet. 'Well, good luck Mr Deadman. You know where we are if you need us. And please keep us informed as to your progress.' He took off his glasses and slipped them into his pocket as he walked towards the door. 'This case has been hanging over us now for many years. I'd like to think we could close the file before I go. Thank you, Mr Deadman, and good day.'

Trubshaw extended his hand to Deadman as he left, the door closing gently behind him. Deadman looked at the file as he stood in the secretary's office.

'A little light reading for bedtime?' enquired Miss Reckless, nodding towards the file.

'You could say that,' replied Deadman, as he took his coat from the stand. 'But never mind the reading material. I'd better go and dig out my best black suit. I've got a funeral to go to.'

3

HERNE CHURCHYARD, KENT, 2013

The journey along the A2 was uneventful, a series of dreary Kentish or rather South London suburbs eventually giving way to the Kentish countryside, the A2 itself giving way to the M2 which wound its way towards Ramsgate and Margate. Deadman's journey would end a good way shorter than these two coastal towns, at the village of Herne, where his silver Alfa Romeo GTV6 pulled up outside its small but picturesque churchyard. Although the main road to Canterbury passed through the village it remained a particularly nice place, with a clutch of very attractive houses, some in the traditional white weatherboard style of Kentish houses. There were also three pubs in close proximity to each other that served a small but evidently thirsty population. There was nowhere to park as several other cars had taken up all the spaces in the adjoining road. Instead, the Alfa backed carefully into the small car park in front of the Red Lion pub, next to the church. Deadman switched off the engine and got out of the car. He pulled up the collar of his dark grey overcoat, tugged on his black leather gloves and looked around. A group of mourners were just beginning to emerge from the church.

Deadman strolled through a traditional arched wooden gate and stood back whilst the group assembled round the grave. A pile of earth lay to one side, whilst a green cloth lay covering the edges. He listened as the vicar began the service.

'I am the resurrection and the life...'

As Deadman listed to the short service he took note

of those who stood silently around the grave, their heads bowed and hands clasped. Deadman could tell there were a few hard cases standing there. The shades were a bit of a giveaway, as were the black shirts. The more respectable mourners were dressed in black suits or dresses. There were no shades, no outward signs that they were anything other than genuine mourners.

'Ashes to ashes, dust to dust…'

With the service finally at an end the coffin was lowered slowly into the grave, Deadman gradually losing sight of it. A few of the mourners bent down to grab handfuls of soil which were cast down into the grave. Then, whilst the vicar shook a few hands, the mourners began to disperse, slowly wandering around the picturesque churchyard or simply making their way back to their cars. Deadman noticed one of the mourners lingering by the side of the grave. He reckoned she must have been about the same age as himself. Her blonde hair was in stark contrast to her black coat, she wore a pair of black stiletto heels, whilst her shapely legs were encased in black stockings. Deadman knew it wasn't the time to be eying her up but thought she was very attractive all the same. She suddenly turned, caught him in her sights and began walking slowly towards him. She stopped and looked back over her shoulder at the grave.

'Dad never spent much time in England during the last few years but he loved coming down here to the seaside.' She turned to Deadman. 'I don't think I know you. Did you know my father?'

Deadman was somewhat taken by surprise. There he was, investigating the possibility that the deceased might have been one of the Great Train robbers when his daughter rather obligingly introduces herself.

'Not exactly,' mumbled Deadman. 'I was more of a

business acquaintance.' It was the best he could manage at the time.

The woman extended her hand towards him.

'I'm Jenny, Jenny Bragg.'

Before Deadman could say anything she laughed softly and rolled her eyes.

'Yes, I think it was Dad's idea of a joke. I think he really wanted a son whom he could name after himself but when I came along he did the next best thing.' She laughed again. 'It was typical of him.'

'Well, I think Jenny's a nice name. Let's face it, it could have been worse. Imagine if his name had been Bert. You don't strike me as a Bertha.' He extended his hand. 'My name's Deadman, Matt Deadman.'

Jenny smiled. 'Well, I'm pleased to meet you. Are you coming to the wake now? We're going into Herne Bay, to the Dolphin Hotel. Sandwiches, some drinks, and all that. I guess everyone's going to be telling the usual stories about dad.'

'And what would they be?' asked Deadman.

'Oh, you know. When he was small he did this and that. And then there's this story that's appeared in the local press about him being one of the Great Train robbers.'

Deadman tried to play dumb. 'The train robbery? You mean the big one back in the early sixties.'

'Has there ever been another?' Jenny started strolling back to her car which was parked in the road. 'I don't know how they got the story but they claimed Dad had told someone he had been one of the robbers who got away with it. I don't believe the story's true. Dad loved to spin a yarn. Mind you, I always wondered why he was so reluctant to return to England. We rarely came back here as a family. I suppose that living in Spain meant there was no need for us to come back here. I mean, the beaches here are nothing compared to the ones where we live.'

'Where you live? You mean you still live in Spain?' Deadman suddenly became interested again.

'Well, my Mum does. We live there for about half the year. Look, why don't you come to the hotel. We can talk there. The others are starting to leave. I'd better go. Just follow me into town. It's only five minutes.'

'Sure, why not,' replied Deadman. 'I'll see you there.'

Jenny Bragg returned to her car, leaving Deadman to walk the short distance to the Red Lion where his car was parked. He was just about to turn on the ignition when he noticed a black Bentley Mulsanne pull up in the road outside the church. Deadman couldn't help admiring the car as it sat idling by the roadside and wondered whether he'd ever be in a position to indulge in such a luxury. But his admiration turned to curiosity when the chauffeur got out of the front seat and opened the rear door. A tall man dressed in a dark coat, wearing black leather gloves and dark shades stepped out and, looking right and left, made his way through the gate, into the churchyard and to the freshly dug grave, now covered with flowers. He stood there for a few moments before bending down to pick up a handful of earth which he tossed on to the grave. He remained there, deep in thought for a few more moments. He then turned, walked back to his car and, as quickly as he had come, he was gone.

Deadman watched it all from his old Alfa Romeo.

Now, that was very strange. And very interesting too.

He reached into his inside pocket and took out a notebook. He'd been quick enough to note the registration number, which he scribbled into his leather notebook; D326. It was obviously a private number plate, and a strange one too. Still, there was no time to dwell upon it. He had a wake to go to.

For Londoners keen to escape the smoke and grime of Victorian London Herne Bay was the ideal destination. It didn't take long to get there, for the building of a pier in 1832 meant Londoners could steam up the Thames and in an hour or so be sunning themselves on the beach or strolling along the promenade. If they wanted to stay a bit longer they could always check into the Dolphin Hotel, a fine, stylish building that sat at the junction of Dolphin Street and Central Parade. It was a four-storey building, in classical square Victorian style, and offered sumptuous rooms to its residents and a good dinner to boot. However, the coming of the railway to Herne Bay in 1861 all but killed off the steamships but allowed even more people to visit, particularly those from south London and west Kent.

By the time Matt Deadman strolled through the main entrance to the hotel things had well and truly changed. The Dolphin Hotel was a tired and very pale shadow of its former self, and was in dire need of updating. The elegant Victorian and Edwardian visitors were long since gone. Today, visitors to the hotel were more likely to find the place playing host to rock bands on weekends and to hordes of 'DHLs', or 'Down From London' types as the locals called them, who were down for a day in the amusement arcades, and a fish and chips lunch with a few beers afterwards. But there were always the function rooms which played host to a variety of groups and organisations as diverse as the Women's Institute and the local train spotting society.

Jenny Bragg was in the middle of a small group of people when Deadman entered the room in which the wake for her father was being held. She spotted him the moment he entered and, with a smile, excused herself and went to greet him.

'It was good of you to come. Would you like a drink? Help yourself to a sandwich.'

'Thanks.' Deadman took a glass of orange juice from a table covered in white linen. He sighed. 'I'm driving and all that.'

Jenny smiled. 'Yes. Oh well, better to be safe than sorry.' She took a sip of white wine from the glass she was holding. 'So, tell me about yourself. How did you know Dad?'

'Oh, I didn't really know him that well to be honest. My Dad knew him when they were kids. They worked together for a while after they left school. I remember meeting him once in some sort of lock-up when I went out with my Dad one morning.' Deadman was struggling to keep his story going. 'It was somewhere off the Old Kent Road.'

Jenny smiled. 'Yes, that sounds about right for Dad. He was always up to something back then, usually on the wrong side of the law.' She sipped some more wine. 'Still, I don't ever remember Dad mentioning your own Dad, and I can't remember him ever coming to the house.'

'The house?' asked Deadman.

'Yes, our place in Spain. Dad was always entertaining old mates. Some of them were a bit of the unsavoury sort, if you know what I mean, but they never gave me the impression of being anything other than old mates. It wasn't until all the Brits started to come down to Benidorm and the Costas in the late 1960s that they began to show up. They'd have a few beers and talk about old times, but that was it. When Dad met Mum he said he'd made a fortune from property deals in England. That was good enough for her and was good enough for me. We had a roof over our head, food on the table and clothes on our back. We enjoyed a good lifestyle. We still do. I suppose to the outsider the idea that he was one of the Great Train Robbers would seem to fit but it's just nonsense. Dad, rubbing shoulders with the likes of Ronnie Biggs and Bruce Reynolds? No, it's rubbish.'

Deadman tried to change the subject.

'So, what about your Mum? Does she still live in Spain?'

'Yes. She wasn't well enough to travel. She's at home now with some of the family. You know, I'm half Spanish. My Mum was working in an office in Alicante back in the early 1960s when Dad showed up enquiring about property for sale. Carmen Maria de Laspara was her maiden name. I must admit, it sounds a bit better than Carmen Bragg! In Franco's Spain this was quite something. Don't forget, it was well before the holiday boom of the mid-sixties. Anyway, they hit it off and the rest is history. I came along in 1967.'

As Jenny continued to give a brief outline of her family's history Deadman was making careful calculations in his head. It all seemed to fit. If Lenny Bragg had indeed been one of the robbers the dates would certainly tally. If he had showed up in Spain in the early 1960s it almost certainly would have been because he was on the run. It wasn't exactly the Costa del Crime back then but things would have been very difficult for Scotland Yard to bring him back to England, even if they could find him in the first place. Deadman decided to delve a little deeper.

'So you say your Dad never returned to England much?'

'No, not really, not until he was getting on a bit. I suppose he just wanted to see a bit of the old country again. It wasn't until the early 1990s that he started visiting this part of the world again. He used to bring us here, and to the other little towns along the Kent coast, you know, Seasalter and Whitstable. He loved Whitstable and he loved his seafood. He always said there was nothing quite like cockles and whelks from Whitstable. Okay, he could get oysters in Spain but for an old cockney you couldn't beat Whitstable.' Jenny laughed. 'It was a long way to come for a pint of cockles!'

'Yes, it's not exactly a trip down the road.' Deadman finished his orange juice and put the glass on a table.

'Look, I'd better be getting along. Can I ask a favour? I'd like to write to your Mum to pass on my condolences. You know. For old times' sake and all that. I don't have your address.'

Deadman took out a small notebook and started writing as Jenny spelt out the address. It was a small village close to the town of Lliber in Spain.

'Font D'Axia is the street or rather village. It's only a tiny place. You only have to ask for the house where the Englishman lives and the locals will know what you're talking about.'

'Thanks Jenny. I'll drop her a line.'

'Yes. I'm sure mum would like that.'

Deadman put away his notebook and gave Jenny a soft kiss on the cheek. 'I'll see you around.'

And with that he turned, collected his coat, and was gone.

'Can't you see? It all makes sense.' Matt Deadman poured himself a third glass of Solberano brandy as he sat in the living room of his flat in Gloucester Gardens, Paddington. An impressive early Victorian building, the flat also doubled as his unofficial board room where he chewed over his ideas and theories with his old friend, Jack Moscroft.

'Lenny Bragg did a runner with his share of the loot

from the Great Train Robbery. The cops didn't know who he was, didn't have an idea of his identity. They probably never had any evidence against him anyway. He was able to slip away to Spain and live out the rest of his days in obscurity, posing as a successful businessman.'

Deadman sighed and took another sip of his brandy.

'What I'd really like to do is to get at the original police files, but most of them are closed until 2045, and we can't wait that long! And in any case, I need to check out this Bragg fellow before delving into official records and all that.'

Moscroft sat and listened to Deadman's theory. Moscroft was Deadman's trusted ally, quartermaster and general fixer. He was also a good mate to have around in any tight spot. The two had met some years before in the army when they were serving in Germany. Deadman was still plain Lance Corporal Matt Deadman, of the Corps of Royal Military Police, at the time, whilst Moscroft was a captain in the Queen's Yorkshire Regiment. The two men had bumped into each other, literally, during a bar room brawl in one of Düsseldorf's more notorious nightclubs, when Deadman and his unit had been called in to break up a fight. It was Moscroft who hauled a couple of squaddies off of Deadman after they had backed him into a corner. The two men had remained firm friends ever since.

'But surely Bragg's family would have known who he was? I mean, you couldn't keep something like that a secret, could you? I certainly couldn't. I'd want to let every bugger in the neighbourhood know I was the man who knocked off the mail train.'

'Yes,' replied Deadman, leaning forward in his armchair, 'but that was just the point. Bragg had to keep it a secret otherwise he'd have had the cops down on him in a flash. I mean there's not much honour amongst thieves. Don't forget about the reward. One careless word and it wouldn't have taken long for someone in the underworld to hear about it. Money talks, as they say.'

Moscroft laughed. 'Ironic when you think about it. Bragg couldn't brag…'

'Oh, very funny.' Deadman sat back in his chair and took a sip of his brandy. 'Well, I guess I'd better pay Bragg's widow a visit. If anyone knows the truth it'll be her.'

'But what makes you think she'll let on?' asked Moscroft.

'Well what's the bloody point of keeping it a secret any longer? I mean, they can't exactly dig him up and put him on trial can they?'

'Well, that's what they did to poor Oliver Cromwell,' replied Moscroft.

'Well, this ain't the fucking seventeenth century is it?'

Deadman got up and walked round the room. 'No, if anyone knows it'll be her. I mean, come on, surely he couldn't have kept it a secret from her all these years? Didn't she ever wonder how he got his money?'

'But he told her he made it from property deals in England. Why should she question it?' Moscroft had a point which Deadman conceded. He sighed.

'Well, I've got to go anyway. I've got hardly anything to go on at the moment. She's my only link with the robbery.'

'Assuming Bragg was telling the truth and wasn't simply spinning a yarn,' replied Moscroft.

'Well, there's only one way to find out.' Deadman drained the last drops of his brandy. 'You know, this makes a nice change from gin and tonic.'

Moscroft raised his glass. 'Well, where you're going, old boy, you'll be able to bring back a couple of bottles of the good stuff. Cheers.'

4

ALICANTE, SPAIN, 2013

Matt Deadman's black BMW cruised along the A7 motorway, heading north from Alicante. The car, on hire from Avis, was as smooth and as quiet as his old Alfa Romeo GTV6 back in England was rough and raw, with the impact of every bump, manhole cover and London pothole being sent shuddering up the steering column. The BMW was much smoother. It was an easy drive too, with barely any traffic on the road, most Spaniards choosing the back roads rather than the pay the increasingly heavy tolls. The sun was up, the sky was deep blue, and the Mediterranean sparkled away to the east. Perfect. Except Deadman was on a mission, and a strange one at that.

As he drove north from Alicante one thought continued to creep back into his mind; he was on the trail of a dead man who had claimed to have been one of a gang that had carried out a robbery over fifty years ago. There was no evidence, nothing to corroborate the man's story, nothing, save for a brief article in a local newspaper, written by a hack who was obviously trying to make a bit of a name for himself with the scoop. Okay, it hadn't filtered through to any national newspapers but it had at least landed on the desk of Trubshaw and Goat, solicitors, who considered it worthy of further investigation which was why Matt Deadman was now speeding his way north into the Gata de Gorgos hills, to the north east of Alicante.

The BMW exited the motorway at Benissa before heading inland towards Lliber. Before entering the small town the car took a sharp right and began heading up into the hills. The narrow road twisted and turned every hundred yards or so, and was barely wide enough to allow two cars to pass. Every now and then a local, more familiar with the road, would come hurtling round one of the many bends, causing Deadman to either swerve or suddenly brake, both actions usually being accompanied by a tirade of abuse in the usual cockney manner.

I must be bleedin' mad coming all this way on a bleedin' wild goose chase. And where the fucking hell am I?

Deadman was struggling. The GPS system in the BMW had taken him up the long and winding road from Lliber but ten minutes later the trail went cold. He was actually looking for a place or street called Font D'Aixa, although he hadn't a clue what this meant. He spun the car around and was just on his way back down towards Lliber when he spotted an old wooden sign hanging on a post by the roadside. It said simply 'Font D'Aixa.'

Jesus, no wonder I didn't spot it.

Deadman took the turning and immediately found himself crawling along a road or rather a track, down a steep hillside until he came to a dry river bed. An old stone causeway had been fashioned across it, wide and strong enough for wheeled vehicles. He edged the BMW steadily across it before making his way up the opposite hillside. Houses began to appear on both sides of the track, outside one of which an old woman was busy with a scythe, hacking away at the weeds. Deadman wound his window down.

'Por favour, dónde vive el ingles?'

The old lady looked up and straightened her back. She turned and simply pointed towards the end of the track.

'Al final del camino, a la izquierda.'

At the end of the track, on the left.

'Muchas gracias.'

A couple of minutes later and Deadman was standing in front of an imposing iron gate with the full array of security lamps, an entry system and, more worryingly, three very large dogs.

Bloody hell. This is more like Fort Knox.

Deadman rang the buzzer and waited. Nothing. He was just about to press the buzzer again when there was a sudden click, and the gates slowly began to open. He swung himself back into the car and eased it through, parking it in the gravel drive where a large olive tree offered some shade from the increasingly hot sun.

The three dogs, two Alsatians and an Irish Setter, came slowly towards him, eyeing up their prey.

'Oh, don't worry about them. They're three old softies.'

Deadman looked round as saw the familiar face of Jenny Bragg, who had just emerged from the front door. He breathed a sigh of relief.

'Oh, well that's good news. I've become a bit sick and tired of dogs hanging on my arse.'

'Oh, so you make a habit of this do you?' Jenny asked, smiling.

Deadman ignored the question.

'It's a nice place you've got here.'

The house was very smart but was showing signs of wear and tear. Deadman reckoned it dated from the early 1960s, which fitted nicely with Jenny's story. It was a long, two storey house, which looked as though it was divided into two sections. A long veranda ran the full length of the house, with tables and chairs placed at intervals. It was an ideal place for *al fresco* eating. Traditional blue and white tiles adorned the walls. There was nothing particularly fancy or modern. It was simply a very traditional, white, Spanish house.

'I didn't expect to see you here, but come in.' Jenny gestured towards the front door which led into a long passageway running left and right. She led Deadman a short way to the right before entering one of the rooms off it.

'Come in. Make yourself at home.'

The room was furnished with white leather armchairs and sofas, which surrounded a large raffia rug that lay on the traditional stone floor. A round glass table stood in the centre of it. Oak cabinets stood on either side of the room, with family photographs scattered on one of the sideboards. A fireplace stood at one end of the room as a reminder to visitors that it was not always scorching in Spain. A large, flat screen television was the only apparent concession to the twenty-first century. Deadman sat down on one of the sofas.

Jenny stood in the centre of the room. 'Right then. Tea, coffee, or something a little stronger?'

'Tea please. Milk no sugar,' replied Deadman.

He glanced around the room. There were no obvious signs that this was the home of a wanted criminal. There was none of the bling or glitz that adorned many a crook's home on the Costa del Sol further south. Jenny re-appeared a few minutes later with a tray which she placed on the glass table. There was a teapot, two cups with saucers, a small jug of milk and a sugar bowl.

'Shall I be mother?'

She poured two cups of tea, took one of them and gave it a stir. She sat back in one of the sofas.

'So, what brings you here to our neck of the woods? It's a long way to come just to pass on your condolences to my Mum, isn't it?'

Deadman could sense he'd been rumbled. It was time to get everything into the open. He leaned forward and put his cup down on the table.

'Well, I suppose I might as well come clean.'

He took a deep breath, not certain how Jenny would react to her Dad being accused of being a Great Train Robber.

'I'm not a policeman or anything like that, but I am a private investigator. I've been employed to look into the possibility that three of the gang that robbed the mail train in 1963 got clean away with it. The man who led the hunt for the gang died in 1970 but left a legacy in his will to anyone who could find and bring these three men to justice.'

Deadman waited for Jenny's response.

'And that's why you've come here,' she said, leaning forward. 'You've come all the way from England believing Dad's confession, believing that he was one of the gang?'

She started laughing.

'I could have saved you a wasted trip. I mean, if you'd had told me all of this in Herne Bay I could have saved you the trouble of coming out here. Dad, a train robber?' She continued laughing. 'And in any case, it was fifty years ago. Do you really think anyone really cares about it? I mean, it's like ancient history, isn't it?'

'Well, I must admit I asked myself the same question. Still, my employers believe it's still worth it. And they have a point. If a crime was committed and the culprit is still on the loose it doesn't really matter how long ago the crime was committed, does it? I mean, if everything had a time limit we'd have stopped looking for Nazi war criminals.'

Deadman had suddenly remembered the argument which Trubshaw had put forward when he'd met him in his chambers at The Temple.

Suddenly, a woman appeared in the door. Jenny looked around, still laughing.

'Mr Deadman, may I introduce my mother, Carmen? Mum, may I introduce Mr Deadman? He's come all the way from England thinking Dad was a master criminal.'

Deadman shook his head. 'I didn't say that.'

'But it's the same thing isn't it?' said Jenny,

becoming more serious.

Jenny's mother sat down and looked at Deadman.

'Look, what's this all about?' she asked, in a mixture of rapid Spanish staccato and thick cockney drawl. 'My husband is dead five minutes and you come here making allegations? And stupid ones at that.'

She got up, walked to the sideboard and picked up a photograph of her late husband.

'Leonard made a good living from his property deals in England before deciding to come to live in Spain. He was an honest man, and was a good father and husband.'

She walked over to Deadman and showed him the photograph.

'Look at him, Mr Deadman. Do you really think this is the face of a train robber?'

Deadman didn't answer. He was in a difficult spot. He was a guest in someone's house and he was effectively accusing the woman's late husband of being a crook. He looked at the photograph but said nothing. He'd met crooks before who looked as though butter wouldn't melt in their mouth. An angelic face was no proof of innocence.

Deadman had come a long way to investigate Lenny Bragg and certainly wasn't going to go away without having put a few questions to Bragg's widow.

'Look, I don't wish to be offensive. I've seen the confession and in the eyes of my employers some aspects ring true. There were certainly one or two details that only one of the gang would have been privy to.'

'I don't care, Mr Deadman. Leonard was no thief.'

Deadman pressed on with the interview. 'Tell me, Mrs Bragg, or may I call you Carmen? When exactly did you meet Lenny?'

Carmen seemed to calm down a bit.

'We met in 1965. Leonard walked into my office one

day, enquiring about properties in the Alicante area. I showed him a few and during the few days he was here we seemed to hit it off.'

'You must have heard about the Great Train Robbery though?'

'Mr Deadman, we were only allowed to see the sort of things that the Generalissimo wanted us to see.'

Jenny interrupted. 'My mother means General Franco.'

'So the crime wasn't reported here?' asked Deadman.

'No, why should it? Tell me, Mr Deadman, have you ever heard of Lucio Urtubia?'

Deadman conceded the point. 'No, I'm afraid I haven't. I suppose you're going to tell me he was a famous Spanish bank robber?'

Carmen didn't have to answer the question. 'So you see what I mean?'

Deadman sighed. 'And you believed him when he told you his wealth was down to property deals he'd done in England?

'Why shouldn't I?

The conversation was going nowhere.

'Did he ever have friends come out from England, men who may have had criminal connections? Was there anything at all that may have given you reason to suspect that Lenny's money had come from other means?'

Carmen got up again and walked to the sideboard. She put the photograph back in its place. 'I think you'd better leave now, Mr. Deadman. I've told you everything I know. My husband was not a thief, nor did he have any friends who might have been. Of course, I can't vouch for everything he did before I met him, or the men he knew, but I can tell you this; he was not a criminal. Now, if you don't mind…'

Jenny stood up.

Deadman had hit a brick wall. There was no point in going any further.

'Well, thanks for your time. I'm sorry to have bothered you.'

He turned to Jenny as he walked back to his car.

'Thanks for the tea.'

Jenny said nothing, but pushed a button and the iron gates glided slowly open. Deadman turned the key in the BMW's ignition and the car moved slowly forward, with the sound of gravel crunching beneath its tyres. The car disappeared slowly round the bend and was gone, leaving the gates to close slowly once more.

Back in the house Carmen Maria de Laspara, better known as Carmen Bragg, picked up the phone and began dialling 00 44 for England.

5

STAPLEHURST, KENT, 2013

Back in London, Matt Deadman was mulling over his options with Jack Moscroft. The Alicante lead had drawn a blank although Deadman's senses told him that Jenny and her mother had been stonewalling him.

'Something wasn't quite right. I don't know what it was but something didn't quite ring true.'

Deadman was back on the Solberano brandy again.

'Well, you've been pretty spot on about these things in the past, old boy.' Moscroft thought he'd better chip in with a word or two of encouragement. 'What else did Trubshaw tell you? Didn't he say Grappler had a daughter down in Kent?'

'Yes, that's right. In Staplehurst. The details are in the file. I suppose I ought to go down and speak to her.'

'Good,' said Moscroft, perking up. 'I could do with run out to the country.'

'Who said anything about you coming along?

'Come on, old boy. You know what they say, two heads are better than one!'

'Yes,' sighed Deadman, 'although in our case it's usually been a case of too many cooks.'

'Or too many crooks!' Moscroft laughed. 'Come on Matt. We can have a good lunch somewhere along the way. You need the company.'

Deadman finished his brandy and placed the glass on the table.

'Oh, alright then. I'll give her a call and we'll go down tomorrow.'

It was a fairly straightforward drive to Staplehurst. Deadman and Moscroft left the teeming streets of the capital and were soon cruising along the M20 into Kent. The county was once known as the Garden of England, although large swathes of north Kent were now part of London's urban sprawl. Still, it was a pleasant drive all the same. Deadman's Alfa Romeo GTV6 exited the motorway at the Leeds Castle junction, passing through Leeds village itself, before heading deeper into the country. Sutton Valence was passed before Deadman's Alfa Romeo descended the hill and continued along the Headcorn road. A right turn was made which took them along a pleasant country lane which threaded its way through green fields, with oast houses and traditional white weather boarded houses and cottages dotted here and there. Finally, the road arrived at the A299 and the village of Staplehurst.

The Alfa Romeo would its way through the village and out the other side before pulling into a drive on the left hand side of the road. A wooden sign said 'The Old Vicarage.' The car crawled along the narrow drive with tall hedges on either side before emerging in front of a very impressive red brick house.

'Well, this is very nice,' said Moscroft, emerging from the passenger's side of the car. 'Queen Anne, I should say, probably early eighteenth century. It's a fine building.'

Deadman was out of the car now, stretching after the drive from London.

'Well, we haven't come here to admire the architecture. Come on. Miss Grappler is expecting us.'

The front entrance to the house was impressive; a classical Queen Anne design, with a stone arch above the door, and ivy growing all over it. Two glass panels in the door allowed Deadman to peer into the hall. It was long and dark, and the passageway lined with all sorts of framed prints. A dark shape suddenly moved in the recesses of the passage and a few moments later a woman appeared. She looked carefully through the door at Deadman and Moscroft before opening it.

'Good morning, gentlemen. You've come about my father's obsession, I think.'

The two men looked at each other.

'Er, we've come about your father's legacy, if that's what you mean,' replied Deadman.

'Well, as far as I'm concerned, they were one and the same thing. Believe me Mr…'

'Deadman, ma'am, Matt Deadman, and this is my colleague, Jack Moscroft.'

Moscroft stepped forward and offered his hand to Grappler's daughter, a thin, bespectacled and grey haired lady. Moscroft guessed she was about sixty.

'Hello. My name's Betsy Grappler. Do come in gentlemen.'

Deadman and Moscroft stepped into the hall before passing into the passageway beyond. A couple of pairs of green Wellington boots lay in the corner, along with some walking sticks and umbrellas. A life-size paper-mache butler stood motionless, as if waiting for orders. The two men followed Betsy into the front room. It was sparsely but comfortably furnished with classical English furniture. A mahogany table and sideboard, comfortable sofas and a couple of armchairs, a drinks cabinet and an Adam fireplace which looked as though it hadn't been raked over for quite a while. An elegant chandelier hung from the ceiling.

Deadman looked around. 'It's a very nice room, ma'am, if I may say.'

'Well, father had reasonably good taste and saw to it that the house was well furnished. Would you like something to drink?'

Moscroft glanced at his friend. Both had noticed the port, sherry and brandy decanters on the table.

'Two glasses of sherry would be nice,' replied Deadman, thinking it would seem more civilised to have sherry than ask for something a bit stronger.

Betsy poured the sherry into three delicate glasses, handed two of them to Moscroft and Deadman, and took one for herself.

'Your good health,' proposed Moscroft.

'Now then, you've come about the men who got away.' Betsy Grappler came straight to the point. She continued before Deadman had a chance to reply.

'You know, you're not the first to come knocking on my door, chasing these men. Ever since my father died people have been coming down here, asking me questions. Well, not that many, but enough.' She took a sip of sherry.

'My father was obsessed with catching the criminals, obsessed. Do you know, when we went on holiday to the seaside, he would take a pair of binoculars with him and would spend the day scanning the beaches in the hope of spotting one of the gang. He was obsessed, absolutely obsessed.'

She finished her sherry and poured herself another glass.

'I still blame my father for my mother's early death. She couldn't stand it anymore. Of course, they said it was cancer, but I knew. It was his obsession with catching the gang that drove her to an early grave. She was only forty-two when she died, just forty two, God rest her soul. Of course, my father didn't last too long afterwards anyway. You can visit him if you want'

Deadman and Moscroft shot puzzled glances at each other.

Betsy went on. 'Oh, yes, he's buried in the churchyard just down the road.'

The two men relaxed again and sat back in their armchairs.

Deadman thought he'd better cut in. 'Look, Miss Grappler.'

'Betsy. Please call me Betsy.'

'Of course, Betsy. Now, did your father keep any papers, any notebooks or private material relating to the Great Train Robbery?'

Betsy Grappler gulped down the last of her sherry, placed the empty glass on the table and stood up.

'Follow me, gentlemen.'

Deadman and Moscroft quickly finished their drinks and got to their feet. They followed Betsy up a wide, wooden staircase that creaked beneath their feet. The stairs led to the first floor. A further flight led to the second. Then, just when it looked as though the stairs came to an end, Betsy opened up a small door, revealing a smaller staircase. She turned.

'This one leads to the attic. Mind your heads as you go up.'

And with that she began climbing the staircase that led to the attic.

Deadman followed her up. The wind rustled in the rafters, whilst a lone pigeon fluttered its way out through a hole in the roof. The attic was large and roomy but was crammed with all manner of boxes, piles of books, children's toys, and all sorts of discarded items which had long since ceased to be any use.

'I'm afraid my parents were a pair of real hoarders.'

Moscroft was now up, standing with his head bent low against one of the rafters.

'Yes, I can see that. It's a good job your father had

the good sense to install some good flooring, otherwise this lot would probably have given way.'

Betsy edged her way into a corner where a pile of boxes sat gathering dust.

'I think these are what you're looking for. Some people came a couple of years ago to look at them but didn't find anything that they didn't already know.'

Deadman and Moscroft dragged the boxes to the staircase and started taking them downstairs. It was easier to consult them on the landing where the light was much better.

The boxes contained all manner of papers, ledgers, scrapbooks and notebooks, all relating to the cases which Thomas Grappler had been involved in during his long and very distinguished career. Betsy Grappler stood there with her arms folded, looking down with dismay at the boxes.

'Well, I'll let you two get on with it. I'll put the kettle on in a while. Call me if you need anything.'

And with that she went downstairs, leaving Deadman and Moscroft to start ploughing through the series of boxes. There was very little that was of use to them. Charge sheets, newspaper cuttings were bundled up in piles.

'Crikey, shouldn't these charge sheets be with the police?' asked Moscroft.

'Probably, but who gives a shit now. Just keep looking.'

An hour passed. Boxes were opened, examined and closed afterwards. Cups of tea came and were drunk. But the boxes yielded no clues. Sure, there were plenty of papers and cuttings relating to the Great Train Robbery, but there was nothing to indicate the existence the three men who were supposed to have gotten away with it.

Deadman sat back, sighed and wiped his forehead. 'Well, that's about it then. There's bugger all here. What a fucking waste of time.'

Moscroft said nothing but wiped his head too.

'Come on,' said Deadman, getting to his feet. 'We might as well take them back to the attic.'

The boxes were manhandled up the stairs, back to the attic and one by one stacked up in a corner.

Deadman stood erect and stretched his back. 'Well, I can understand now why nobody else ever found anything. What a bloody waste of time.'

Moscroft was just pushing the last of the boxes into the corner when he noticed a rather nice doll's house stuffed behind an old rocking horse. 'You know, I always envied my sister having a doll's house,' said Moscroft, moving the rocking chair from in front of the house.

'Wasn't Action Man good enough for you or something?' laughed Deadman.

'Oh bugger off. And wasn't Action Man a doll anyway?' Moscroft moved the rocking horse and opened the front of the doll's house. The inside was rather nicely kitted out in the style of the 1930s.

'Come on Moscroft,' said Deadman, wearily. 'Playtime's over.'

'Hang on a minute. Strange, but the roof usually opens on these things.'

Moscroft tried to lift up the roof of the doll's house but it seemed to be stuck. He took out a penknife from his pocket and inserted the blade beneath the roof and the ceiling of the doll's house's top floor. There was a small crack and the roof finally gave way.

'That's better,' said Moscroft, gently lifting the roof. 'Now, what have we got here?'

'Unless you've found hidden jewels I'm going to be bloody annoyed. Now, come on, let's go.' Deadman was losing patience with his friend.

'Ha!'

Moscroft turned slowly. There was a huge grin across his face. He was holding an old leather notebook in his hand.

'Matthew, old chap, I do believe I've just found what we've been looking for.'

Deadman was speechless for a moment, but suddenly found his voice.

'You jammy bastard! Is that what I think it is?'

'It certainly is,' replied Moscroft, triumphantly. 'Let's get it downstairs.'

The notebook was the very thing Deadman and Moscroft had been hoping for. It was an old leather notebook, with a lace tied around it. Moscroft quickly undid the lace and opened it. It was a bit damp and had suffered the unwanted attention of the odd bug or two over the years. There were cobwebs between some of the pages. Moscroft blew hard on it, brushed away some dirt and opened the notebook at the first page. There, staring at the two men, and written in fine bronze copperplate, were the words, 'Private Notes Relating to The Mail Train Robbery of August 1963, Thomas Grappler.' It was as though Deadman and Moscroft had won the lottery.

'Shit', exclaimed Moscroft, 'Grappler must have kept a private record of interviews and other pieces of evidence.'

'He must have wanted the glory for himself,' said Deadman. 'I mean, look at this stuff. Shouldn't this be tucked away in the archives with other police records?'

'Absolutely right,' said Moscroft, flicking through the pages. 'There are names in here that I've never seen mentioned before. And look at this, police informers. Christ, there were a lot of jealous crooks around in late 1963. No wonder they say there's no honour amongst thieves.'

Moscroft passed the notebook to Deadman, who

went suddenly quiet as if studying a book in a library. Moscroft remained silent. He knew his friend was on to something. What seemed like an eternity passed before Deadman finally broke the silence.

'Shit....this is it....it's what we've been looking for!'

Deadman closed the notebook.

'They were bullshitting me.'

'Who?' asked Moscroft.

'Those cretins in Spain, the Braggs. Take a look.' He handed the notebook back to Moscroft, who read the relevant page. He looked up.

'So, Grappler was right all along. There really were three others who got away with it.'

'Yes,' replied Deadman, sighing, 'and Lenny Bragg was one of them.'

About halfway through the notebook was a page with a list of names on it. Grappler had written NAMES SUPPLIED BY INFORMERS at the top of the page. A quick scan was all that Deadman needed in order to realise the Braggs had been lying to him. Grappler had a list of sixteen names, twelve of which were well known. Reynolds was there, as was Biggs, Goody, and Edwards. Then there were the lesser known gang members, such as Jimmy White, Roy James, John Daly, Roger Cordery, Robert Welch, Tommy Wisbey, and James Hussey. Grappler had also written the words, 'two Post Office workers; unknown'. But there, written just above these two, were the names that Deadman was looking for most of all; Jimmy Damon, Danny Higgins and Lenny Bragg.

'Damon, Higgins and Bragg. So, these are the ones that Grappler reckoned had got away with it.'

'Well,' said Moscroft, 'it's one down, two to go, if you know what I mean.'

'Yes,' replied Deadman. 'Bragg is dead now

anyway, so it's pointless going back and dealing with those two in Alicante. Bollocks. I bet they're having a right laugh now.'

'Oh, I wouldn't think so. I mean, if they know you're onto them they're probably shitting themselves, waiting for the Guarda Civil to knock on their door at any moment.' Moscroft was trying to look on the bright side.

'Yes, I guess so. Still, I hate the thought of them getting one over on me.' Deadman sighed again. 'So, what do we do now? We have no leads, nothing to go one.'

'Oh I wouldn't say that,' said Moscroft. 'We need to pay a visit to the register of births and deaths people. We need to find out whether these other two blokes, Damon and Higgins are still alive. I mean, Grappler may well have been right, but if they're both dead the case is over anyway.'

'Yes. Well, we'll cross that bridge when we come to it. Come on, let's get out of here.'

Deadman turned to Moscroft. 'Here, give me the notebook. That's coming with us.'

And with that, the two men went downstairs. They found Betsy Grappler in her kitchen making yet another pot of tea.

'Are you staying for tea? Did you find what you were looking for?

'I'm sorry, Betsy. I guess you were right. We found nothing that the other guys didn't already find. Just a load of case notes really.' Deadman did his best to look disappointed.

'Oh well, I did warn you. Never mind. I'm glad to have been of help. Are you sure you won't stay for tea?'

'No thanks,' replied Moscroft. 'We really must be getting back to London.'

The two men said their goodbyes on the doorstep before getting into Deadman's car. Then with the gravel crunching beneath its wheels the Alfa Romeo made its way back down the drive and out onto the A229.

'Right, let's get back to London,' said Deadman.

Moscroft was deep in thought.

'What's up Jack?'

'It's the notebook,' replied Moscroft. 'I mean, are you absolutely sure Grappler was right. I mean, we only have his word, or rather his notebook. Suppose he was wrong?'

'Yes, I know what you mean. The thought had crossed my mind too.'

Deadman shifted into fifth gear as he sped along the A229.

'But there's one way to find out. We need to consult the original police files that are in the National Archives.'

'But didn't you say they were closed until 2045. I mean, we can't wait around that long. We'll be dead by then.' Moscroft laughed.

'Don't worry, Jack, I've thought of that one too. Yes, the files are indeed closed until 2045 so we'll have to get a look at them.'

'And how do you propose to do that? Are you going to walk in and steal them?'

Deadman laughed. 'No, I'm not, but I know someone who will.'

'Please tell me you don't expect me to do it.'

'No, don't worry. It's not you. But I know someone who might be able to get them out for us. Trust me....'

6

LONDON, 2013

'Hello? Yes, can you put me through to Angela Deadman please? Thanks. Sure, I'll hold.'

The Ministry of Defence was a difficult place to get through to at the best of times, but Matt Deadman was in luck today. The lines were not as busy as usual and the operator surprisingly friendly.

'I'm just putting you through now, sir. Go ahead…'

'Hello, Angie? It's me, Matt.'

A woman's voice crackled over the telephone line.

'Oh, it's you, and what do you want now. Another favour I suppose?'

'Oh, come on Angie, don't be like that. Listen, what time do you get off work?'

The Two Chairmen pub in Dartmouth Street is one of the oldest pubs in London and one of the most atmospheric too, its old world charm bringing in local office workers, builders and tourists alike. It was a great place to meet. Situated about ten minutes' walk from the Ministry of Defence building in Whitehall it was also a handy place for Deadman to meet up with his ex-wife, Angela. It was Friday night, and there was no rush to get home, and unlike lunchtime meetings there was no rush to get back to the office either.

The Deadmans had been married for four years before the split came. There was nothing acrimonious, no fights, no arguments. It was just that their work took them further and further apart. Their relationship began to stagnate and then broke down altogether. With no real reason to cling together any more the best and cleanest solution was to call it a day. The split had come five years ago but Matt still saw Angela every once and a while, usually when he wanted a favour, but provided it wasn't too outrageous she did her best for her ex-husband. But as he sat at the bar in The Two Chairmen, waiting for her to turn up, he wondered whether he was pushing his luck this time in asking her to go well and truly beyond the call of duty.

Deadman was just ordering his second pint when Angela walked in. She looked as attractive as ever, her long brown hair cascading down the back of a smart beige trench coat. Deadman, always a sucker for a pair of good legs, couldn't help glancing down at Angela's and at the high heeled shoes she was wearing.

'Okay, stop gawping. Put your tongue away.' She leaned forward and allowed Deadman to plant a kiss on her cheek.

'Sorry Angie, but you know how it is. Times are hard when you're a single bloke.'

'Pull the other one, Matt.'

'What'll it be? Don't tell me, you're still drinking Mother's Ruin?'

'Just get me a glass of white wine, you idiot.'

The drinks arrived.

'Shall we sit down?' asked Deadman, gesturing towards a free table in the corner. He followed Angie towards it and they sat down.

'Right, what's it all about then? You wanted a favour.'

Deadman took a couple of gulps of his beer and went for it.

'Okay, it's like this. I need to get hold of an old police file. The problem is that it's closed until 2045. I'll probably be dead by the time they open it up. It's kind of urgent.'

'So, where do I come in?' Angie took a sip of her wine.

'Where do you come in? Well, don't you still work in the archives at the MOD?'

'Yes, but we don't keep Scotland Yard's files. You know that.'

'Yes,' replied Deadman, sighing, 'but some of your files are housed in the National Archives at Kew, aren't they?'

Angie could sense what was coming. Her job at the MOD involved maintenance of various archives and her work often took her to Kew where she had special clearance to consult top secret files and other restricted documents.

'Yes, we do.' She paused. 'Please don't tell me you want me to steal one of the files for you. That's not it is it?'

Deadman said nothing.

'Oh, Christ. It is, isn't it? You want me to nick a bloody file for you!'

'Look, keep your voice down.' Deadman glanced over his shoulder. 'It's only for an hour or so. You'll have it back the same evening and you'll be able to slip it back the next day. Nobody will know that it's gone.'

'Oh, come on Matt, it's more than my job's worth. If they find out I've taken the file they'll go nuts. That'll be the end of my career. I'll be right up the swanee.'

She paused and took another sip of wine. She said nothing for a few moments but then sighed.

'I'm going to regret this.'

Deadman rubbed his hands and grinned.

'Thanks Angie. I knew I could count on you.'

'Well, get me another glass of wine and tell me what this file is all about.'

On the following Monday evening the buzzer rang in Deadman's flat in Paddington. He glanced at the small black and white monitor and saw Angela standing there.

'Well, are you going to let me in then?' she snapped.

Deadman pressed the buzzer and she stepped through the front door of the building. A few minutes later the buzzer on Deadman's own front door told him that Angela was outside. He opened the door to find her out of breath.

'You know, you really ought to consider moving to the ground floor. Those bloody steps...'

Deadman laughed. 'Yes, Moscroft says the same thing.'

Angela entered and took off her coat.

'And how is Jack? I haven't seen him for ages.'

'Oh, he's okay. He's out somewhere at the moment. Probably at the theatre or some cultural thing. Anyway, never mind him. Have you got the file?'

Angela reached inside her bag and produced a dog-eared cardboard file. A huge sticker with the words NOT TO BE OPENED UNTIL 2045 was stuck on the front of it.

'This had better be worth it!' she said, handing it over.

For once, Deadman fell silent. Angela noticed the serious look of anticipation pass across his face. He gently opened the file and began carefully turning the sheets of paper inside. There were police statements, witness statements, details of interviews, surveillance operations and all manner of reports relating to the pursuit of the Great Train Robbers. Suddenly, Deadman drew back. A smile came across his face.

'Bingo. This is what I was looking for.'

One of the confidential reports gave the names of

three men Scotland Yard believed to be part of the gang that held up the mail train. The report said the Yard was ninety-nine per cent certain, and that surveillance operations had shown the men to have been in frequent contact with members of the gang who had since been arrested, charged and sent to prison. Deadman then read out the names; Jimmy Damon, Danny Higgins and Lenny Bragg. It was the confirmation he needed to corroborate the secret list which Grappler had compiled himself.

The problem was that there was no evidence to link Higgins to the crime, although he had been named by an underworld grass, a man who was known to be very accurate with any intelligence he passed on to Scotland Yard. Bragg and Damon, meanwhile, were wanted for questioning, but although the Yard was certain of their involvement in the robbery, the two suspects could not be found anywhere. Thus, detectives were forced to bite their lips in frustration, not having any way of proving Higgins's guilt in a court of law or being able to find the other two.

Angela could tell her ex-husband had discovered something very important and asked him what the names meant.

'You know all about the Great Train Robbery don't you?' asked Deadman.

'Well, I don't remember it personally but, yes, of course I've heard of it.'

'And all of the robbers were captured and sent to jail. Yes?'

'Well, yes, eventually. I seem to recall Ronnie Biggs led the police a merry dance. Didn't he come home a few years ago?'

'Yes, but never mind Biggs. What about the rest of the gang? You said they were all arrested and put away?'

'Yes,' said Angela, 'they all received very hefty

sentences.'

Deadman sat back in triumph. 'Well, actually, Scotland Yard didn't catch all of the gang. Three of them got clean away with it.' He brandished the sheet of paper aloft. 'And these are the names of the three men.'

Angela could scarcely believe it. 'What, three of them really did get away with it? Well, well done them!'

Deadman went on to explain how he'd been given the job of tracking down the three men and bringing them to justice. He told Angela about the Grappler Legacy and the discovery of Grappler's notebook at his daughter's house in Staplehurst.

'That's fantastic. But will anybody believe it?'

'They will when I've done with it. It'll be great publicity if I can nail these blokes. Of course, Bragg is dead now. As for the others, well, at least I have it confirmed that Scotland Yard believed the three men to have been members of the gang. All I've got to do now is trace the two others.'

'And where are you going to start?' asked Angela. 'I mean, it'll be like the proverbial needle in the haystack.'

'Well, not quite. I mean, I only have to consult the register of births and deaths and I'll know whether the other two are still alive or not. This report gives their last known addresses, so I'll have that to go on also.'

'But the report is over fifty years old now. They'd have moved years ago.'

'Well,' said Deadman, 'I've got to start somewhere. I'll pick up more information somewhere, don't worry about that. In the meantime, you'd better take this.' He placed the report back in the file and handed it back to Angela. 'Make sure it gets put back safe and sound, and for gawd's sake don't let anyone see you do it.'

He finished off his drink, looked across at Angela and grinned. 'Okay, what shall we do now… ?'

Angela said nothing but finished her own drink. She put the glass on a table and looked at her watch. 'Some of us have got to work, you know.' She got to her feet, walked over to her ex-husband and planted a kiss on his cheek. 'I'll call you tomorrow.'

'Well, you can't blame a guy for trying,' said Deadman, with a rueful look on his face.

'Goodnight, Matt, and have fun hunting your train robbers.'

7

LONDON, NOVEMBER 1963

'Jimmy, have you read this?' Lenny Bragg slid the morning's copy of *The Daily Mirror* across the table to his old mate. 'They've nicked Roy now. That leaves just the three of us, plus Bruce, Buster and Jimmy White. We're the only ones left now.'

Lenny and his two best mates, Jimmy Damon and Danny Higgins, were tucking into a full English breakfast at Ted's Café in Albany Road, Peckham, just a stone's throw from Jimmy's home in Silcote Road. The three friends were taking a bit of a risk as Scotland Yard had been keeping tabs on Jimmy's home for a few days now, ever since a copper's nark had fingered him and put him in the frame for the train robbery.

Following the raid on the train in August the police had gone into overdrive, picking up suspects, arresting anyone remotely connected with the robbers and generally causing London's criminal elements to go to ground. Indeed, the crime rate in post-train robbery London showed a mark reduction. One by one the men who had attacked the train on the morning of 8 August had been picked up, either through their own carelessness or following tip-offs from members of the underworld who were only too keen to divert the heat away from themselves. And then, of course, there was the reward. A staggering two hundred and sixty thousand pounds, about ten percent of the total haul, was up for grabs and members of the public and criminals themselves were not shy in coming forward to stake their claim.

Roger Cordery had gone into the bag first of all, barely

six days after the robbery, along with the unfortunate William Boal, a man who had nothing whatsoever to do with the robbery. He just happened to be in the wrong place at the wrong time when Cordery was arrested. Charlie Wilson was next, being arrested on 23 August, and by the end of September Ronnie Biggs, James Hussey and Tommy Wisbey were in the bag as well, along with Brian Field and Leonard Field who, although not actually being present at the raid itself, were involved in the planning. Gordon Goody was fitted up and arrested in October, as was Robert Welch, followed on 3 December by John Daly. Roy James' arrest, seven days later, left just six of the original fifteen robbers on the run.

Danny Higgins read the report.

'What are we going to do now, Jimmy? I mean, it won't take them long to find us. It's obvious someone has grassed us up. The boys are going down like ninepins.'

Jimmy was deep in thought as he sipped from a mug of hot tea.

'Well, I suppose there are a few options on the table. For a start, we could chuck ourselves in.'

He let the words hang in the air for a moment, allowing the shock to sink in with his two mates. He suddenly laughed.

'Nah, of course not. I ain't never doing that. Never. They'll have to catch me first.' He sipped some more tea. 'We could try to get away, you know, leave the country. I see they're asking for Brits to go to Australia. You know, they're calling us Ten Pound Poms.'

Lenny looked puzzled. 'What do you mean, Ten Pound Poms?'

Danny cut in. 'It means it will cost us just ten quid to go to Australia. They've come up with a cheap fare. They reckon it will get loads of us to go to Australia and help build things. You know, all that sort of thing.'

'Yeah, Danny's right,' said Jimmy, 'although I'm not sure I want to go all of that way, just to escape the law. I mean, it's the bottom of the world ain't it?'

Lenny laughed. 'Well, it's not as if we can't afford it now, is it?'

Jimmy went silent again. 'Of course, there is another way out, but it's not a good one.'

Lenny and Danny leaned forward.

'Look, I've spoken to Billy Bates.'

'You mean the copper's nark?' snapped Danny. 'I wouldn't trust him as far as I could chuck him.'

'Shut up, Danny. Listen. Billy says he can speak to the coppers. He's on drinking terms with Frank Hawkins,'

'You mean that bloke at Scotland Yard? Ain't he with the Sweeney?' asked Lenny.

'Yeah,' replied Jimmy, 'he's with the Sweeney but he's alright. You can trust him. Billy reckons that if we give the money back it'll give us freedom from prosecution, you know, they'll lay off of us. They won't give us any more bother.'

Danny and Lenny went quiet. Sure, they were being sought by the police and the heat was well and truly on. But the prospect of handing back around one hundred and forty thousand pounds each was too depressing to contemplate. After all, none of them was ever likely to be able to lay their hands on that much cash ever again in the lives, not unless one of them was lucky enough to win the Football Pools.

Jimmy continued. 'The only other way is to lay low for as long as we can and hope the heat dies down. It's a long shot but it's an option. That's all I've got. It's up to you.'

Lenny was first to speak.

'Well I'm certainly not gonna hand myself in, and I ain't gonna hand the money back neither. I mean, fucking hell, I didn't go through all this just to give it all back again.'

'Yeah, but think of it,' said Danny, 'they'll throw the book at us if they catch us. I mean, we've got to be looking at a fifteen year stretch if we go down. At least. I'm buggered if I'm going to spend that long inside. Bollocks to that.'

Jimmy had sensed from the minute they'd pulled off the robbery that Danny was getting cold feet. True, he'd been in from the start and had gone at it a hundred per cent during the robbery. But the excitement had turned to fear, fear of being hunted down and driven from one hideout to the next, until the inevitable came. The pressure was getting to him. If anyone was likely to hand back the money it was Danny.

'Look,' said Jimmy, 'we don't have to decide right now. Let's split and meet up later. If anyone has a better idea they'd better be quick and it had better be a good one. Otherwise, I can't think of anything else. They'll be watching the Beckett. I'll see you in the Lord Nelson tonight.'

The police were making a clumsy attempt to look inconspicuous outside Jimmy's home in Silcote Road. A Post Office tent had been erected over a manhole cover across the street, but a closer inspection would reveal that the two men inside enjoying their tea and sandwiches knew nothing about telecommunications. They were simply a pair of flatfooted coppers. Knowing this to be the case Jimmy was staying with a friend, Stan Tanner, in Bagshot Street, not far away. 'Stan the Man,' as he was known, lived alone and could be relied on to keep quiet.

The three friends met up that evening as agreed in the Lord Nelson in the Old Kent Road. Danny ordered three pints of bitter. They sat in a corner, glancing every now and then at the door and keeping a wary eye on the other customers. Rumours were going round of their involvement in the robbery, although the recent assassination of President

Kennedy had, for the time being at least, become the main topic of conversation.

'Well,' asked Jimmy, 'what do you think? What are we gonna do?'

Danny hesitated but finally blurted it out. 'Look, I don't care about the money any more. I'm not going down. I'm gonna speak to Billy Bates and get him to set up a meet with Mr Hawkins.'

Lenny and Jimmy sat back and looked at each other. They said nothing sipped their beer.

Danny went on. 'I mean, it's not like we ever had the money before is it? What you don't have you don't miss.'

He was trying hard to convince himself it was the right thing to do. He gulped down his beer. 'I'm not going inside, not for no one or nothing.'

'Well that's it then, isn't it? So much for The Three Musketeers and the all for one and one for all thing we had at school, eh? I suppose it's every man for himself now.' Jimmy finished his beer and put the glass on the table.

'If you're sure it's what you want. It's up to you, Danny.'

'I'm sure.'

'Right then, I'll let you see to the arrangements. You know where Billy is. Talk to him and sort it. But get this straight; if you breathe a word to the cops about me and Lenny…' Jimmy tailed off.

Danny looked disappointed. 'Come on Jimmy, you know I wouldn't do that. How long have we known each other now? Yeah, they did call us The Three Musketeers at school, and, yeah, it's still one for all and all for one. You know that. Trust me.'

'Well just make sure it stays that way, that's all I'm saying.' And with that Jimmy left, with Lenny following close behind.

'Do you think he'll squeal?' asked Lenny once he'd got outside.

'Who, Danny? Nah, he won't say anything. His bottle's gone but he wouldn't grass us up. I'm off now. Got some thinking to do. I'll see ya later.'

And with that Jimmy Damon disappeared into the thick grey fog of another winter's evening in South London.

A week after their meeting in the Lord Nelson the three friends met again.

'So, how did it go? Did it all go to plan?'

Lenny was anxious to know whether Hawkins had been as good as his word when Danny had handed in the cash.

'Well, I didn't see Hawkins myself. Billy made the arrangements and I sat in the car whilst he took the holdalls inside.'

'What,' asked Lenny, 'you mean you sat outside Scotland Yard while the deal went down? Shit, they might have nicked you first.'

'Nah, Billy had it all sorted. No problem. I've been coming and going now without any hassle from the cops. I reckon it's done the trick.' He sighed. 'Okay, I might be a few quid down…'

'A few quid?' exclaimed Lenny.

'Well, you know what I mean. The money's gone but I ain't going inside. The heat's off.' Danny looked relieved to have got rid of the money.

Jimmy had listened to Danny with great interest. He knew the cops were after him. They wanted to bring him in for questioning and it was almost inevitable that at some point his alibi would fail and he'd wind up like the others who were now awaiting trial. Jimmy had other ideas however. He had a plan which, if successful, would get the cops off his back for good, but would still allow him to keep his share of the cash. He needed to make sure his plan would work first of all, and the fact that Danny was now being left alone proved his plan would work.

Detective Inspector Frank Hawkins had evidently been as good as his word in taking back Danny's share of the money and in dropping him from the investigation. Jimmy had no intention of handing in his share of the loot but couldn't help thinking it would be a good way of getting the cops off his own back. The problem was, he didn't want to give up his share. And then the thought hit him; he didn't have to give up his share of the loot. He could hand back John Daly's share and say it was his own. It made perfect sense. John Daly had asked Jimmy to look after his share of the robbery because he didn't want to upset his pregnant wife, who was bound to wonder where all the money was suddenly coming from. But having been put in the frame by an informer Daly had gone to ground and hadn't come to Jimmy for his money. Having now been arrested, he was unlikely to come for his money. All Jimmy had to do was to go round to his Gran's house in Kelvington Road, dig it up, and do the same deal with Hawkins that Danny had done, except he'd still have his own share of the loot, and would be free to spend it. It was perfect.

The staff at Scotland Yard were preparing for their Christmas parties and there were just a few days to go before the big day itself. Despite the ongoing hunt for the train robbers who were still at large even Grappler and Hawkins mucked in. Even coppers had to enjoy themselves once and a while.

Frank Hawkins was laughing and taking a drag on a

cigarette. A glass of whisky rested in his other hand. Suddenly, his phone rang. He put the glass down and took the cigarette from his mouth.

'Yes, Hawkins here.'

Hawkins listened for a few moments, seemingly unable to comprehend what he was hearing. The shouting and laughing in his office was too loud and he struggled to hear.

'Oi, you lot, keep it down a minute will you?'

His colleagues shouted back at him, but lowered their voices anyway.

'And where did you say the phone box is? Hang on a minute, let me get this down.'

Hawkins scribbled some details on the back of an envelope on his desk before hanging up.

Grappler came wandering over to him.

'What's up Frank? You look like you've just been speaking to a ghost.'

'It's Jimmy Damon.'

The office went silent.

'He says he'll leave his share of the train robbery loot in a phone box, provided we get off his back and drop him from our investigations.'

Grappler was astonished.

'Bloody hell, he must be getting desperate if he's offering to hand over his share of the money. Did you get his number?'

'Yes, here.'

Hawkins handed to Grappler.

'He says I've got five minutes to phone him back, otherwise he'll scarper.'

'Christ, Frank. It looks like Christmas has come early this year. Give me the phone.'

Grappler and Hawkins had been trying to find Jimmy since he was put in the frame by a grass. But as much as they wanted to arrest him they thought it better to get the money back. After all, nine of the gang were already under arrest awaiting trial. They would have to do for now. But very little of the money had been recovered.

Hawkins looked disappointed at Grappler's eagerness to do the deal. After all, he'd been after Jimmy for some time now.

'Come on Frank, cheer up. We'll get the money back and nick him for something else later on. Two birds with one stone and all that.'

There may have been no honour amongst thieves but at times it seemed as though there was even less amongst the police.

Jimmy Damon was stood shivering in his large, grey overcoat outside one of Gilbert Scott's classic red telephone boxes in Great Dover Street, at the junction of Black Horse Court. Now and then a red bus crawled past, and Jimmy couldn't help thinking everyone on board was looking at him, as though they knew what he was up to. He paced up and down, every now and then taking a drag from a cigarette. His dark blue Ford Anglia was parked close by, with two sacks, stuffed full of used banknotes on the back seat. Suddenly, the phone rang. Jimmy dropped the cigarette and stubbed it out with his foot. He rushed to answer the phone.

'Mr Hawkins?'

Jimmy listened for a few moments.

'And I have your word you'll leave me alone? I mean, Danny's done the same deal, hasn't he? I want the same. Do I have your word?'

Jimmy Damon and Frank Hawkins operated on very different sides of the fence but there were times when a truce, albeit a fragile, uneasy one, had to be called, and this was one of those times.

'You've got my word Jimmy. Now, leave the cash, and for Christ's sake don't let anyone else take it!'

'Well then, you'd better get one of your boys here as quickly as possible, hadn't you?'

And with that Jimmy hung up. He went to his car and hauled two large, heavy sacks from the back seat. He dragged them to the phone box and left them there, propped up inside. Then, looking around to make sure he wasn't being watched, he drove a short distance up the road, just to make sure nobody else took the money instead. What a waste that would be.

The light was beginning to fade when, about ten minutes after Jimmy had made the call, a black Jaguar Mark II came speeding up the road, screeching to a halt outside the phone box. Jimmy smiled and took a drag from his cigarette.

'That ought to do the job.'

He started his motor, released the handbrake and drove slowly away.

On 20 January 1964 the trial of the Great Train Robbers began in Aylesbury in a blaze of publicity. There was massive interest in the case, of course, and the crowds were enormous. Onlookers waited patiently in the rain to get a glimpse of the infamous defendants as they were led from the back of a black Maria to the courthouse, not that they would have seen much for each member of the gang had a blanket covering his head. The trial was, of course, big news and the next day headlines were splashed all over the front pages of the national newspapers.

Jimmy Damon, Danny Higgins and Lenny Bragg

were back in their old haunt at Ted's Café. Bacon sandwiches were being munched and mugs of tea drained.

'Just think,' said Danny, 'that could have been us.'

'Well it could still be me and Lenny,' snapped Jimmy, 'I mean, you're in the clear aren't you?'

'Yeah,' replied Danny, 'and I'm fucking skint too.'

'Well we did warn you,' said Lenny, slurping his tea. 'You might be skint but at least you've not got the old bill on your tail day and night.'

Jimmy kept silent. Ever since he'd handed in John Daly's share of the loot he'd pretended to be on the run like Lenny. He hadn't told either of his mates what he'd done. True, they were best friends, but even they would have been appalled by the idea that Jimmy had double-crossed one of the gang. And double-crossed the police too. Lenny, on the other hand, really was on the run, and continually took chances to meet up with his mates around Albany Road. Whenever he came out with a story about a close shave with the police Jimmy would match it, often embellishing it with dramatic details. It was all part of his secret game.

Danny was free but skint, whilst Lenny was lying low, his money running lower by the day as a result of having to pay minders, and 'friends', or to stay holed-up in safe houses. None of his friends or associates would give him away to the police but they made damn sure they fleeced him all the same in return. Jimmy, on the other hand, was not only free from prosecution, but was extremely wealthy. He just had to be careful how he handled his money. After all, if he started splashing the cash it would be bound to raise suspicions.

The newspapers continued to cover the story, although by the middle of February interest had begun to wane. The trial entered its fourth week with the respective defence and prosecution teams arguing their cases. Lenny Bragg continued to lie low, emerging every now and then to share a drink or a breakfast with his two mates Danny Higgins and Jimmy Damon. All three of them were drinking one lunch time in the Lord Nelson pub. It was St Valentine's Day and the three friends were talking over their plans for the evening.

'What are you up to tonight Danny? I suppose you're on a promise with that blonde you've been seeing.' Lenny laughed. 'What's her name again? Enid isn't it?'

Jimmy laughed too. 'Enid?'

'Well, no actually. We're off to the pictures. Down the ABC. We're seeing that new film everyone's going on about, you know, *Zulu*.'

'Oooo, Zulu!' Jimmy and Lenny laughed.

'Oh, fuck you, you stupid bastards. I supposed you've got hot dates, or are you staying in with your Mums?' It was Danny's turn to laugh.

Before Jimmy could answer Lenny gasped.

'Fucking hell! Here, have you seen this?'

He was flicking through the morning's copy of *The Daily Mirror* when one of the stories on the inside jumped out at him.

'Daly's been let off. He's out!'

Jimmy was dumbstruck. 'What? Here, let me see that.' He stubbed out his cigarette and grabbed the paper. His blood froze in his veins. 'Shit! Bollocks!'

Lenny and Danny looked surprised.

'What's up Jimmy? It's great isn't it? Maybe there's hope for the rest of the lads?'

Jimmy mumbled something.

The newspaper report was true. When the gang had left their hideout at the farmhouse they'd left behind one gigantic clue in the shape of numerous fingerprints left on ketchup bottles, bath rails, window sills, tins of beans and, curiously, on a Monopoly set. The prints were quickly and easily matched with those held in the Criminal Record Office. John Daly's prints had been found on the Monopoly board but his defence team argued, very shrewdly, that they could have been placed there at an earlier date. After all, Bruce Reynolds, one of the known robbers and one of those yet to be caught, was Daly's brother-in-law. Daly's team argued that Reynolds had played the game at Daly's house and had subsequently taken the board to the farmhouse. This explained how Daly's fingerprints came to be on the board. It was nonsense, of course, for Daly had indeed been present with the rest of the gang at Seers Crossing. But, remarkably, the judge accepted the argument and ordered Daly to be dismissed without charge. It was the best St Valentine's Day gift his wife could have hoped for.

The release of John Daly may well have been a godsend to his wife but to Jimmy Damon it was nothing short of a disaster, for the first thing Daly would want to do would be to get his share of the loot back. Jimmy needed to think quickly. Any day now Daly would get in touch, wanting his money. Worse still, if word got out that Jimmy had double-crossed Daly by using his share of the money to get the police off of his back it wouldn't be too long before someone grassed him up in revenge. The police would soon be on his trail once more. Hiding out from the police was one thing, but hiding out from Daly, with all of his criminal connections and informers, was quite another. Jimmy weighed up his very limited options. There was only one thing for it. He would have to become a 'Ten Pound Pom.'

There was a frantic knocking early one morning on the door of the flat above the dry-cleaners in Albany Road. A bleary eyed Lenny Bragg opened the door of his latest hideout an inch or two to see who it was that had disturbed his sleep. He rubbed his eyes.

'Jimmy? What do you want this early in the morning? Blimey, it's only just six o'clock.'

'Yeah. Sorry about that Lenny. Look, can I come in?'

A few minutes later and the kettle was boiling away as Lenny prepared a couple of mugs of tea. He poured some milk into the mugs and offered one to Jimmy who was sitting on a sofa in the small living room.

'So, what brings you here at this hour? Have the Old Bill been round?'

Lenny still had no idea that Jimmy had used Daly's stash to get the cops off his back.

'Well, sort of, yeah. Listen, you remember all that stuff I told you about going to Australia?'

'Oh, you mean that 'Ten Pound Pom' stuff? Yeah, I remember it.' Lenny drank some of the tea. 'Don't tell me you've changed your mind? You mean you're off Down Under?'

'Yeah, well sort of.' Jimmy fumbled with his excuse. 'Things ain't been quite right round here lately, and the cops are getting a bit too nosey, if you know what I mean. I was thinking; why don't we stick our money somewhere, get someone to put it in a bank or Swiss Bank Account, you know, a place where they don't ask questions, and we can fuck off to Australia. The Aussies have been advertising for bricklayers and labourers to go down and work on something called the Snowy Mountain Scheme, or something like that. No one's gonna notice us down there with all these other blokes.'

Lenny remained deep in thought for a few moments.

'Well, I can't say I haven't thought about it myself. I've been living like a bleedin' dosser for these past few months, ever since I got word that the Old Bill were looking for me. He sipped some more tea.

'Mind you, Jimmy, what are we gonna do when we get there? I mean, what do we know about being brickies? We've never built anything in our lives.'

'Oh, for fuck's sake, Lenny. How difficult can it be to build a fucking wall? Have you seen these blokes on the building sites? They're as thick as shit. How hard can it be? Anyway, we'll skive off, duck and dive, you know, the way we always play it. Come on Lenny, it'll be fun.' He gulped down some tea. 'And it'll get us both away from this shit here in England. What d'ya say?'

Lenny continued to mull over the prospect.

Jimmy leaned forward as Lenny started mumbling.

'Well, I suppose so. I mean, it's not like I've got anything to lose here, no family or anything like that. I suppose Australia is as good as anywhere for someone who wants to lose himself.'

Jimmy grinned. 'Yeah, that's what I thought. I mean, they used to send convicts down there in the old days. We'd be carrying on a tradition!'

The two friends laughed. Lenny stood up and raised his mug as a toast.

'Here's to a land fit for thieves!'

8

SOUTH LONDON, 2013

Matt Deadman was staring at the screen of his computer, studying a map of South London, and the Old Kent Road in particular. He was on the trail of three men who were almost certainly Great Train Robbers, but whom had never been caught. With the help of an old notebook and a file 'borrowed' from the National Archives Deadman had been able to establish their names; Jimmy Damon, Lenny Bragg and Danny Higgins. His search for Lenny Bragg had taken him to the picturesque churchyard in Herne where he witnessed for himself Bragg's funeral. It had also taken him to Spain to meet Bragg's daughter and widow, both of whom vehemently denied that Lenny was anything other than a hard-working man who had made his fortune through property deals in the late 1960s. That was obviously a lie, but with Bragg dead there was no point in pursuing that line of enquiry any further.

His enquiries had also established that Danny Higgins, the man who handed back his cash in return for freedom of prosecution, had died in 2008. This left just Jimmy Damon as the only possible survivor of the gang of three. But where on earth was he? Deadman had no clues whatsoever as to his possible whereabouts. He wasn't even sure he was alive, although the Register of Births and Deaths had turned up only his birth certificate, so maybe he was. The only way Deadman was going to find Damon was to do things the old way, by getting out onto the streets and putting in a good few hours of legwork.

Things weren't as bad as they seemed, however, for Deadman at least had one or two things hidden up his sleeve which might yield results. The file that his ex-wife, Angela, had 'borrowed' from the National Archives gave the addresses of all three men. In late 1963 and early 1964 these were staked out by Scotland Yard almost constantly, day and night, in the hope that one or all of the three suspects would turn up. So, at least Deadman had something to go on. He would have to pay a visit to the addresses in the feint hope that someone, at one of them, may be able to steer him in the right direction. True, the robbery was over fifty years ago, but this didn't mean to say that any of the three didn't return home some years later, when the heat had died down. At the very least Deadman hoped somebody would remember them, or that a relative was now living at one of the addresses. It was a long shot but he had bugger all else to go on.

Of the three men suspected of being train robbers Jimmy Damon was the only one still alive, or at least Deadman hoped he was. His address was listed in one of Grappler's reports in the secret file Angela had obtained for him. It was 5 Silcote Road, Camberwell, London, SE5. The problem was, Silcote Road didn't appear to exist any more. Deadman scanned Google Maps, looked in the A-Z, consulted other maps but couldn't find it anywhere. Then he came across a forum on the internet. There were some old photos of Silcote Road, taken in the early 1980s, all of which bore the caption, 'Silcote Road, prior to demolition to make way for Burgess Park.' It was true. Silcote Road, along with one or two other nearby streets, had been completely obliterated to make way for Burgess Park, off Albany Road. What the Luftwaffe failed to do the Greater London Council succeeded in doing. The park was now an oasis in an otherwise residential desert, with a large lake sitting in the middle of it. On hot summer days, local kids would go to the park to sail their model boats, or to sit by the water's edge, while the children of the 80s' Yuppies took their own kids to the park to fly their designer kites or see them tumble into the water. Otherwise, the locals just tossed their empty McDonald's wrappers into it. It was one of those places. Still, Damon's original home address slotted nicely into the story, with the Thomas A Beckett pub and Albany Road being situated close by.

Danny Higgins' address was listed as 91 Albany Road. This too, fit the bill nicely, as it was situated very close to Silcote Road. As for the late Lenny Bragg, he had been living in a variety of safe houses after the robbery, but his home address was still officially listed as being 35 Longcroft Road. This was now situated on the other side of Burgess Park. It was also very close to Cobourg Road School, where all three robbers had first met as seven-year-old kids in 1947. The school still stood in Cobourg Road, as did the old Victorian church opposite, although this was now The Peckham Mosque. Times had certainly changed since 1963. There was nothing for it really, but to take a trip down the Old Kent Road, into the badlands of South London.

There were no tube stations in the area around Burgess Park, the nearest being New Cross, and that was miles away. Deadman would have to take his car. It wasn't a long trip. Straight down the Edgware Road, down Park Lane, around Buckingham Palace and down to Westminster Bridge. Once across the bridge Deadman passed the General Lying-In Hospital in York Road. It was here that Deadman himself was born. On a good day you could just about hear the bells ringing in distant Bow Church. Deadman was always proud to claim that this made him a true Cockney, even though the hospital was on the south side of the river. The road continued on to the Elephant and Castle, where some of the train robbers had once operated. The Elephant effectively marked the beginning of The Old Kent Road.

Once an area of dockers, market traders, Millwall supporters, gin palaces and good old-fashioned Cockneys, it was now largely inhabited by immigrants from the Commonwealth or from new Europe, churches had become mosques, pubs like the famous The World Turned Upside Down, had closed due to a lack of custom, whilst traditional greengrocers, butchers, haberdasheries and gentlemen's clothes shops, had given way to internet cafes, to fried chicken and other fast-food joints, Turkish and Caribbean restaurants, to Al Halal butchers and generally to shops whose business it was to send money half way round the world to the new inhabitants' families back homes. Where once you could have enjoyed a right old knees-up, you were now more likely to hear a burst of reggae music or the cry of the local imam. It was a far different world from that which existed at the time of the Great Train Robbery.

Deadman negotiated the midday traffic in the Old Kent Road, which was never anything other than busy. He passed the Thomas A Beckett pub at the junction of Albany Road before swinging his Alfa Romeo right into Trafalgar Street. It wasn't possible to turn right into Cobourg Road so he had to take a detour and approach Longcroft Road from the south. There wasn't much left of it, just six of the original houses being left high and dry by the Burgess Park development.

Christ, they really slaughtered this area back in the 1980s.

Lenny Bragg's old house was number 35, or second from the end. The houses began with number 33, the others having been pulled down to make way for the park. The house was a substantial looking grey-brick terraced house, dating from the late 1880s. There were two bay windows, one on the ground floor and one on the first. It looked tidy enough. Deadman got out of his car and stared at the house for a moment. It was hard to imagine this had once been the home to one of the three men who had avoided arrest. Not knowing what he was about to discover Deadman took a deep breath and rang the doorbell. Hopefully, he'd find a relative or an old local who remembered Bragg living there some years before. There was a noise from within. The door opened and Deadman found himself looking down at a short Indian woman.

Bollocks.

Two minutes later Deadman was back in his car, driving back up Cobourg Road. The lead had come to nothing. The Indian woman tried to be as polite as possible but she hadn't a clue who Lenny Bragg was. The woman said her family had lived there for seven years and added that a Nigerian family had lived there before them. It was a dead loss.

With Damon's own house having long since been wiped off the map of London, it left only Danny Higgins's old house, number 91 Albany Road, as the only possible lead. Fortunately Deadman was in luck.

Danny Higgins's old house was almost identical to Bragg's. Deadman guessed the entire area must have been covered in them. In fact, when he was scanning an old map of London the area where the three robbers had once lived was enclosed within a border, with the words UNITED MISSION SERVICE in capitals, which suggested the houses had been funded by a Christian organisation. There were two storeys, again each with a bay window. The only obvious difference was that the house in Albany Road had a front garden, or at least it used to before it gave way to a parking place for the owner's car. Deadman parked close to the house, got out of his car and walked slowly towards number 91. A man, presumably the owner, and a man about the same age as Deadman himself, was busy raking some weeds from beneath the bay window. He turned when he saw Deadman standing there.

'If you're going to tell me it used to look much nicer, please don't bother. Some one has beaten you to it.'

Deadman was taken aback and puzzled by this curious story.

'Sorry, what?'

The man straightened his back and groaned.

'I'm sorry. I didn't mean to be abrupt. It's just that some old guy who lives round the corner always seems to catch me when I'm digging around. He has a habit of stopping for a chat, not that I mind much. He's harmless really. It's just that he used to know a guy who once lived here. He reckoned the garden back then was immaculate. "Oh, Danny did this, and Danny did that." I must say he goes on a bit. Now how can I help you?'

A huge grin had already spread across Deadman's face.

'You already have. The old guy, the one who you say stops for chat now and then. Did he say the bloke who used to live here was named Danny?'

'Yes, that's right. I could hardly forget it. You'd think he was still around the way that the old chap goes on. I swear one day there'll be a knock at the door and this Danny bloke will be standing there, offering to do some gardening!'

The man looked around. 'Well, look at it. There's not much left now, just some weeds and a place for the car.'

'Do you happen to know where this old chap lives? You say it's round the corner?'

'Yes, in Bagshot Street. It's just a few yards down the road. First turning on the right. I don't know the number but I know he's always drinking in the Duke of York. It's also in Bagshot Street. I guess you can ask in there.

The man stretched again. 'Just ask for Stan Tanner.'

Matt Deadman looked at his watch. It was almost

one o'clock.

The regulars will be drinking by now.

Deadman walked back to his car and drove a short distance before turning right into Bagshot Street. About halfway along the road was the Duke of York pub, built in the usual Victorian style, solid and square, with the names of various drinks etched onto the frosted glass windows. The pub had defied the best efforts not only of the Luftwaffe, that had caused much damage in the area during the Blitz, but also Hitler's much-feared Vengeance weapons, the so-called V1 and V2 rockets. The houses across the street hadn't been so lucky, however, for on 17 December 1944 a V2 rocket had a direct hit on the west side of the street, destroying twenty-five houses and damaging a further fifteen beyond repair. Fifteen people were killed and scores more injured. A row of nondescript council flats now sat where a very attractive terrace once stood.

The few drinkers in the Duke of York glanced around as Deadman entered the pub, much like cowboys were wont to do in a western whenever a stranger walked through the swinging half-doors. A few workmen, enjoying the end of their day's work, were playing at the snooker table, whilst two other men were busy losing money on the fruit machine. A couple were sitting in the corner, chatting away and barely noticing anyone else. A few other men were drinking at various tables, but it was the man sitting at the bar who caught Deadman's attention. Wearing an old tweed jacket and cap, grey trousers and brown leather boots, polished to perfection, the man was finishing off his first pint of the day.

'Let's have another one then, Billy!' He held his pint glass aloft.

'Here, let me get that. I'll have the same please mate.'

The man swung round in his stool and found himself looking at Matt Deadman. He was naturally suspicious of the stranger. After all, it wasn't often that complete strangers bought him a drink.

'Do I know you?'

The drinks arrived. Deadman paid for them and began supping his.

'Cheers.'

The man raised his glass. 'Cheers, and thanks.'

'My pleasure. I wonder if you can help me?'

A wary look came across the man's face.

'I'm looking for a bloke named Stan Tanner. He lives in this street, I think? You wouldn't happen to know him would you?'

The man turned away and sipped his beer. 'It depends who's asking.'

'The name's Deadman, Matt Deadman. Relax, I'm not a cop or anything like that. You wouldn't happen to be Mr Tanner by any chance would you?

The man said nothing but continued to drink.

'Yeah, I guessed as much. Look Stan, I can call you Stan can't I? Look, I'm trying to trace a man who used to live round here some years ago. I understand you knew him, Danny Higgins?'

The man continued drinking and said nothing. Then, placing his drink on the counter, he turned to Deadman. 'We'd better sit down.'

There weren't many people left in The Duke of York pub when Stan Tanner began recalling the old days and his time spent with Damon, Higgins and Bragg.

'Yeah, I remember them well. I mean, it wasn't that long ago that Danny was living in Albany Road. Five years, I think. We were all at school together, although I was never really one of the gang. They called themselves The Three Musketeers. I liked to think of myself as the fourth musketeer, although I never got involved in any of their shenanigans afterwards. We all left school when we were fifteen. I got a job in the drinks factory round the corner, you know, R. Whites. I didn't really see them much after that. Sure, we'd meet each other here or in the Lord Nelson from time to time. East Street market was another place where we always seemed to bump into each other, but that was about it.'

This trip down memory lane was all well and good but Deadman had really come to discover what happened to Jimmy Damon. He ordered another pint of beer for Tanner.

'The lads called me 'Stan the man,' back then. But it was a long time ago.'

Deadman decided to move things along.

'Stan, tell me about Jimmy Damon. Do you know what happened to him?

A look of concern and dread came across Stan's face at the mention of Damon's name. He glanced around the pub.

'Jimmy Damon? Phew. There was a time when you wouldn't be heard mentioning his name in public, not in here.' Stan gulped down some of his beer. 'The last I saw of Jimmy was way back in 1964. He'd been staying with me for a while. The cops were looking for him in connection with the mail train robbery, you know, the Reynolds one. There were those who said he'd done it, that he was one of the gang, Danny and Lenny too. Anyway, he never told me anything and I never asked. It was a dodgy business. I mean, if they'd had found Jimmy at my place I'd have gone down too for hiding him.'

Stan supped his pint again. 'Bollocks to that. I ain't

going down for no one or nothing.'

'So he never spoke about the robbery, never mentioned it?'

'He didn't have to, son. It was written all over his face. I knew. I'd known him since we were nippers playing together. I tell ya, I knew Jimmy had done it. And Lenny and Danny.'

'And yet Danny stayed here, living in the same house. Why didn't the police simply pick him up?'

'Well, the word was he'd done a deal with The Yard, you know, had a word, like. They reckon he gave his share of the loot back. That way, he was free to come and go as he pleased. The cops would leave him alone.'

Deadman sat back and sighed.

'Jeez, he handed it all back? You know how much his share would have been worth in today's money don't you?'

Deadman didn't wait for Stan to answer.

'Nearly two and a half million, that's how much.'

'Gor blimey. That much? So the total haul must have been…'

'Between forty and fifty million.'

Deadman waited for the figure to sink in.

'Bloody hell. I think I would have tried to lie low if I'd had had that much dough, I can tell you.'

'Stan, tell me. When was the last time to saw Jimmy?'

'Well, it's like I told ya. It was in 1964. Lenny came round one day to see Jimmy. The heat was getting too much for them so they decided to make a run for it, you know, leave the country. Jimmy knew a bloke who said he could get them on a ship to Australia. I don't suppose you remember it, but back then they were selling cheap fares to Australia. It was to try to get us to go down under to help all sorts of new building projects.' Stan laughed. 'Ten Pound Poms, they called 'em. Anyway, Jimmy managed to set it all up. It cost them both a few quid, but that's how it was back then. You didn't get anything for nothing.'

'Well, nothing's changed then,' said Deadman, sarcastically.

'And don't forget, neither Jimmy nor Lenny could lay their hands on dodgy passports. They didn't have time. The ship was sailing and they had to be on it. They paid the man and there were no questions asked. You know what I mean? They paid the cash and it was *bon voyage!*'

Deadman sat back in his chair and took a sip of his beer. If Jimmy had gone to Australia there'd be little or no chance of ever finding him. But how come Lenny never got there? He turned up in Spain, so something must have happened along the way. A change of mind, or an argument. Something must have changed Lenny's mind.

'Stan, you know Lenny never made it to Australia. He went to live in Spain.'

Stan finished his beer and wiped his mouth on his sleeve. 'Yeah, of course I know.'

Deadman looked surprised. 'You knew?'

'Yeah, of course I knew. I saw him a couple of times when he used to come back to visit. Course, he had to keep his head down. I mean, the robbery was a long time ago, but you never know who's watching you. Don't forget, the reward was bleedin' massive.'

Deadman was astonished. 'You mean he came here, to this pub? When?'

'Not only to this pub, but to the Beckett and the Lord Nelson. I saw him in there a few times over the last few years. He used to come over and go to the seaside down in Kent. You know, cockles, whelks and all that. You can't beat them. Not like that Spanish shit. Nah, he loved his seafood. I reckon he must have had a dodgy passport by then. I mean, he'd never get into the country otherwise would he?'

Stan's story had the ring of truth to it. Lenny returning during the last few years, trips to the seaside, and cockles and mussels. All it needed was Molly Malone, *alive, alive oh!*

'Tell me about Danny, Stan.'

'I will if you stand me another pint.'

Deadman laughed, got up and went to the bar. A few moments later he was back at the table and Stan was supping his third pint. He put down his glass and shook his head.

'Poor Danny. He died a few years ago.'

'Yeah, in 2008, so I believe,' replied Deadman.

'They said it was an accident but there are those what say he was done in. A road accident or something like that. I was away down me sister's at the time, down in Dymchurch. They say Jimmy had come back and done it when he heard Danny was threatening to sell his story to the papers.'

'Jimmy? Back here? Surely not?' Deadman didn't believe this one. It was too fanciful to be true.

'Well, that's what I heard at least, I can tell you. I never saw Jimmy after he left in 1964. I don't believe he ever came back. Mind you, Danny was on his uppers, skint, you know. I mean, if he'd had wanted to tell his story he could have made a fortune. You know what these papers pay nowadays for these sort of stories.'

Stan gulped down his beer. 'Anyway, why would Jimmy come back? We don't even know if he's still alive. I mean, he'd be seventy-three now, the same age as me. I reckon he's still in Australia one way or the other, you know, either dead or alive, but gawd knows where.'

Deadman finished his own drink.

'Thanks Stan, you've been a great help. Here, have a few more on me.'

And with that, Deadman handed Stan a twenty pound note. He was about to leave the pub when he suddenly stopped in the doorway. He turned and walked back to Stan who was busy stuffing the note into his pocket.

'I know this is gonna sound crazy, but can you remember the name of the ship that Jimmy and Lenny boarded for Australia?'

Stan laughed. 'Oh, I remember that alright. That's easy. It was the *Adele*.'

Deadman was stunned. 'Are you certain? I mean, it was almost fifty years ago. How can you be so sure?'

A huge grin came across Stan's face. 'Did I ever tell you about a girl I once went out with? Ah, she was a smasher, had it all. Looks, clothes, money. Trouble was, she didn't want me. Her name? Adele! That's how I know!'

Deadman laughed. 'Cheers, Stan. You're a diamond.'

9

GIBRALTAR, 1964

There was little mistaking the mighty Rock of Gibraltar when it loomed out of the mist as the *Adele* sailed into its harbour. The rock rose out of the sea, towering above the narrow streets, shops and houses that clung to its base. It was said to be one of the Pillars of Hercules, with the mountains of North Africa, only fifteen miles distant, as the other. Gibraltar was a piece of old England, stuck on Spain's southern coast, and despite the unwanted attention of Franco and his government and the pressure they put on the place the Gibraltarians remained fiercely loyal to Her Majesty. It was fish and chips, Woolworths, English Bobbies on the beat, Watney's Red, and, more important, the good old British pound. The only thing missing was the drab English weather.

It was the middle of March, 1964, when the *Adele* steamed into Gibraltar carrying its cargo of 'Ten Pound Poms.' The ship had endured a rough time whilst crossing the Bay of Biscay, something that was not uncommon at that time of the year, and more than a few of the passengers were looking worse for wear when the ship docked. The *Adele* would remain at Gibraltar for three days in order to take on fresh water and provisions and go through the usual customs formalities when allowing the passengers to go ashore. New passengers would also join the ship. It would then continue on its way across the Mediterranean, through the Suez Canal and out into the Indian Ocean before steaming on to Australia.

'I'm not going back on that fucking ship! Never. I don't know what I was thinking.'

Lenny Bragg was helped from the *Adele* by his old mate, Jimmy Damon. The journey had been worse than Lenny had expected and he'd hated every minute of it, spending half the time with his head in a bucket, or hanging over the side, puking his guts up.

'Come on, Lenny,' said Jimmy, trying to sound sympathetic. 'Even Nelson got seasick.'

'Oh, fuck Nelson. I really couldn't give a shit about him. I knew I shouldn't have come. I can't even take the Woolwich ferry without feeling sick.'

Jimmy laughed. 'Look, come on. There's a long way to go yet. You've got to get with it. I mean, you can't go on like this all the way to Australia.'

The thought of the long journey that lay ahead made Lenny feel even worse.

'I'm telling ya, I'm not going back on that ship. It's fucking torture.'

Jimmy was losing patience with his mate. 'Look, just get a fucking grip will ya? We don't want to draw attention to ourselves.'

Jimmy Damon and Lenny Bragg were on the run, and on the run from both the police and one of the members of the gang that robbed the mail train in August the previous year. Lenny didn't know this, of course, as Jimmy was still keeping his double-cross a secret. He saw no point in letting on, no reason to tell Lenny about him having stitched up John Daly by handing back to the police Daly's share of the loot in exchange for freedom from prosecution. Mind you, this hadn't done any good. By now even Scotland Yard had sussed Jimmy's ruse, that he had used another robber's share of the loot to try and get them off his back. Either way the plan had misfired. The two men were travelling on their own passports. There hadn't been time to organise fake ones. It was unlikely that the authorities in Gibraltar were watching for them but they couldn't take any chances.

By the early afternoon Jimmy and Lenny were holed up in The Clipper Inn, an old pub in Irish Town, one of Gibraltar's darker areas. The beer was cheap, the food good, and it offered Lenny the chance to regain his senses. The two men were already halfway through their third pint of Watney's Red bitter.

'This is more like it, isn't it Lenny?' As always, Jimmy was trying to be optimistic. 'Two more days and we'll be on our way again. We'll be in Australia before you know it. Sunshine, plenty of beer and girls. It'll be great.'

'I don't think there'll be any girls where we're going, Jimmy. I mean, when did you last see a bit of skirt on a building site?'

'See, there you go again, always looking on the negative side of things. Listen, once we're in Australia the cops will give up looking for us. They'll never find us. We can stick around for a while on these building sites, earn some cash and then clear off when the coast's clear. I hear the beaches are great down there. It'll be like one great big fucking holiday.'

Lenny wasn't so enthusiastic. Sure, Australia would take him beyond the reach of the long arm of the law. Even Scotland Yard had its limits, or so he thought. But it was a bloody long way to go. It had been bad enough getting to Gibraltar, what with the storms in the Bay of Biscay and the general rocking and rolling of the ship every day. The prospect of sailing across thousands of miles of open sea filled him with dread.

The two men passed the afternoon and evening in The Clipper Inn, before moving off to find something to eat. The restaurants in Irish Town were basic and cheap, but the food was good. Steak and chips washed down with more beer was just what they needed.

It was late when Jimmy and Lenny tumbled from the restaurant into the dimly lit streets of Irish Town.

Lenny yawned and stretched his arms above his head. 'Oh, fuck it. Let's not go back to the ship. Look, there's a hotel here. They'll have a couple of rooms. We can doss down here for a night or two. Nobody will miss us on the *Adele*. It's not gonna sail for a couple of days yet.'

Jimmy agreed. The Bristol Hotel was a smart three-star hotel, far too smart for the likes of Jimmy and Lenny. But not now, not when they had a pile of cash at their disposal. Although they had deposited most of their share of the robbery in overseas banks they still carried a fair amount on them for occasions like this. The woman in the smart, marble floor reception looked at the two men with disdain. They looked like a pair of drunks after a night on the town, but their money was just as good as the next man's and a few minutes later they were staggering up to the rooms on the first floor.

The next morning Lenny was as right as rain again and ready to do some sightseeing. Gibraltar may well have been tight, cramped and desperately short of space, but it had more than enough interesting places to see and things to do to make it far more than it really was, one of the Royal Navy's most important stations. When Jimmy came down for breakfast he found Lenny flicking through some tourist leaflets while he was tucking into a full English breakfast.

'You know, they reckon there are more cars than people in Gibraltar.'

''Really? said Jimmy, sarcastically, 'I didn't know that.'

'Yeah, really.' Lenny smiled and sat back in his chair. 'I reckon I'll take at look at these caves while I'm here, have a look at those monkeys and all that.'

'Now, I didn't know about the cars but I can tell you

that they're actually apes.'

Jimmy had also been reading some leaflets, in his room before coming down to breakfast.

'Yeah, I'm all for that. I knew a bloke who served here during the war. He said the Rock is riddled with caves and tunnels. Plus we can get a look at Spain from up there. It'll be great.'

On the evening of the second day in Gibraltar Jimmy and Lenny were entrenched once again in The Clipper Inn. By now they were on first name terms with the barman, Harry, who wasn't shy in extolling the virtues of the place, of the weather, the low cost of living and just how much better it was generally than the old country. Sure, the Spaniards made life difficult but it was a small price to pay for being able to enjoy life on the Rock. Lenny listened with great interest. He'd already seen for himself how good life was for the Gibraltarians. The cost of living was indeed much cheaper than in England, not that this was something that was likely to bother him any more, not with his share of the robbery money. Although his share had been significantly reduced as a result of having to shell out for minders, safe houses and other things for which he was fleeced mercilessly by his so-called 'friends' Lenny still had more than enough money to be able to enjoy the good life in Gibraltar, Australia or wherever he chose to lay his head.

'Well, I suppose we'd better be getting back to the ship.' Jimmy sighed as he finished his breakfast at the Bristol Hotel. The *Adele* was due to sail at eleven that morning and he didn't want to miss it. Lenny said nothing but drank his tea. He was strangely silent.

It was just after ten when the two friends strolled back to the docks where the *Adele* sat, idling at the quay, with thin wisps of black smoke drifting from its two funnels. There was the usual hustle and bustle on the quay.

Passengers were getting back on board local suppliers were getting off, whilst an assortment of Royal Navy and merchant navy personnel idled around or busied themselves with final preparations prior to the ship finally getting underway. The two men approached the gangplank when suddenly Lenny stopped.

'I'm not going, Jimmy. I can't go back on the ship.'

Jimmy turned, confused. 'What?'

'I'm staying here in Gibraltar. I'm sorry Jimmy, but I'm not gonna spend the next couple of weeks on that thing, and I don't want to spend the rest of my days in Australia in the middle of nowhere.'

It was not the time or place to be arguing. Jimmy grabbed Lenny's arm and pulled him away. 'You've got to be kidding? It might be fucking sunny here but these people are still British. They're like us. They'll nick you as soon as they find out who you are. Come on, they'll never find us in Australia.'

'I don't care. I've been up all night thinking about it and I've made my mind up. I'm staying put. Sorry Jimmy.'

Jimmy had known Lenny long enough to know that once he'd made up his mind there was no going back. He knew the journey had been a tortuous one for Lenny and the odds were that he would probably end up chucking himself overboard long before they hit Australia. There was no point in Jimmy arguing any longer.

'Well, I think you're making a big fucking mistake but it's your call. I'm going to Australia, with or without you.'

'That's fine by me, Jimmy. You'll go on without me then.'

Jimmy turned and walked up the gangplank. Lenny followed a few moments later. He had to collect his kit. Five minutes later the two were back on the quayside, saying their farewells.

'Are you sure you won't change your mind?' asked Jimmy.

'You know the answer to that. Look, we've had a good run and I intend keeping it going, but not in Australia. You know I couldn't face another trip at sea. It'd do me in.'

Jimmy extended his hand.

'Well, old mate. I suppose this is it then. Keep ya chin up and don't let the bastards find you. We haven't come all this way for you to get nicked in some poxy place like this.'

Lenny shook Jimmy's hand and gave him a hug.

'The same to you. Mind how you go down under, and watch out for the kangaroos!'

Jimmy turned and walked up the gangplank, stopping at the top. He turned, gave a brief wave and called out to Lenny.

'Cheerio mate!'

He turned around and that was it. He was gone. Lenny was left standing on the quayside with his kit as other passengers pushed their way around him as they boarded the ship. He picked up his kit and strolled slowly into town. There were digs to find and maybe even a job. It was the start of a new life, hopefully a long and free one. As he strolled into the streets of Irish Town he heard a ship's horn blasting away in the morning air.

Well, I suppose that's it now. You're on your own now mate.

10

GIBRALTAR, 2013

The Straits of Gibraltar looked no wider than the Thames estuary as the British Airways 737 approached Gibraltar. As Matt Deadman peered out of the window he found it hard to believe that it was actually two different continents that lay on either side of the narrow stretch of water.

Suddenly, a voice crackled over the loudspeaker, informing everyone that the plane would be landing in ten minutes. Deadman sighed. He'd never been to Gibraltar before and he wondered what it was like. A piece of old England stuck on the end of Spain. Still, he hadn't come for a holiday. He was on a mission, or, as his old friend Jack Moscroft had put it, a wild goose chase.

Deadman's visit to South London and his chat with Stan Tanner had been enlightening to say the least. But it had left him with a few unanswered questions. He now knew that both Jimmy Damon and Lenny Bragg had sailed to Australia, apparently using their own passports, under cover of the 'Ten Pound Poms' scheme, as it was popularly known. The problem was that Lenny never arrived. Somehow he'd gone to Spain and had been living there since 1965. Something had happened along the way and Deadman's hunch was that it had happened in Gibraltar.

After returning from his visit to the badlands of South London Deadman had met with Moscroft and had told him Tanner's story, that the two fugitives had set sail for Australia but only one of them had arrived. Moscroft duly pointed out, however, that there was no real evidence that either of them had arrived. Okay, Lenny Bragg had certainly not gone 'Down Under', for not only had Deadman visited his family in Spain, where he had corroborated the story, but he'd been present at his funeral in Herne, Kent. But what of Jimmy Damon? There was no evidence that he had arrived in Australia either, or that he was even still alive. Some more investigations would be needed and Moscroft knew just the place to start.

After a quick delve into the world of the internet Moscroft discovered the *Adele* had been a P&O ship. He assumed it would take just a quick visit to the company's old archive office in London to check the passenger list and to establish whether or not Jimmy and Lenny had actually boarded the ship for Australia. A quick thumbing through the registers was all it took the ever diligent Moscroft to find the men's names, hand written in ink, amongst the passenger manifest. What Moscroft thought was remarkable was that the two men had boarded the ship using their own names. This, of course, owed much to the bribe pounds that they'd handed over to the captain for a 'no questions asked' passage. Moscroft also thought it likely that, with the trial of the robbers in progress and with eight months having passed since the robbery itself, the police were starting to take their eyes off the ball. Anyway, he could at least establish the fact that both men had boarded the ship at Southampton in March 1964. The problem was, however, that when Moscroft checked the registers he found that although the *Adele* was indeed bound for Australia the passenger list only gave the names of those who were travelling as far as the first stop en route. At this point, the captain would have to submit a further list of those passengers who were travelling on the next leg of the journey, and so on, until by the time the *Adele* reached Australia the captain would have filled out about half a dozen lists, depending upon how many stops the ship made.

It must have been a tiresome business for the captain, thought Moscroft. But what intrigued him more than anything was the first port of call en route to Australia. It was Gibraltar.

There was only one thought on Deadman's mind as the plane started its descent towards the runway, and that was that it didn't land in the Mediterranean. The sea was getting mightily close as the plane descended, whilst there was no sign of the runway. Then, suddenly, the edge of the runway appeared a few yards beneath him. There was the usual shudder and screech as the plane hit the ground, followed by a roar as the pilot attempted to bring the plane to a halt. Deadman could feel himself gripping his seat tighter by the second as the end of the runway started to get closer and closer.

Fuck this. Hurry up with those bloody brakes!

Deadman needn't have worried, however, for the plane was brought steadily to a halt, albeit with just a few yards to spare. He relaxed.

The runway at Gibraltar was one of the strangest Deadman had ever seen, completely crossing the isthmus which connected Spain with Gibraltar from one end to the other. It was strange watching British policemen, in their uniforms, holding up the traffic in order to allow the plane to land. Welcome to Gibraltar.

Deadman walked into the smart new terminal, flashed his passport and collected his bag from the carousel. He didn't anticipate staying too long but thought he'd come prepared anyway. The last time he'd taken just a bag, for a trip to Minsk, he'd ended up travelling halfway across Europe, ending up on the Black Sea coast. He hailed a taxi and ten minutes later was standing outside the Hotel Caleta, wondering whether Moscroft had made a mistake for a change. It wasn't often that Moscroft booked the wrong hotel but finding himself on the eastern side of the Rock, cut off from the town itself, began to make Deadman think he'd got it wrong for once. However, when he stepped out onto the balcony of his room he could see why Moscroft had booked the hotel. Away to the right he could see the glint of cars moving about. These were actually driving along the roads in Ceuta, in North Africa. Away to the left Deadman looked down a good length of the Costa del Sol. Straight in front of him the sea sparkled in the midday sun, whilst numerous ships and tankers waited patiently to be allowed into port to refuel or unload their cargoes. It was all quite spectacular. True, Deadman hadn't come for a holiday, but he figured he may as well make the most of it whilst he was there. If the records had been online he wouldn't have had to come to Gibraltar anyway. Still, here he was, gazing out to sea and ready to go to work.

Having unpacked Deadman took a light lunch in Nuno's restaurant in the hotel before calling for a taxi to take him into town. Ten minutes later he was standing in Irish Town, in front of the old Lloyds Shipping office in Irish Town Street. An imposing four-storey building, decorated in yellow tiles and with shutters on the windows on the top floors, it bore all the hallmarks of officialdom, with its large sturdy ground floor windows and double oak door. Deadman thought it looked more like a bank.

A tanned and very attractive looking girl looked up from her desk. Deadman reckoned she was Spanish, which was confirmed the minute she began to speak.

'Good afternoon, sir. Can I help you?'

Deadman leaned over the desk and explained that he was looking for passenger lists for ships arriving in Gibraltar in March 1964. That was about as much of the story he was prepared to tell her. The girl frowned. A series of questions followed but Deadman was not prepared to give anything away. He gave the girl some bullshit about it being a matter of urgency and that he was working for the state. The girl gave way.

'1964? Well, I'm pretty sure we still have those particular ledgers. We'd better have a look hadn't we now.'

She got up from behind the desk and took some keys from it. Deadman looked around. There didn't seem to be anyone else working in the office. The girl sighed.

'Yes, they're all at lunch, most likely in the pub.'

She walked to the door and turned the sign from 'Open' to 'Closed.'

'Better to be safe than sorry. If my colleagues decide to come back from the pub they can ring the bell. It'll serve them right. Okay, let's go.'

Deadman couldn't really believe his luck. The girl's attitude made a refreshing change. A visit to an archive or record office usually involved a series of letters and applications prior to the visit and security checks, supervision or a reader's ticket. This was completely different, although Deadman suspected it had more to do with the fact that the girl was pissed off at being left on her own to man the office and deal with odd strange requests like this. She led him up some stairs to the first floor. A door on the right was marked 'Private.'

'If we've got what you're looking for you'll find it in here. Otherwise, I'm afraid you will have had a wasted journey.'

The girl smiled as she unlocked the door and swung herself into the room. She was polite but efficient, and wasn't the sort of girl who would take any nonsense from anyone. She waved her hands at some ledgers.

'Right. Here we are then. They're all yours. The old dusty ones date back to the First World War. 1964 will be at this end. Can I leave you on your own for a while? Just call me if you need anything.'

And with that she quickly disappeared out of the room and down the stairs, leaving Deadman alone in the quiet of a records office in Gibraltar.

Well, this makes a change. Right here we go then.

The ledgers were huge, were bound in leather and were very heavy, each volume representing a vast number of ships that docked in Gibraltar each month. Deadman opened the volume for March 1964 and began to go through its large, blue-lined pages. It didn't take long before he found what he was looking for. There was an entry for 12 March 1964. The *Adele,* bound for Adelaide, Australia, had docked in Gibraltar for three days to take on food and water and half a dozen passengers. Scores of names were neatly written in brown ink. He ran his finger down the list until he found what he was looking for, DAMON, JIMMY.

So, he went on to Australia after all. Jimmy didn't stay in Gibraltar.

There was no entry for Lenny Bragg, not that Deadman expected to see one. After all, Deadman had already been to Spain to speak to his widow and daughter, whilst Stan Tanner's story only served to confirm that Lenny had ended up in Spain. Lenny had stayed in Gibraltar, whilst Jimmy had gone onto Australia. Deadman carefully closed the huge ledger and placed it back on the shelf. He closed the door behind him, went downstairs and after thanking the girl, smiled and left.

Deadman strolled along Maine Street, deep in thought. The street teemed with tourists who had been unloaded from one of the huge cruise ships that regularly docked in Gibraltar. The street offered tax free purchases, although most of them seemed to be jewellers, and Deadman wasn't sure just how many Rolex watches a man needed, but they seemed to be selling them everywhere. It was now the middle of the afternoon and he sat at a table outside one of the many bars and cafes and ordered a pot of tea. He needed to think.

Lenny had stayed in Gibraltar for some reason or another, not that it was important. After all, he showed up in Spain the following year and was dead now anyway. He must have remained in Gibraltar for a period of time before crossing the border into Spain. He'd met Carmen, his future wife, and they'd taken it from there. End of story. He was gone now. So was Danny Higgins, who had died in 2008. This left just Jimmy Damon. What had happened to him? Was he still alive?

Deadman sipped his tea and started to think. If Jimmy had gone to Australia there was no way he'd ever be found, at least Deadman didn't think so. With so many Brits emigrating in the 1960s and with the country being so vast Damon could easily have slipped away into the country to enjoy a quiet life for the rest of his days. Then, of course, there was the possibility, unlikely as it was however, that Jimmy had left the *Adele* at Cairo or Aden, two ports where the ship docked en route to Adelaide. The trail had gone cold. There was no point in hanging around Gibraltar any longer. It was time to go home.

11

LONDON 2013

'Well, I did warn you it would be a wild goose chase, didn't I?'

Julian Moscroft took a sip of Brandy from the glass that Matt Deadman had just handed him. The two had enjoyed a good dinner at Deadman's flat in Paddington, during which the two had discussed the result of the visit to Gibraltar.

'Yeah, I know, but it wasn't entirely wasted. On the contrary, we've established for certain now that whilst Damon left Gibraltar Bragg didn't, but chose to stay behind. At some point he crossed the border into Spain. The rest is history.'

'Agreed,' said Moscroft, 'but it was a long way to go just to find that out.'

'I don't agree,' countered Deadman. 'The records are not online and I certainly wasn't going to mess around phoning them and asking them to go through the ledgers for me. I've done that before and it proved quicker to go myself. No, it was worth the trip.'

He took a sip from his own glass.

'And besides, Gibraltar's an interesting place.'

'Well, said Moscroft, frowning, 'I hope you're not planning to do a day trip to Australia, just to check to whether or not Damon made it to Adelaide.'

'No, don't worry about that. I have some contacts Down Under. One of them owes me a favour. He'll sort it.'

He took another sip of brandy.

'And in any case, I'm almost certain Damon continued on to Australia. I mean, do you really think he got off at Cairo or Aden? No, he went alright. All that money, the status, all that sort of stuff? It'd be worth nothing in those shitholes.'

'Oh, I don't know,' said Moscroft, raising his eyebrows, 'with the sort of money Damon had he probably could have bought Cairo and set himself up as the new pharaoh in town! A harem, dancing girls every night…'

'Yeah, and a fucking great tomb stuck out in the middle of the desert!'

Deadman laughed and shook his head.

'No, Damon went to Adelaide alright. Trust me. I'll give it an hour or two then I'll phone my man. I don't think he'll appreciate a call this early. Right now I reckon it'll be about eight in the morning out there. I'll make the call at ten, our time.'

Given the circumstances of the case which Deadman was investigating, it was a curious irony that the father of his contact in Australia was himself a 'Ten Pound Pom.' Tired of post-war austerity in England and tempted by the prospect of a new life in Australia Archie Smith had left his home in Dartford, Kent, in 1950. Five years later he married an Australian girl, Kay, and a further five years after that they had a son, Richard. Having joined the Australian army, Richard became part of the Multinational Force attempting to keep the peace in the Middle East and it was during this mission that he came into contact with the small British contingent, one of whom just happened to be Lance Corporal Matthew Deadman, of the Corps of Royal Military Police. The two became good friends during their time in Sinai and remained in contact on and off in the years that followed. Whereas Deadman went into the private investigation business when he left the army, Richard Smith joined the Australian Federal Police and now enjoyed the rank of Commander.

It was just after ten o'clock at night when Deadman called his old pal in Australia. Smith was pleased to hear from his old mate and the usual pleasantries followed before the two men got down to business. Deadman explained what he was after. It was a fairly straightforward request to discover whether or not a certain Jimmy Damon arrived in Adelaide on the *SS Adele,* which had sailed from Southampton in March 1964. Deadman reckoned it would have been about April by the time the *Adele* reached Adelaide.

'No problem, mate,' was Smith's reply.

'Consider it done. I'll have someone check the records and I'll email you this evening.'

Deadman turned to Moscroft.

'Now all we have to do is wait.'

The email from Australia was waiting for Deadman when he booted up his computer the next morning. It confirmed what he suspected. Jimmy Damon arrived in Adelaide on 5 April 1964. The bad news was that Smith had also checked other records including deaths, marriages, the electoral register and social security records, but the name Jimmy Damon had failed to turn up. It was a mystery. Smith wasn't going to spend much time on the case but said he'd let Deadman know if anything turned up. Otherwise, Damon appeared to have disappeared once he arrived in Australia, the only assumption being that he had assumed a new identity.

Moscroft had stayed the night and was tucking into a bowl of porridge. He looked up between mouthfuls. 'Well, it's not as if he couldn't have afforded to buy a new identity, is it? I mean, the scheme must have been a perfect way for all sorts of scallywags and scoundrels to escape the long arm of the law here in England.'

Deadman agreed. 'Yeah, but it certainly makes the job much harder. We now have no idea what his name is, where he is or whether he's even dead or alive. There's not much to go on.'

Moscroft finished his porridge and put down his spoon. 'If I were you I'd go back and speak to that old chap in South London again. Let's face it, he's the only real link here with Damon isn't he?'

'Well,' replied Deadman, 'I suppose there's always the robbers themselves. I mean, how many of them are still alive?'

'Four, I think,' said Moscroft, 'although you could hardly call Biggs alive. Have you seen the state of him? He looks about a hundred and twenty years old now.'

'Which leaves Goody, Welch and Wisbey as the only three effectively still with us.'

'And they're unlikely to tell you anything are they?' said Moscroft, sipping some tea. 'I mean, they've remained silent now for fifty years. They're hardly likely to start singing now.'

'You're right,' said Deadman with a sigh. 'I suppose there's nothing for it. I'd better get myself back down the Old Kent Road.'

He laughed and started singing.

'Chim chimenee, chim chimenee…'

The Duke of York was half full or half empty when Deadman rolled up just after lunchtime. There was no sign of Stan Tanner. He ordered himself a pint of beer. This was not the sort of place to be ordering non-alcoholic beer or fancy drinks like tonic water or gin and tonic. The barman, a man in his mid-twenties and wearing a Millwall football shirt, was washing some of the glasses and tidying up the bar in between serving the customers.

''ere mate,' said Deadman, affecting a thicker than usual Cockney accent, 'has Stan been in today, you know, Stan Tanner?'

The barman was stacking some pint glasses on the shelf above the bar.

'Haven't you heard, mate? Stan got killed the other day. Yeah, knocked down by a car.'

Deadman was stunned.

'Knocked down?'

'Well, they say he was knocked down but one bloke saw it and said it was a hit-and-run job, reckoned the car went up the pavement and hit him. Why, was he a friend of yours?'

Deadman hesitated.

'Er, no, actually, well, yeah, in a sort of way. Dead? Phew, that's a turn up.'

The barman continued stacking the glasses.

'Yeah, a bit of shock round here. I mean, Stan's lived here all his life. Gets through the blitz and all that and gets run down by a bleedin' car. Poor bastard. His funeral's two weeks from today. They have to do a post mortem and all that. Can I get you anything else?'

Deadman finished his drink and made a note of the funeral on his phone.

'No thanks mate. Cheers. Thanks.'

Deadman stepped into the street, stunned by what he just heard. Stan Tanner, dead. There were a couple of bunches of withered flowers tided to a lamppost in Bagshot Street.

I guess that's where the old fellow got hit.

Call it intuition but Deadman began to hear alarm bells. The word 'dead' seemed to be cropping up a bit too often now, and usually where Jimmy Damon was involved. First Danny Higgins and now Stan Tanner. Was there a connection?

Five minutes later Deadman found himself ringing the doorbell to number 91 Albany Road, Danny Higgins's old house. The door opened.

'Oh, hello there. Didn't we speak last week?'

It was the same man who'd been scraping away at his weeds the week before.

'Yeah, sorry to trouble you again. The guy who lived here before you, Danny Higgins. The old chap in Bagshot Street...'

'Oh yes. What a shock that was. Poor man. Walking home after a night in the pub and then...bang.' The man smacked his fist into his other hand.

'Yeah,' replied Deadman. 'Well, that's what I've come about. Stan told me Danny had died as a result of a road accident.'

The man laughed. 'That's if you believe what they say. Listen, I spoke to the solicitors handling the sale of this house. Higgins had no next of kin, no relations or anything. They were handling the sale. According to the solicitors the police didn't think it was an accident.'

The man looked left and right along the road.

'They reckon it was a hit or something like that. You know, the sort of thing you see in films.'

'What gave them that idea?' asked Deadman.

'Well, for a start it was in broad daylight, with no other traffic around. Then there was the witness.'

'The witness?'

'Yes. This Eastern European fellow saw it. I think he was from Latvia, Lithuania or somewhere like that.

Anywhere, he made a statement claiming the car had been parked but suddenly pulled away and deliberately seemed to drive at Higgins. The strange thing was, though, that the man disappeared before the inquest could be held. Or maybe it's not so strange. You know the way these people move about. I'm surprised he gave the statement to the police in the first place.'

Or simply kidnapped.

'So what happened?'

'Well, nothing happened. They passed it off as a possible hit-and-run by a person or persons unknown. That was it. Without the witness the police had nothing to go on. That's about all the solicitors knew.'

It was also more than Deadman knew, but a picture was now beginning to form. First Higgins and now Tanner. Something wasn't right. Deadman shook the man's hand and thanked him for his trouble and for the information.

'Ah, Mr Deadman. Please come in a take a seat please.'

Deadman sat down and adjusted his cufflinks.

Cornelius Trubshaw sat back in his comfortable leather chair and clasped his hands. 'So, how are things going?'

Deadman was back in the office of Trubshaw and Goat, in London's Temple. It had been a few weeks since their first meeting and Deadman was here to report on his progress so far. And ask for a little help.

Trubshaw was delighted to hear the progress Deadman had made, that he'd established the identity of the three Great Train Robbers who had got away with it, Damon, Higgins and Bragg. He took out a pen and drew a line through these latter two names.

'Well, that's two rogues we won't be chasing any more.

But what about this fellow Damon? Any luck.'

Deadman squirmed a bit. 'Er, no, not really. Well, what I mean is, I tracked him as far as Australia and it appears that he arrived there in April 1964 and then completely disappeared. I have no idea if he's still living there or if he's even alive.'

Trubshaw stroked his chin. 'Hm. So it's a case of two down, one to go.'

'Yes, if you put it like that,' replied Deadman. 'The thing is, I think something odd has been going on in relation to these three men.'

Deadman went on to tell Trubshaw about the very similar deaths of Higgins and Tanner. Trubshaw agreed that it was indeed strange but could merely have been a coincidence. Deadman disagreed. He'd seen far too many of these sort of things before. It was a possibility but it was unlikely.

'So you suspect foul play?' asked Trubshaw.

'Yes, which is why I thought you might be able to help. I mean, did Grappler ever give you any other papers, any documents or anything else relating to this case?'

Trubshaw said he'd received nothing, other than what Deadman had already been given. But then he turned and pulled a dusty old file from a shelf. He took it down and handed it to Deadman.

'I'm not sure if this will help. It contains details of all the known robbers that took part in the Great Train Robbery.'

Deadman opened it and gave the documents a cursory glance. Trubshaw allowed him a few moments to look at them before speaking.

'Of the known twelve robbers, four, Welch, Biggs, Goody and Wisbey, are the only ones alive today. Reynolds, Cordery, Daly, Hussey, James and White all died natural deaths.'

He then leant forward in his chair.

'Wilson, Edwards and Field all died in, shall we say, unusual circumstance.'

Deadman looked up suddenly and closed the file.

'What do you mean, unusual? And if my maths serves me right, you've named thirteen robbers. I thought there were only twelve?'

'Yes, but Brian Field is said to have been the man behind it all. Reynolds simply put the gang together.'

'Well,' said Deadman, 'as I said to Moscroft, my associate, the survivor is hardly likely to say anything now. And why would they? It's been over fifty years, and if they'd not piped up before they're hardly likely to do so now.'

'In which case all I can suggest is that you examine the file a little closer to see if there's any connection between the deaths of Field, Edwards and Wilson, and your two men, Higgins and Tanner.'

Deadman sat back and sighed. He knew where this one was going. He was going to have to call in yet another favour, this time from one of his mates at Scotland Yard. He got to his feet and shook hands with Trubshaw.

'Well, there's no time to waste then. I'd better get cracking. I need to pay a visit to The Yard.'

There wasn't much time left in the day when Deadman arrived at New Scotland Yard to be greeted by an old mate, Mervin Rabble. The two went back quite a long way, when both were serving as MPs in the army.

'What are you now Merve? You must be Chief Inspector or something,' asked Deadman.

'Chief Inspector it is, and not before time either. Now,

what can I do for you?'

Deadman wasn't about to let slip the story about Higgins, Bragg and Damon, not just yet anyway. Grappler had kept things pretty close to his chest and Deadman didn't want to stir things up again until he had sufficient proof to be able to go after the last remaining fugitive, Damon, assuming he was still alive. Instead, Deadman came out with some excuse about wanting to see the Yard's reports on the deaths of Field, Wilson and Edwards.

'Well, for a start,' said Rabble, 'I don't think we'll have much on Wilson. If I remember rightly, he was shot dead in Spain, so it's unlikely we'll have anything on that particular case. We ought to be okay with the other two however.'

Rabble led Deadman to a room on the fifth floor of the Met's home in St James's. After explaining how the system worked he began sifting through some steel cabinets, pulling out the odd file and placing them back again. This went on for a few minutes until an evidently bored Deadman finally piped up.

'Is everything okay, Merve?'

'Well, actually, now that you ask, it isn't. The files dealing with Edwards and Field have both been filtered out and there's a record sheet instead, which says they've been sent to the National Archives to be collated with the existing files on The Great Train Robbery.'

Rabble slammed the steel draw shut and turned to Deadman.

'I'm afraid someone has moved the file to Kew. They've been designated Closed Files. You won't be able to get access now until 2045 when they'll be open to public scrutiny. Sorry.'

Deadman couldn't believe it. Another secret file.

Bollocks.

A sense of massive irritation came over him, not so

much because he'd been thwarted by red tape and officialdom, but by the fact that he was going to have to ask his ex-wife, Angie, for yet another favour. The last one had been pushing it somewhat. He was now going to have to ask her to repeat the exercise.

Mervin Rabble showed Deadman to the door of New Scotland Yard. Deadman shook his old mate's hand and thanked him for his trouble. He stepped in to the street, pulled out his mobile phone and dialled a number.

'Angie? Hi, it's me. Listen, I need another favour…'

For once, Angie Deadman seemed interested in what Matt Deadman was up to. In the past she'd shown little interest in her ex-husband's work. Indeed, it had been one of the reasons the two had drifted apart, not that he had taken much interest in Angie's career. But now, having been told the reason why the files had been 'borrowed' from the National Archives, she seemed more than a little interested in things.

Angie turned up at Deadman's flat in Paddington early the following evening. She took off her coat and made herself a coffee.

'Oh, make yourself at home,' said Deadman sarcastically.

'Listen, if it wasn't for me you'd be stuck up that tree out there wouldn't you?'

She gestured towards one of the trees in the communal garden to the rear of the block of flats. Deadman rolled his eyes but conceded the point.

'Right then. So belt up.' Angie stirred her drink and sat down.

Deadman was going through the sheath of documents in the file. Angie sat back, crossed her legs and smiled.

'Well Sherlock, have you got it yet?'

Deadman looked up. Angie was already grinning, as though she'd already discovered the secret Deadman was looking for. 'You mean you've already looked at them?'

'Yep, and I think I've found what you're after.'

Angie sat back with a look of self satisfaction on her face. Deadman closed the file.

'Okay then. What have you found?'

'Look,' said Angie. 'You're trying to find a possible connection between the deaths of Field, Edwards and Wilson. Yes? Add to these Higgins and Tanner.'

Deadman knew he'd been outwitted.

'You always were one step ahead of me.'

'Right then.' Angie put her coffee down and took the file. 'There's nothing on Tanner, of course, it's too recent. And in any case, he's an innocent party, or at least I don't think he's got any connection with the others other than knowing too much.'

'What do you mean, knowing too much?'

'I took a look through these files this afternoon when I was alone in the office. I think I may have found the common denominator. According to the police reports in this file they believe Field, Edwards and Wilson had all approached a national newspaper with a view to revealing the identities of the men who got away. This is based on conversations with one of the top crime reporters at the time. From what you've told me Higgins may have been about to do the same. Let's face it, all of them were on their uppers and in need of cash. Tanner had no intention of going to the press but it's obvious that whoever is behind all of this thought poor old Stan knew too much and had him silenced.'

'But Higgins was one of the men who got away.

That scuppers that theory,' said Deadman.

'Except that he gave his share of the robbery back, didn't he? At least that's what you told me.'

Deadman went on. 'But how would this 'Mr Big' character know that these blokes intended going to the press? I mean, he'd have to be working for one of the papers or know someone who did, or something like that. No, it doesn't make sense. Why on earth would a reporter want these men silenced?'

'Who said anything about it being a reporter?' replied Angie. 'I mean, it could be an editor or owner. And as for knowing about the stories, let's face it, Fleet Street wasn't exactly tight-lipped back then was it? Reporters only had to get a sniff of a story and it would spread quicker than butter on a hot crumpet.'

Deadman sat there thinking for a few moments before dismissing the idea.

'Nah, it doesn't make sense. A newspaper bloke? Okay, he…

'or she..' interjected Angie,

'Get real Angie. *He* may have known that the robbers had approached the papers but what possible motive could he have had for killing all three of them?'

'Or four, if you include Higgins,' replied Angie.

'Okay, four, then?'

'Well,' said Angie, 'that's all I've got, and, to be honest, I think you'll find it's the only connection between the four murders. Stan Tanner never intended going to the press but someone got wind of the fact that you'd been talking to him. They must have known that sooner or later Tanner was going to say too much.'

'But this is like the shit you get at the pictures. You'll be telling me the Mafia are involved next.'

'Oh come on, Matt, for God's sake. How long have

you've been doing this bloody job? These things happen, don't they?'

Deadman fell silent again. 'So that's our theory, eh? Four robbers are killed by person or persons unknown because they were about to reveal the identities of the two robbers that got away.'

'In a nutshell,' replied Angie, smiling. She got up and placed her mug on the worktop in the kitchen. 'Now, are you going to cook dinner or shall I?'

A taxi arrived three hours later to take Angie home. It had been an enjoyable evening but she had to be back at work early the next morning, and she had to get to Kew first in order to return the file to its proper place. She gave Deadman a peck on the cheek and said goodnight. Deadman watched as she disappeared down the stairs. He closed the door and returned to his sitting room to pour another brandy. The file had at least moved the case on a little. If Angie's theory was correct the killings of Edwards, Field, Wilson and Higgins, were indeed connected, although the notion that someone connected with the press was behind it was only a theory, and a rather tenuous one at that. Still, it was a step forward. He decided to call it a night. It had been an enjoyable evening and a profitable one too. Tomorrow was another day, though, and he would have to give some thought as to how he would go about investigating the link with Fleet Street.

Deadman was up bright and early the next morning and was munching away on some toast when his phone rang.

'Shit! I'd forgotten all about that. Okay, I'll bring it

in this morning.'

He'd been so wrapped up in the case that he'd forgotten that his Alfa Romeo GTV6 was due for its annual check up and service that morning. It was fortunate that one of London's leading Alfa specialists, Ramponi's, was situated just around the corner. He'd finish his breakfast and get it round there in no time before heading into the City.

Fifteen minutes later Deadman was skipping down the four flights of stairs to the ground floor, twirling his car keys in his hand. Old Bill, who lived on his own in the ground floor flat, was just picking up the morning paper when Deadman walked by with a brisk 'morning Bill.' He stepped out into the private drive in front of the terrace of elegant early Victorian houses and looked around. The garden separating the drive from the main road had just been tidied up and the bushes trimmed. *Nice.* It was going to be a good day. Deadman hadn't parked his Alfa in its garage at the rear of the block of flats but had left it outside the front door. The scramble for the limited parking spaces was always a mad one but Deadman had been lucky. His silver Alfa sat there, the morning dew glistening on the bodywork.

Old Bill was back in his kitchen, and was just taking a sip of tea when his flat was rocked by a tremendous explosion. One of the doors flew open, the windows shook and a picture fell from the wall, crashing on the floor. For a moment his mind flitted back to the Blitz of 1940. Outside in the street bystanders ran to try and help the man in the burning Alfa Romeo that was completely engulfed in flames. Debris lay everywhere, the tidy gardens being littered with pieces of metal and burning upholstery. Taxi, car and van drivers ran from their vehicles to try and help but it was useless. The heat was so intense none of them stood a chance of getting anywhere near the car, nor did the man inside it have any chance of survival.

12

LONDON, HEATHROW AIRPORT, 2013

There was a gentle crush of reporters on the cold, grey morning at Heathrow Airport. Photographers jostled with each other, while police officers kept a good humoured watch on proceedings. Curious onlookers gathered to see what the fuss was all about. Was it a pop star or rich footballer? Maybe it was a film star. Suddenly there was a blaze of flash bulbs. It was rapid fire from the ranks of photographers as a group of passengers emerged from behind the sliding doors leading from the customs area. The onlookers craned their necks to see who it was but were left to shrug their shoulders in disappointment. There was no celebrity, no sports or film star, just a couple of men in suits with a small entourage tagging along behind. There were a few shouts from the reporters. Some microphones were thrust into the face of the tall man wearing dark glasses but these were quickly swatted away by a couple of burly minders, who also wore black shades. The tall man kept his head down and made quickly for the exit, pursued eagerly by the pack of reporters. The man and his entourage hurried through the glass doors and were hustled into the backs of two waiting black limousines. Five minutes after they had emerged into the arrivals area they were gone, speeding off down the M4 towards Central London.

'So, how was Bermuda, sir? A good deal warmer than England I imagine?'

'Yes, Johnson, it was. I should have bloody stayed there, coming back to all this. The country's in a mess, the weather's bloody lousy and I still can't get a minute's peace. And I've only been away a week. I should have stayed in

Bermuda. So what have we got?

'Not a lot really, sir. You've got a press conference lined up this afternoon to announce the purchase of Channel 6 TV, but apart from that it's the usual administrative stuff and a briefing from the heads of departments on how things are progressing across the board generally.'

Sitting in a navy blue, three-piece suit, light blue Oxford shirt and dark blue tie, Neil Johnson had the usual look of an efficient personal secretary about him as he took some copies of the morning's newspapers from his black leather attaché case.

'There's not a lot else at present. Here are this morning's newspapers.'

Johnson handed them to his boss who took out a pair of wiry reading glasses from inside his black woollen overcoat.

'There's nothing of any great importance really. The usual silly stories, scaremongering about immigration, overpaid MPs, the usual stuff. Oh, this story's been getting a great deal of coverage in the press and on television.'

He pointed to a story on the front pages of *The Daily Telegraph*. There'd been an explosion the previous morning in Paddington.

'It appears a bomb exploded beneath a car. The vehicle burst into flames and was totally destroyed. The poor chap inside didn't stand a chance.'

'Burned you say?'

'Done to a crisp, sir.'

Johnson's boss gave a wry smile, but said nothing.

'The police haven't got much to go on. They think it may be the work of terrorists. The dead man…' Johnson allowed himself a discreet laugh. 'The dead man's name was Deadman.'

Johnson's boss took off his glasses and rested the

newspaper in his lap.

'Deadman, you say? Is that some sort of joke?' He laughed.

'Well, at least that's what the papers are reporting. They think the explosion may have been connected to the man's line of work.'

'And what was that?'

'Oh, he was a private investigator. He had links with Bahrain and the Middle East. They think this may have something to do with it, although they can't be sure.'

Johnson's boss said nothing but stared out of the window at the gloomy West London rooftops. At least the sun was out now. The limousine glided easily over the Chiswick flyover and was soon embroiled in Central London's traffic.

There were more reporters and a couple of TV crews waiting when the limousine pulled up outside Dugdale Media's shiny head office in Canary Wharf. Johnson emerged from the car and immediately found himself confronted with a barrage of cameras and microphones. He tip-toed and glanced over the heads of the reporters and gave a brief wave towards the front entrance of the building. Three men in black suits, dark glasses and wearing ear-pieces immediately emerged and made straight for the limousine, clearing a path for Johnson's boss who stepped into the sunlight before making quickly to the entrance without stopping to answer any of the reporters' questions. Neil Johnson walked backwards, keeping them at arms' length. He stopped when he arrived at the revolving doors leading into the building. He held up his hands.

'Lord Dugdale will be making a statement at the news conference this afternoon. It'll begin at two o'clock. Now, if you don't mind, ladies and gentlemen…'

And with that, he turned and disappeared into the

building leaving a posse of disgruntled reporters behind him.

Lord John Dugdale was one of the most powerful media moguls in Britain. He was now in his seventy-fourth year but his appetite for gobbling up newspapers and television channels was as great now as it had been when he bought his first newspaper, *The Bungendore Bugle,* a small provincial newspaper in the Australian Capital Territory, back in 1974. *The Canberra Chronicle,* a much larger newspaper followed a couple of years afterwards. Dugdale turned round the fortunes of these ailing newspapers and soon established himself as one of Australia's leading businessmen. One of Australia's leading news networks then fell beneath his spell and by the end of the 1978 Dugdale controlled almost thirty per cent of Australia's media outlets. It was an astonishing rise to power.

When Dugdale arrived in England in 1979 he was feted as a captain of industry, but his eyes were already fixed upon his next prey, *The Daily Chronicle,* one of Britain's most popular daily newspapers. By the end of the century Dugdale controlled a huge slice, not only of Britain's media but North America's also. His achievements had not gone unnoticed by successive British governments who were only too quick to cultivate his friendship and, more important, his influence. Indeed, it was said that one particularly scathing headline in *The Daily Chronicle,* had been instrumental in swaying a dithering British public on the eve of the 2001 General Election which saw the Labour Party, under Anthony Bland, gain power after years in the wilderness. Dugdale's reward for his influence, and for being a major party donor, was a peerage, awarded to him in 2004, the year after the dossier emerged.

Rumours were rife in the City when Dugdale returned from Bermuda following his short holiday in the spring of 2013. Shares in Channel 6 TV had already begun to rise steadily when rumours of a takeover by Dugdale began to circulate. Not for nothing had dealers in the City given him the nickname, 'Mr Midas.' These same dealers listened eagerly to the press conference that Lord Dugdale duly gave that afternoon, announcing his takeover of Channel 6 TV. It was a major coup for his company. But whilst the dealers in the City, and indeed DDM's own shareholders, watched the conference, there were those amongst the media watchdogs who watched with a sense of growing apprehension as Dugdale's grip on the British media appeared to tighten even further. Nevertheless, there was nothing now to stop the Dugdale steamroller. Channel 6 TV was now part of DDM.

Not everybody was interested in news of Dugdale's newest acquisition. Chief Inspector Mervin Rabble pushed his way through the double doors leading to one of the private wards in St Mary's Hospital in Praed Street, Paddington. Two constables were sitting dozing outside one of the rooms. When they saw Rabble suddenly burst through the doors they got to their feet, hastily straightening their uniforms.

'Alright, stand down. It's not a bloody inspection.'

He flashed his badge and opened the door to the room which the two officers had been guarding.

'Well, you look a right state.'

He went into the room and closed the door behind him.

'Well, I reckon you'd look like this if a fucking bomb went off under your fucking car!'

Rabble laughed. 'It's good to see you haven't lost your sense of humour.' He sat down and helped himself to a grape from a bunch that sat beside the bed. 'So, are you going to tell me what happened?'

'I've got no idea, really.' Matt Deadman sat up in his bed and groaned as he moved. 'My car was due in for servicing that morning and I'd forgotten all about it. Anyway, when I stepped outside to get in the car Steve Smith was standing there. He's the guy who services my car. He works for Ramponi's. They're only round the corner and he thought it'd save time if he came and picked the car up. I chucked him the keys and walked away. There was this fucking great bang and everything went pink. Next thing I know I'm in this hospital bed being looked after by one of the nurses, and a very pretty one too, I tell ya, I thought I'd died and gone to heaven.'

Rabble helped himself to another grape. 'Well, you very nearly did, from what I hear. The poor bloke in the car didn't stand a chance. Burned to death in an instant, that's if the explosion didn't kill him in the first place. Anyway, there's good news.'

'Good news?' asked Deadman, 'what, like I'm alive.'

'No, nothing like that. The papers seem to think it was you that got fried. It means…'

'…it means,' said Deadman, interrupting, 'that whoever did this thinks I'm dead.'

'Exactly, which means we, or rather you, can go underground and do your stuff without being rumbled. They think you're dead. You're back in the shadows again. It's worked out quite well, don't you think?'

Deadman scoffed. 'Not if your name was Steve Smith.'

'Well, there's always the unexpected.'

'Oh, shit!' Deadman suddenly stirred in his bed.

'Whoever did this isn't the only one to think I'm dead. I'd better phone Angie before she has a fit, Moscroft too. Neither of them knows I'm here. Bollocks.'

Mervin Rabble laughed. 'Look, Matt, I'll leave you to it. I'll be back later today to make sure you're still in the land of the living. See ya later.'

And with that, he grabbed the last of the grapes which he'd been picking and disappeared through the door.

Two days later a taxi arrived at St Mary's hospital to take Deadman home. He was still a bit bruised and feeling a little worse for wear but there was no point in being waited on hand and foot any longer. He needed to get back out into the field, to start trying to find out what the hell was going on. What was essentially a historical missing person's case seemed to be spiralling out of control into something much more sinister.

It took the taxi only five minutes to reach Deadman's flat in Gloucester Gardens. It still cost him a fiver, however, even for the relatively short journey. He decided it would be safer to get the driver to drop him off in Gloucester Terrace, so he could use the back entrance to the building. He stepped out onto the street and walked up to the back door which led from the communal garden. There was a sudden shout from behind him. Deadman looked over his shoulder and saw the Filipino gardener, Joe, standing with a rake in his hand, looking as though he'd just seen a ghost.

'Jesus save us! Mr Deadman! I thought you dead.'

Deadman looked anxiously around and placed his finger over his lip, beckoning Joe to come over. He pushed him hurriedly inside the building.

'Joe, for Christ's sake, keep it down.'

The gardener was still in a state of some shock and was trying unsuccessfully to catch his breath.

'Please, Mr Deadman. What happened?'

'Look, Joe, the papers say I'm dead right? Well, let's just keep it that way for a while. Okay?'

'Sure thing, Mr Deadman. You dead. Okay'

'Yeah, right. Look, there are some people out there who would prefer it if I weren't around. You understand?'

Joe understood perfectly. Although he was somewhat lacking when it came to the finer points of correct English grammar he knew perfectly well what Deadman was telling him.

'Sure, no problem. Mr Deadman. You mean like the ones who were hanging round your car the other day?'

Deadman had turned and was about to go up the stairs to his flat when he stopped dead in his tracks. He turned around again.

'What do you mean, the people who were hanging around my car? You mean when it blew up?'

'That's right, Mr Deadman. I remember now because the car, it had a funny plate.'

'What sort of funny plate? Can you remember what it was? It's important.'

'Sure, it was GOSS 1P.'

'GOSS 1P?'

Deadman stroked his chin as he always seemed to do when he had thinking to do. He smiled to himself.

Well, at least someone has a sense of humour.

'Have you told this to the police? Have you told anyone at all?'

Joe was a Filipino, and a Filipino with dodgy paperwork. The last thing he was going to do was to go to the police and get involved as a witness to a murder case, particularly as it had terrorist undertones. Scotland Yard took a dim view of exploding cars on the streets of London.

'No, no, of course not. I stay silent.'

Deadman patted him on the shoulder.

'Well, just make sure you stay that way. It could get a bit awkward if people think I'm still around and come snooping. I mean, you wouldn't want to get involved now, would you?'

Joe needed no encouragement to take the hint.

'My lips are sealed.'

13

LONDON, 2013

'Hello, Matt? It's me, Mervin. Listen, I've got your car but not your man.'

Matt Deadman listened as Mervin Rabble's voice crackled over the telephone.

'The car's registered to the DDM Group.'

'The what?'

'The DDM Group. It's stands for Dugdale Media.'

'So shouldn't that be DM Group?'

'Look, if you're gonna split hairs…'

'Sorry Merve. Go on.'

'The DDM Group. They're out at Canary Wharf. The car's registered to the company but not to any one person in particular. I've got nothing more for you right now. It's over to you.'

'Cheers, Merve. Thanks. I owe ya.'

Deadman put the phone down and turned to Moscroft. The two men were having a brainstorming session in his flat in Paddington. The debris had been cleared up whilst Deadman had been recovering in hospital. Joe the Filipino had seen to that. A black bottle of Hendricks gin sat on the table alongside a half-empty bottle of Solberano brandy.

'DDM eh?' said Deadman.

Moscroft was already on it. He was Googling the company on his iPad. He hummed as he scanned his tablet.

'Right, the DDM Group. Okay. Well, it's impressive stuff old boy. Newspapers, television channels, some small communication companies. Fingers in every pie really.'

'You say newspapers? Any in particular?' Deadman

took a sip of brandy.

'Well, there's *The Daily Chronicle* for a start. Then there's *The Morning Star.*'

'Blimey, what strange bedfellows,' commented Deadman. The two newspapers were at totally opposite ends of the social spectrum. He sat up. 'Now we know why the car had such an odd number plate, GOSS 1P. Get it? Put the two halves together and you have GOSSIP. I suppose that's somebody's idea of a joke.'

'Well, there's your connection,' said Moscroft. 'Remember what Angie said about the killings possibly being down to a newspaper, one of its editors or a reporter. We've got no proof but the car bomb has certainly put DDM in the frame.'

It certainly was a lead. Four of the men connected to the Great Train Robbery had died in suspicious circumstances, and all four – according to police sources – after threatening to sell their stories to the press, stories that would reveal the identity of the robbers who got away. The question was; why would a newspaper or any of its staff want them dead? Surely it was in the interests of the newspaper to print these stories, particularly *The Morning Star,* a Sunday tabloid newspaper notorious for its Sunday morning exposés. Moscroft and Deadman were puzzled. They couldn't figure it out.

'You know,' said Moscroft suddenly, 'why don't we find out who was reporting on the case at the time? I mean, they may know something. If they were around at the time of the robbery and of each of the killings they might know something.'

'Crikey, they'll be getting on a bit now won't they?'

'Well, we won't know until I find out who they were.'

Deadman was dreading the thought of having to

visit the British Library to check back issues of the newspapers. He'd need to get a reader's ticket, mess about ordering copies piecemeal, and spend ages rubbing shoulders with stuffy academics. Moscroft, however, was already ahead of him.

'Of course, we don't have to go to the British Library or anywhere like that to check the old newspapers do we?' He grinned. 'Remember, Grappler's daughter had a complete file of the newspapers in her father's archive.' He smiled. 'Looks like I'm on for a trip back to Staplehurst again.'

The following evening Deadman and Moscroft were back round the table with their drinks. Moscroft's return visit to Staplehurst to see Grappler's daughter had been a profitable one and he'd come up with the names of four reporters who had worked for *The Daily Chronicle* and *The Morning Star* who had covered the Great Train Robbery in August 1963. There still remained the task of discovering where the former reporters lived, assuming they were still alive today.

'I've already checked,' said Moscroft with a smug look on his face. 'Three of the reporters are dead. I checked them out. Two of the men were such renowned crime reporters that they were listed on Wikipedia, their pages giving the dates of their respective deaths. I found the obituary of the third reporter on *The Morning Chronicle*'s online archive. This left just one reporter, Harold Slater, as the only possible survivor. Slater was not the main reporter at the scene of the robbery at Sears Crossing but had been a junior reporter at the robbers' trial in February 1964.'

'So we need to find the bloke and speak to him.' Deadman winced a little as he sat forward. The injuries suffered in the explosion were still giving him some pain.

'Well, that's easier said than done,' replied Moscroft.

'What do you mean? Don't tell me he's dead too?'

'Not exactly. It's just that he's disappeared. Off the radar, off the map. Nobody has seen him for about nine years.'

Moscroft sat back and allowed a feint trace of a grin to break across his face.

'You know where he is, don't you, you crafty bleeder.' Deadman grinned too.

'Ha, I wondered when the penny would drop.' Moscroft laughed and rubbed his hands.

'When I asked Betty Grappler about the reporters she couldn't really help. She'd met so many over the years. However, she remembered Harold Slater quite well. He was a little older but she said they developed a bit of a friendship over time, not that it ever came to anything. Anyway, Betty said Slater came to see her one day,
it was in September 2004. He told her he was going away for a while for health reasons and that he was retiring from his work with the newspaper. She said there was an unusual look about him, as though something more serious was worrying him. She couldn't quite put her finger on it. Anyway, he gave her an address and said he could be contacted there if she ever wanted to get in touch, adding that she was on no account to give the address to anyone. That was the last she ever heard of him. She never saw him again nor did she ever feel the need to get in touch. Slater simply vanished.'

'I don't think it's suspicious though,' said Deadman, 'I mean, people disappear without trace all the time. Just because a bloke decides to retire somewhere and take it easy doesn't mean something has happened to him, does it?'

Moscroft said nothing. Deadman sighed and rolled his eyes.

'And I take it you've got the address?'

Moscroft grinned and slowly held up a slip of paper. 'Seek and thou shalt find.' He got up and picked up his jacket. 'Come on, we've got an old hack to find.'

'Hold on a minute. I'm still a bloody invalid you know.' Deadman winced again as he got to his feet. 'And where are we off to?'

Moscroft laughed. 'We're off for a breath of fresh air. I hope you like oysters!'

One hour later Deadman and Moscroft were just clearing the suburbs of south London and were breaking into open space on the A2 heading south into Kent. Moscroft was behind of the wheel of his Ford Mondeo whilst Deadman stared silently out of the window, eventually dropping off into a comfortable sleep. Ten minutes later they crossed the River Medway and were cruising along the M2. About twenty minutes after that they turned off in order to take the coast road towards Seasalter.

Moscroft guided the car easily along the road that turned and twisted as it wound its way through an unspectacular countryside with rolling grassy uplands to the right and the sea wall to the left. There was little to be seen save for the hundreds of sheep that busied themselves munching on the lush grass. Deadman suddenly stirred from his sleep and sat up. He looked around and suddenly realised where he was.

'Here, I came down here for Lenny Bragg's funeral. Herne Bay isn't far is it?'

'No, not really. Whitstable is only just up the road. They do lovely oysters there, unless you prefer fish and chips.'

'Look, we haven't come all this way just to sample the local seafood.' Deadman was quick to remind his friend why they'd come to Kent.

'Well, maybe after we've found Slater.' Moscroft wasn't about to let the opportunity slip.

'Yes, Herne Bay isn't far. I came down here for the funeral. You don't think there's a connection?'

'I wouldn't have thought so. I mean, this part of Kent has always been popular with Londoners wanting to get away for a bit. It's probably coincidence.'

The high bank of the sea wall gradually gave way to a row of beach houses. Some were mere chalets whereas others were proper houses. Moscroft slowed down as he approached them.

'What exactly are we looking for?' asked Deadman.

'We're not,' replied Moscroft, bringing the Mondeo to a halt. 'We're here.'

Nestling between a couple of clean, white chalets was a light blue one, with a navy blue door and navy window frames. Whereas other chalets were used only at weekends or during the summer holidays, the light blue chalet was obviously lived in permanently. It was clean and very well kept. A large television aerial was fixed to the side of the chalet whilst a small metal chimney poked out from the tarpaulin roof.

Moscroft parked the car outside the chalet on a piece of hard standing.

'Well, let's hope he's in.'

Deadman walked up to the door and rang the bell. There was no reply. He rang it again, slamming the letterbox at the same time. Still nothing.

'You'll not find him in this morning.'

Deadman and Moscroft turned to find an old man

standing there in a check shirt, brown corduroy trousers and wearing green Wellington boots. He was carrying an old bucket.

'If you're looking for Harold you'll find him out on the beach. The tide's out at the moment, and he'll be picking up shellfish. Good day.'

Moscroft raised his eyebrows. 'I must say, they're a bit polite around here aren't they?'

'Never mind that. Come on, let's go and find our man.'

The two men walked between a couple of the chalets and found themselves staring out at the great expanse of the sea, or rather they would have done had the tide been in. Instead, there lay before them a huge beach, a mixture of shingle and sand, stretching out about half a mile to the sea. Here and there people were bending down with their buckets busily gathering in odd shellfish.

Moscroft scratched his head. 'Which one is ours? I mean, how are we going to recognise him?'

'Don't be stupid. Our man will have a ticket marked 'Press' tucked in his trilby.'

'Very funny,' replied Moscroft.

'Well, how the hell am I supposed to know what he looks like? An old newspaper reporter I suppose.'

The two men started walking out to sea and quickly realised that it wasn't shingle beneath their feet but millions of old shells which crunched and sank as they walked over them. A few people were beginning to make their way back as the tide began to come in. Suddenly, Moscroft noticed an old man crouched down by his bucket, picking up shells and examining them.

'My money's on that chap over there.'

'Done,' said Deadman. 'A tenner says it isn't him.'

As they approached him the man stood up and

groaned as he stretched his back.

'That looks like hard work,' shouted Moscroft.

'It's bloody hard work actually. Still, it's not been a bad morning's work.' The man looked down at his bucket which was half full of mussels and whelks. 'They'll make a nice supper tonight once I've boiled them all up.'

Deadman decided to take the bull by the horns and simply come out with it.

'Would you be Harold Slater by any chance?'

The man froze for a second but quickly relaxed. He put his hands on his hips.

'It depends whose asking.'

'Look, don't worry. We're not the cops or anything like that. We're friends really. We're following up a story and think you may be able to help. We're not from the newspapers or anything like that. We just want a word.'

'Where's your ID?'

Deadman sighed. 'Look, Harold, I don't have any. I don't work for anyone. I'm freelance.'

There was a moment or two of silence.

'In a few minutes the tide will be in. You two will get wet feet.' He picked up his bucket and started walking towards his chalet. 'Come on, this way.'

They reached the chalet and after looking nervously around Slater unlocked the door.

'You'd better come in. If you had said you had ID I would have told you to get lost. It would have meant you were working for someone.'

Slater waved his guest through into a small living room. A small stove sat in the corner, whilst an old 1950s-type mirror hung by a piece of wire. Two old armchairs faced each other across the small room, whilst an oak sideboard rested against a wall. Deadman thought it was cosy at best.

'It ain't much, but then I don't need much these days. Then of course, I've been on the move for some time. I only rent this you know, can't afford to buy a place, not that I'd want to. They'd find me that way, and I can't be taking any chances nowadays.'

Matt Deadman introduced himself as 'John Cheeseman'. He needed to remain dead for the time being. Slater might appear to be a harmless old hack, on the run from somebody, but experience had taught Deadman not to trust anyone. He eased himself into an old armchair. He was feeling fit enough now to be able to get out on to the streets once more.

While Moscroft and Deadman sat down Slater put the kettle on. He took off his Wellington boots and slipped into a pair of old slippers. A couple of minutes later he entered the small sitting room with a tray bearing three mugs of tea.

'There's milk and sugar if you want it. Personally, I never touch the stuff.'

Deadman took one of the mugs from the tray and took a sip of tea. He leaned forward.

'Right now, Harold, what do you know about all of these deaths?'

'Deaths? I'm not sure what you're talking about. I only know about one death.'

Deadman was disappointed but not surprised. He'd been in the game too long now and knew when a contact or witness was clamming up. It was only natural.

'Come on Harold, there was more than one death.'

Slater sat forward in his chair and clasped his hands tightly together.

'Look Mr…'

'Cheeseman, John Cheeseman.'

'Look, Mr Cheeseman, there was only one death. I

reported on it myself. It caused a huge scandal; you must have read about it or seen it on the television.' He sighed. 'It was the last big case I handled.'

Deadman was puzzled.

'But surely you must have covered loads more stories. I mean, you only retired back in…' He glanced down at his notebook. '…when was it? 2004?'

'Yes, that's what I mean. When Davenport died, I wrote one more piece and that was it. The paper didn't seem to want my services any more. And in any case I thought it was a good time to get out. Things were getting a little too hot.'

Deadman was completely confused. He sat forward in his chair.

'Who the hell is or was Davenport? He wasn't one of the train robbers.'

Slater was equally confused.

'Who said anything about the train robbers? I thought you were here to talk about the business with the Iraq dossier, you remember, the one about the Weapons of Mass Destruction, the Dodgy Dossier.'

By now, Deadman's head was completely swimming and thought the explosion must have hit him harder than he thought. Suddenly, he realised he and Slater were talking at cross purposes. He'd come along to talk about the Great Train Robbery, but here was Slater, going on about the controversial 'sexed up' dossier that was one of the main reasons Britain went to war against Iraq back in 2003.

'Look,' explained Slater, 'you must remember. Professor John Davenport was the chap who claimed the government's dossier about Iraq having weapons of mass destruction was simply made up. You must remember? He gave evidence at the enquiry into the Iraq war and was found dead a few days later. They said it was suicide, but I reckon the government had a hand in it.'

'You'd better start from the beginning Harold.'

Slater went on to tell Deadman and Moscroft about the WMD story and his involvement with Davenport. It was all coming back now, the enquiry, the television coverage, the endless interviews and punditry on Sky News and the BBC.

'I had the story and went to the editor to clear it. You can imagine, it was bloody dynamite. It would have blown the whole thing open. I had definite proof from a government insider who he knew the truth behind the dossier, that it had been a work of fiction. I remember when I read some of the stuff he gave me. It was worthy of Le Carre or Fleming. It was one hundred per cent bullshit. The editor needed to be sure, however, and went so far as to consult with the paper's owner, John Dugdale. It was cleared and we were ready to roll.'

'So what happened?'

'What happened? I'll tell you what happened. Fuck all. That's what happened.'

Deadman and Moscroft were all ears by now.

'Dugdale arranged a meeting with the government to confront them with the evidence. You can imagine, you couldn't simply go printing something like that without at least offering them the chance to comment. Well, I couldn't believe what happened. Dugdale went off to see the prime minister, Bland, and came back with a peerage. Well, at least he was given one in the Honours List a couple of months later. He'd been bought off. The story never got printed. Dugdale said it wasn't in the country's best interests. What bollocks. They'd bought him off with the peerage.'

Slater scoffed in disgust.

'Lord John Dugdale. Look at him now, swaggering

around like he's the king or something. Then we had the business with poor Davenport. He knew the real story and was threatening to tell it, but a few days after he gave his first evidence at the enquiry they murdered him.'

Deadman couldn't believe what he was hearing.

'Murdered? Are you sure? I mean, fuck me, if this is true...'

'Of course it's bloody true. That's why I'm in hiding isn't it? D'ya think I'm stuck here on account on my health or something? Do me a favour.'

'You call this in hiding?'

'Well I sure as hell ain't out in the open am I? Fuck it. I had to quit my job and start renting places under false names. That's how fucking paranoid I am? If they find out where I am...'

'And who are they?' asked Deadman innocently.

'What d'ya mean, "who are they?" Who do you think they are? The same bastards that killed Davenport, that's who! They know I had the inside story, the real dirt. For fuck's sake, if they find out where I am I'll be for the chop, and that's no mistake.'

'Phew. Well, that's one hell of a fucking story. And I only came down here to ask you about the Great Train Robbery!'

Slater was walking around the room.

'The what? Oh, that. Christ, that seems like a lifetime ago.'

He sat down again.

'I'd only been working at the *Chronicle* for a few months but the top crime writer, Percy Hancock, took me along. I used to make his tea. He thought I could be useful during the trial. You never had phones or computers in those days. You had to be first to the phones or the other blokes would get their stories out first. They used to call me

'Handy Harry,' because I was always quickest to the phone. You know, I was the youngest. Those old geezers couldn't beat me.'

Deadman asked Slater about Field, Edwards and Wilson.

'Oh, those three. Well, of course they were all rogues, all of 'em. But they were okay really. Nice blokes, you know. Not like the villains today, with their shooters and knives and all that. I remember Field approaching Hancock and offering him a story about two other men who he said took part in the robbery but got clean away with it. It was news to me but he sounded convincing. He said he knew the real identity of one of the men. Well, Hancock had to sanction it with Dugdale. He was the new owner back then. He'd only bought the newspaper a few months before, so Hancock thought he'd better clear it. Of course, it never happened because Field was killed in a road accident on his way to meet him.

'And what about the other two, Edwards and Wilson?'

'Well, funny, I've never really given it much thought. I assumed they were simply unlucky. But I do know that Edwards approached Hancock with the story. They found poor Buster hanged in his garage. The police said it was suicide. You don't reckon it was murder do you?'

By now Slater could see where Deadman was going with his theory. Field and Edwards had both offered a story to the press about the identity of one of the robbers who got away. Both had died in suspicious circumstances. Wilson was shot dead outside his villa in Spain.

'Are you trying to tell me Wilson was silenced too?' asked Slater.

'Well Higgins certainly was.'

'Higgins? Who's he?'

'Oh, you won't know him, will you? Grappler kept a secret list with the names of the robbers on it. They'd been given to him by informers and criminal types. There were three names on it that have never appeared in the public domain. One of them was Danny Higgins. He got off because he handed his money back.'

'Not the cash in the telephone box, surely?'

'No, that's another story. He did a deal and the police let him go. He was killed in a hit-and-run in 2008. A witness said a car went directly for him. It was no accident.'

'Christ,' said Slater. 'We've got a right fucking story here, haven't we?'

Deadman could sense the old fires burning inside Slater as the urges of an old reporter on the trail of a hot story began to surface once more.

'It's not a story, Harold. Remember, you don't work as a reporter anymore. You've got to keep your head down.'

Slater sighed. 'Bollocks. It'd make a great story. They print a load of old shit nowadays. Micro-celebrities and all that. You know. Reality shows on the telly and crap in the papers. Nah, the editors today are just a bunch of old wankers, or at least most of them are. They wouldn't know a good story if a typewriter hit them on the head. Wankers, all of 'em.'

Deadman laughed. 'Don't beat about the bush, Harold.' He looked at his watch and stood up. 'Look, we'd better be going. Thanks Harold and keep your head down. There's something going on around here and we aim to get to the bottom of it. I'm no newspaper man but I can smell trouble a mile off and this business with Dugdale and the papers stinks.'

The meeting with Harold Slater had given Deadman

and Moscroft plenty to think about as they drove back to London.

'That's one hell of a story,' said Moscroft, changing up through the gears.

'Which one?' asked Deadman. 'I mean, on one hand we have a dodgy document that took Britain to war and on the other we have a potential serial killer bumping off former associates from the Great Train Robber, not to mention the hunt for the ones that got away. Which story do we go with?'

Deadman reflected on the fact that his search for Jimmy Damon had now turned into something potentially far more serious. The words Dugdale and death seemed to turn up a little too often for his liking. In fact, the letter 'D' seemed to be quite popular right now; Deadman, Damon, Davenport, Dugdale and death....

It was also clear to Deadman that having listened to Slater's story he was about to pit his wits not only against a very dangerous man in Lord John Dugdale, but also the dark forces of the Establishment and the Secret Service. The Iraq dossier had effectively taken Britain to war but if it was a document of lies then the government would need to see it remained a secret. MI5 and other government agencies were just the people to do it.

14

LONDON, 2013

Now that Lord John Dugdale was probably involved in the case Deadman decided it was time for a change of digs. If Dugdale was indeed behind the car bomb there was no sense in risking being spotted again at his flat. If the newspapers were reporting him dead it seemed better to remain that way, at least for the time being.

Moscroft, meanwhile, was still trying to take in Slater's story about the Iraq dossier. He could scarcely credit it. If it were true and if the dossier was laid before the British – and indeed, the world – public, the storm that would follow could easily be imagined. It would make scandals such as the Profumo Affair which, ironically, had broken in the same year as the Great Train Robbery, seem like a Boys Scouts' tea party that had got out of control. The government would be crucified for taking the country to war on what would certainly be claimed were illegal grounds, whilst anybody remotely connected with the dossier and the decision to go to war was hardly likely to fare any better. Dugdale could be counted amongst the latter group, for although he was not directly responsible for taking the decision he would certainly have stood a good chance of stopping the war by exposing the dossier as a work of fiction. Indeed, the fact that he had sacrificed the country's honour upon the altar of personal gain was likely to elevate him to the top of Britain's most hated list if the truth was ever revealed. It was also bound to make scores of celebrities and even royals who had courted his friendship shift uncomfortably in their seats for Dugdale was one of the most powerful media tycoons in the world. Indeed, him and his wife, and even his daughters, mixed regularly with the élite of British society, with celebrities, sporting heroes and even royalty.

In a word, Dugdale was a powerful and dangerous man and Moscroft and Deadman would need to be on their guard from now on, for although the would-be assassins believed Deadman to have been the man who was killed in the explosion it was safe to assume that darker forces would still be at work, lurking in the background, making sure the reports were true and that the car bomb had indeed eliminated its target. Phones would be tapped, movements monitored and the usual steps taken to ensure the job had been completed. Moscroft needed to find Deadman a temporary home. Fortunately, one of his friends was away, basking on the golden sands in some tropical paradise. Deadman could use his flat for a few weeks.

'Well, this is very nice.'

Moscroft and Deadman stepped out of the taxi in front of number 62 Conduit Mews. It was a typical mews; a row of former stable blocks which were now smart, trendy homes to London's fast set. Situated in a back street Deadman could at least feel relatively secure in his temporary home, it being very difficult to approach the place without being seen. Moscroft put the kettle on and made two cups of tea.

'Well, old chum,' said Moscroft, grabbing his cup of tea,' it looks as though we've got more than we bargained for.'

Deadman sat there, deep in thought. Slater's story raised all sorts of issues, not least of which was Dugdale's probable involvement in both the Iraq dossier and the Great Train Robbery, or at least the deaths of those who threatened to go public with the names of the two robbers who got away, Damon and Bragg.

'So what are we doing now?' asked Moscroft. 'I mean, are we still looking for Jimmy Damon or do we go about trying to shop this fellow Dugdale? Let's face it, I don't think we would have gone to war without the dossier on Iraq. If he knew about it but kept quiet he's certainly got blood on his hands.'

'Yes,' replied Deadman, 'not to mention the blood of the four train robbers who have died in dodgy circumstances.'

The two men drank their tea, deep in thought. With Dugdale on the scene the parameters of the case were suddenly changed. Moscroft was first to speak.

'Do you think Dugdale is shielding Damon in some way? I mean, the two men may have met each other in Australia. They're not that different in age and judging from what you've told me they appear to come from the same background.'

'What do you mean?' asked Deadman.

'Well, Damon was evidently a thief, prepared to betray his fellow gang members, whilst Dugdale, if Slater's story is true, had information that could have saved many lives and yet was bought off with the promise of a peerage. They're both scum in my opinion.'

'But that doesn't necessarily mean they know each other.'

'So why had Dugdale been bumping off anyone who threatened to reveal Damon's identity?'

'Well, that's assuming he's the man behind it.'

'Look,' replied Moscroft, 'almost everything points to him being behind it.'

'So where do we go from here?'

'Where do we go?' replied Moscroft, 'I'll tell you *how*

we go. We go very carefully.'

Deadman passed an easy night in his new, albeit temporary, home. By not having a main road passing by Conduit Mews was a good deal quieter than his own flat and it put him in a good frame of mind when the sun came up the following morning. That was, however, until reality set in once more, as Deadman recalled the events of the last few days, especially the car bomb and his own narrow escape. Was it really somebody from Dugdale Media? Did he have MI5 working for him? After all, by possessing the truth about the dossier he had the ultimate blackmail card, one that would easily enable him to call upon their services if needed. Then there was the possibility that he could be completely wrong, and that the bomb and the mysterious deaths of the train robbers may have been down to somebody completely unknown who just happened to have links with Damon and was doing his or her best to preserve Damon's whereabouts and identity.

He sipped on his first cup of tea.

Dugdale. He's the answer to everything. He has to be.

He was deep in thought when his mobile phone suddenly began to vibrate. He took it out. Ever since the car bomb attack Deadman had stopped using his phone for calls, fearing they may be traced. The alarms and reminders were still working, however, and one of them had flagged up Stan Tanner's funeral. It was later that day.

The service itself was being held at Camberwell New Cemetery but Deadman decided to go to Tanner's house in Bagshot Street. He figured that any surveillance operation, whether it be by Dugdale's people, by MI5 or some other outfit, was likely to focus on the burial and that it was highly unlikely that any of them would go to the house, at least not until the wake afterwards. It was sound reasoning.

Shortly after noon there was a knock on the door of Tanner's house in Bagshot Street. A woman, aged about seventy, and dressed in a black dress, answered the door. Deadman stood there, suitably dressed in a black suit, white shirt and black tie.

'Oh, hello. I've come to pay my respects to old Stan.'

'Oh. You've come to the wrong place really, luv. The funeral's taking place right now, over in Camberwell New Cemetery.'

Deadman did his best to look disappointed.

'Oh, bugger. It'll be over by the time I get there.'

The woman bought the story. 'Why don't you come in and have a cup of tea? I'm sure they'll be back here very soon. You can meet everyone then.'

Deadman shuffled into the tiny front room. Extra tables had been brought in and were covered in white table cloths. Sandwiches, bottles of beer and glasses were piled up on them.

'Looks like you're expecting quite a few people.'

'Nah, not really. They're all gannets really. Some of them were Stan's friends but most of them are coming just because they know there's a free nosh. You know how it is. Here make yourself at home.'

Deadman found a chair and sat down. The woman came back in with a cup of tea.

'I'm Dolly, Stan's cousin. So, how did you know Stan?'

'Oh, we used to have a few drinks together in the Duke of York. We weren't that close or anything like that but my dad knew Stan from a long way back.'

The woman's face lit up. 'Oh, your dad knew him did he? Well, that's nice. Stan kept in touch with a few of his old mates from school. Here, is your dad in one of these?'

She picked up an old photograph album and handed it to Deadman. It was dog-eared and tea stained but the photos were still in good nick. It was stuffed full of old black and white photographs of all sizes. There were some tiny ones, with tiny figures in them, whilst others were the more traditional six by fours. Deadman laughed.

'Cameras have come a long way since the old Box Brownie, haven't they?'

'Well, that's all we could get back then. Bloody awful they were too. Still, beggars couldn't be choosers, as we used to say. And it's better than nothing. I mean, half of Stan's life's in that album.

Deadman continued flicking slowly through the album, carefully turning the pages. Then he saw it. His heart began to beat a little quicker. One of Stan's photographs showed four young men, sitting on the bonnet of an old car outside a school. The caption underneath read; 'Me and the Three Musketeers, July 1956.'

'This is Stan here, isn't it?' asked Deadman innocently.

The woman came over and leant over him.

'Yeah, that's him there on the left. That must be Jimmy Damon, Danny Higgins and Lenny Bragg.' She ran her fingers over the other three in the photo. 'They used to go everywhere when they were at school. Right scallywags they were too.' She blushed slightly. 'I went out with Lenny for a while. My mate Iris went out with Jimmy. We used to double-date, you know, go out for a night down the ABC and fish and chips afterwards. Course, you couldn't get too much back then, what with rationing and all that. Still, we knew how to have fun.'

'Whatever happened to the other three lads?'

'I dunno. I never saw them much after we stopped going out. Mind you, I did hear that they'd been involved in the robbery, you know, the train thing. We never knew really, but the word in the Beckett and the Lord Nelson was that the three of them were mixed up in it. Not Stan, of course. Nah, he always kept his nose clean. Never done nothing wrong, you know? More tea? Good.'

As soon as Dolly disappeared into the kitchen Deadman took the album and slipped the photograph from its page. He had it tucked away in his pocket by the time she reappeared with another cup.

'Well, look, I won't hang around if that's all the same to you.

Dolly looked disappointed but said she'd better get on with buttering more bread. Deadman shook her hand and said thanked her for the tea before walking off down the street. He swung himself into the back seat of a black Ford Mondeo that was parked outside the Duke of York pub.

'Well, old boy? How did it go?'

Deadman brandished the photo in front of Moscroft. 'Say hello to The Three Musketeers.'

The Pride of Paddington pub was pretty full by the time Deadman and Moscroft walked through the door. It seemed safer to mull things over in the local pub rather than spend the evening in Deadman's kitchen, discussing things over drinks. The investigation into Jimmy Damon and his two mates was proving a painfully slow business and a dangerous one too. Still, at least Deadman's visit to Tanner's house had proved useful. Up until then the only photographs he had of Damon, Higgins and Bragg had been those of each of them, taken from the files in the Criminal Records Office. Now, they had a picture of all three of them, plus Stan Tanner. Okay, it wasn't massively useful but it moved the investigation a step nearer to Damon. Moscroft carried a couple of beers to the table where he and Deadman were sitting.

'It's an interesting photo but it doesn't exactly move us any closer does it?

'Just a little, I suppose,' replied Deadman, sipping his beer. I could always call my mate in Australia or ask Rabble to do some more digging around. The problem is, that any enquiry made through an official channel is likely to be flagged. What worries me is that the minute I make the call MI5 will be on to us like a flash. You know the way those crafty bastards work.'

'But Matt, we don't even know if they're involved. You're only assuming they're up to no good.'

'They're always up to no good. That's what they do for a living don't they?' snapped Deadman in frustration. 'The only advantage I've got over MI5, if they're really involved, is that I'm supposed to be dead, and if I stay in the shadows we might get somewhere. The minute I step out into the light again it'll all get a bit tricky. Trust me. If Dugdale or MI5 get the merest sniff of another enquiry from me they'll think Lazarus has come back from the dead. No, we've got to lie low'

Deadman finished off his beer. 'I'm off home for an early night. It's been a long day and I'm knackered. Take this photo and take care of it. Get in scanned. I'll give you a call tomorrow. Cheers.'

And with that, he slid from behind his table, got up and left.

It was only a short walk round the corner to Conduit Mews. It was now evening and the light was beginning to fade. It was raining too and Deadman dashed between the doorways to try to stay dry. It was dark in the mews, with no lighting other than the few lamps that some of the residents had placed outside their houses. Deadman fumbled for his key in the half dark but eventually managed to find the keyhole. He pushed the door open but failed to hear the splashing of footsteps behind him which were drowned by the sound of falling rain, nor did he have time to react before he was bundled into the hallway of his house. He tried to fight back but was pushed to the floor by at least two men. Unable to move his arms or legs he was pinned to the floor and his arms pulled back behind him. Before he knew it a pair of handcuffs was snapped across his wrists and a sack placed over his head. There was no use in resisting any longer and he gave in to the inevitable. He was yanked to his feet.

'Okay. All clear! Let's go!'

He suddenly sensed he was being pushed through a door and felt a man's hand on his head as he was bundled into the back of a van that had just pulled up. There was the sound of a man banging on the side of the van, and with that it sped off into the night.

Deadman sat there in silence and in darkness with the sack still placed over his head. He sighed.

Fuck it.

15

INTERROGATION

There was nothing quite like being busted by the law, especially when you had no idea why; and this was one of those occasions. It was getting late now and Deadman had sat in an interrogation room for over half and hour without anybody giving him the slightest idea why. There was the usual basic wooden and steel table, three uncomfortable blue plastic chairs and a CCTV camera looking down from a corner of the ceiling. Then, of course, there was a large glass window which Deadman knew shielded his would-be interrogators. It certainly wasn't there to give anyone a view of London.

Ten more minutes came and went before the door suddenly opened. Two men in cheap dark suits walked in, one carrying a cup of coffee which he placed on the table. The two men sat down and began staring Deadman in the face. He'd played this sort of game before, often from the other side, so he was well drilled in the art.

'So, Mr Deadman. Can you tell us what you know about Lord John Dugdale? What's your interest? Apparently, you've been asking questions and taking an interest in him.'

A mild shock ran through Deadman's body as he tried to take in what was happening. First of all, he was surprised to know that these people knew he was alive. The newspapers had reported him dead, so how did they know it was someone else in the burnt out car? And then there was Dugdale again. How come they knew he had been asking questions about him? He decided to tough it out.

'What's it to you? Have I broken a law or something? I mean, there's no law against a bloke doing his job is there?'

'That depends upon what sort of job it is?'

'Well, that's for me to know and you to wonder.'

'On the contrary, it's for us to know and you to wonder why you're being held for questioning.'

The man stood up and wandered round the room.

'Lord Dugdale is a powerful man, a pillar of society and a friend of the government. It doesn't pay to go around sticking your nose in where it isn't wanted, if you know what I mean.'

Deadman had played this game before and knew a threat when he heard it.

'Look, I don't know who you are or what you're playing at but either charge me or let me go. I've not been sticking my nose anywhere it shouldn't be. And what's more, I've been here for fucking ages and you haven't offered me so much as a cup of tea.'

The two men got up from their chairs.

Here it comes; this is where I get a shoeing.

'Don't be clever, Deadman.' The man leant close to Deadman's face. 'We could have you out of here and dead in a ditch in no time. Nobody would know. So don't mess with us. Not so much of the old lip. Tell us what you know about Dugdale.'

Deadman sighed. There was no point in playing dumb, but he could at least string it out a bit. Suddenly, a third man entered the room. He was older than the last two. He had a suit carrier with him.

'Here, put this on please.'

He laid the bag on the table.

'What's this? Are we going on somewhere?'

'It'd be a lot easier if you cut the crap and did as you were told. Now put this on please.'

Deadman sensed things were looking up. The man's

tone suggested they'd given up on him, for the moment at least, and that he was about to be taken somewhere. He decided to put on the suit. It wasn't a bad fit. There was shirt and tie to go with it.

'Is there any point in asking where we're going?'

The man said nothing. It was pointless. Five minutes later Deadman was finished. He looked at his reflection in the glass window and gave a sigh of satisfaction as he straightened his tie.

Not bad, not bad at all.

The door opened again.

'This way please.'

And with that Deadman was taken along a narrow corridor to a pair of doors. The men pushed them open and Deadman found himself amongst the dustbins and refuse at the rear of the building. A black Mercedes sat waiting with its engine ticking over. A man got out from the front seat and opened the door.

This is a little more like it.

Deadman swung himself into the back seat and the door closed gently behind him. The car eased slowly forward and emerged onto a busy London street. It was dark now but the capital's streets were still as busy as ever. Deadman took a while to realise where he was but soon realised he was in London's West End. The car negotiated its way through the busy London traffic, edging its way round Trafalgar Square before turning into Pall Mall. A short way along the road the car turned left into Waterloo Place and made its way around the small square before coming to a halt outside the classically ornate Athenaeum Club. The door of the car opened the man beckoned towards the club's front entrance.

'This way sir.'

Suddenly, Deadman found himself being treated

like a human being again, rather than like some sort of criminal. He stepped out of the Mercedes and found himself looking up at four pairs of columns. A double wooden door was framed by the centre pairs. He was escorted up the four stone steps to the door, taking time to wipe his feet on the mat outside. A doorman appeared and opened the door and Deadman was swept into the marble hall before being shown up a magnificent flight
of stairs. He couldn't help being impressed by the surroundings. Portraits of old soldiers, politicians and men of the arts and literature adorned the walls, most of the sitters being former members of the club. Chandeliers hung liberally from the ceiling whilst elegant chairs were dotted around the corridors. But despite the undeniable elegance of the building Deadman's appreciation for the place was tempered by the fact that he was entering the lion's den, for this was very much the territory of the British Establishment, and as he entered the Drawing Room he did so warily. Although his abductors had still not revealed themselves he had a pretty good idea who they were, and his instincts told him they were not the sort of people to be trifled with. It was one thing to walk into a pub in London's East End to confront a local hoodlum but this was something quite different. Deadman would have to be on his guard.

The Drawing Room of the Athenaeum Club was every bit as elegant and traditional as you would expect from one of London's most prestigious gentlemen's clubs. Long, light and airy, the room oozed tradition, with rank upon rank of expensive leather bound books lining the huge mahogany bookcases that flanked the room. Two huge desks, loaded with more books, sat at one end of the room whilst several comfortable leather chairs were gathered around the Adam fireplace at the other. A huge golden chandelier hung from an ornate ceiling. It was all very imposing.

What struck Deadman the moment he walked into the room was that it was deserted, save for a man who was sitting in one of the armchairs at the end of it.

'This way please.' Deadman's escort walked towards the man who was reading a copy of *The Times*.

'Good evening, sir. Here's the man you've been asking for.'

And with that the escort bowed slightly and walked away, leaving Deadman alone with the man, who was tall and slightly thin, whom he guessed was in his late sixties. He wore a dark grey suit, light blue shirt, regimental navy blue and maroon tie, and black leather brogues.

The man looked up, folded the newspaper and placed it on a coffee table nearby. A tray with some porcelain cups, a teapot, a milk jug and a silver sugar bowl, rested on the table also. The man took off his reading glasses, put them in his jacket pocket and gestured to the chair opposite.

'Sit down please, Mr Deadman. Tea?'

It was the best offer he'd had all evening.

'Milk, no sugar. Thanks.'

The man poured some tea into Deadman's cup, added some milk, and handed it to him. He took a few sips from his own cup and stared at Deadman for a few seconds before placing his cup back on the tray.

'My name is Marcus Trelawney. You need not concern yourself with the organisation for which I act. Just be aware that I act in the country's interests.' He leaned forward and sighed, somewhat menacingly. 'And right now your pursuit of Lord John Dugdale is not, I can assure you, in the best interests of this country. I am here merely to ensure that your interest in his Lordship ends now.'

He picked up his cup once more and took a few sips

before settling back in his chair to wait for Deadman's response, safe in the knowledge that the abduction, the interview and now the meeting in the intimidating splendour of the Athenaeum Club had left Deadman in little doubt that he was out of his league, and was meddling with things that were far beyond his comprehension.

Matt Deadman said nothing but simply stared back at Trelawney. He took a couple of sips of his tea and placed the cup back on the tray.

'So what gives you the idea that I'm the slightest bit interested in Dugdale?'

'Oh come now, Mr Deadman. Our intelligence network quivers at the slightest touch and your enquiries haven't so much as set off a quiver but rather more a rumble of thunder. You know how we work or have you forgotten everything you learned when you were in the service of Her Majesty?'

Trelawney leant forward once more, and whispered his threat once more.

'What I'm saying, Mr Deadman, is that you'd be doing yourself a great favour by dropping your line of enquiry. Do I make myself clear?'

Deadman couldn't believe what he was hearing. It was as if he was the naughty boy at school, brought before the headmaster. But this was no school, no prank. Trelawney was being deadly serious, or at least was trying to be. Deadman had other ideas, however, and wasn't going to be frightened by this jumped-up nobody, just because he was reading a copy of *The Times* and had a regimental tie around his neck. No, fuck it. He wasn't having any of it. He sat forward and launched his counter-attack.

'From the regimental tie you're wearing round your neck you're obviously ex-Brigade of Guards, probably Grenadiers. I'd say you did your service but never made it to the top, probably retiring as a Major whilst your contemporaries went on to make Colonel or even General. I reckon some of your mates went on to senior positions on the General Staff. Frustrated, you joined Military Intelligence, a contradiction if ever there was one, and now you find yourself working for MI5. From the state of your highly polished shoes I'd say you still having to try to impress your bosses. You're not a field agent but you like to flatter yourself that you hold a senior position whereas in reality you're nothing but a glorified messenger who's trying to put the frighteners on me. You've got exclusive use of this room for the evening and are trying to give the impression of power whereas in fact if I take out my cheque book I could hire this very room for myself and some of my friends for a piss up.'

By now Trelawney was beginning to squirm and boil over with anger, whilst the vein in his head looked as though it was about to pop any second. Deadman continued.

'Now, unless you're about to charge me with anything I'm going to get up and walk away from here. And I don't expect to be followed. I know how the system works, Trelawney. Your cloak and dagger stuff might frighten some people but it doesn't scare me. I've been in tighter situations than this and have met far bigger villains than you, even if you are MI5. So, you can go back and tell your masters that, no, I'm not the slightest bit interested in Dugdale. You're barking up the wrong tree. And, yes, I'm gonna find out who tried to kill me, and if it is Dugdale, then he'd better watch out. Got it?'

And with that, Deadman finished his drink and stood up.

'Thanks for the tea. Oh, and will you be wanting this suit back? It fits me rather well, don't you think?'

By now Trelawney was boiling over with rage, his

fists shaking with anger. But there was nothing he could do as Deadman walked away except send one of the cups flying across the room. Deadman stopped and grinned as he reached the door. He looked back at Trelawney.

'That'll cost you a few bob. Should I send up a waiter?'

And with that he left the room and walked downstairs, brushing the shoulder of the escort who was on his way up.

'You wanna watch that bloke,' said Deadman, 'he's got a bloody awful temper.'

The man turned and hissed back. 'Piss off.'

Deadman laughed as he passed through the front door to emerge onto the damp and dark London streets. He hailed a passing taxi and sped off back to his temporary home in Conduit Mews. Deadman loosened his tie and sighed with relief as the taxi cruised along the capital's streets. True, it had all been a bit of fun, but as he stared out of the window he reflected on the fact that he' been lucky, and that the situation could have been far worse. Such bravado would only serve to increase MI5's interest in him and Moscroft and that he would have to tread even more warily if he were going to turn his attention towards the activities of Lord John Dugdale.

16

SEASALTER

'Right then. Something tells me we're going to need new digs.'

Matt Deadman was back in his temporary home in Conduit Mews giving Moscroft an account of what had happened during the previous few hours. Moscroft listened in disbelief as Deadman related his kidnapping and his subsequent interview with Trelawney at the Athenaeum Club.

'You said what to him?'

'Listen, Moscroft, you weren't there. I wasn't gonna hang around and let this idiot read the riot act to me. I've been in the game long enough now to know when to start pushing back the barriers and how far you can push them.'

'Yes, but all the same, it looks as though we've now got MI5 on our case as well as Dugdale's people, and I think we now have to assume he's mixed up in this whole Damon business somehow.'

'Well, that's why I reckon it'll be safer to think about moving again.'

'But we'll have nowhere left to run if you go on pissing people off like this.'

'Ah, fuck 'em! More to the point is why MI5 wants us to lay off of Dugdale.'

'I would have thought that's obvious isn't it?' replied Moscroft. 'I mean, look at it.'

'Enlighten me,' said Deadman, sighing.

'Oh, come on Matt. What did Slater tell us? It's the Iraq dossier isn't it. It has to be.'

Moscroft got up and walked around the room.

'It all makes sense. Yes...Dugdale knows the truth about on the Iraq dossier. It's why the government gave him a peerage.'

'Okay, but so what?'

'So what? Dugdale is effectively immune from prosecution, that's what.' Moscroft snapped his fingers. 'Let's face it, with the inside story tucked safely away somewhere at Dugdale Media nobody is going to lift a finger against him. I mean, he hasn't done anything wrong has he? Okay, he accepted a peerage in return for his silence but there's no law against that. I reckon half the peers in the House of Lords have done something sleazy to get their titles anyway. But Dugdale is a different kettle of fish. The government daren't move against him. Imagine it; he's got them in the palm of his hand, and things will stay that way until Bland's government is voted out.'

Moscroft continued walking around the room, deep in thought.

'On the other hand, Dugdale won't want to play his trump card unless he has to. He can only play it once.'

Moscroft was right. It was no Monkey's Paw, no Genie's Lamp; it couldn't be used three times. No, the truth about the Iraq dossier and the alleged presence of Weapons of Mass Destruction could only be used once, and Dugdale knew this, for the consequences, once the truth was revealed, would be far reaching and fatal not only to the government but to the British establishment generally, as well as those individuals and institutions that had sided with the government over its decision to go to war with Iraq. In effect, if Dugdale went down, for whatever reason, he would take the whole rotten lot with him. Thus, it was a weapon that he would resort to using only in the most extreme of circumstances. And so an uneasy truce existed between

Dugdale Media and the government; the media mogul keeping the great secret up his sleeve for the rainiest of rainy days, whilst the government, paranoid and in a state of almost perpetual fear, worked hard through its agencies – and in particular MI5 – to ensure the dark secret remained a secret. Between them they were sitting on a giant powder keg and it needed just a single spark to set it all off.

'So we've got a stalemate,' said Deadman.

'I'm afraid so. All the time Dugdale has the truth about the dossier the government won't lift a finger against him. MI5's main concern is to keep the thing secret, and let's face it, Dugdale isn't stupid enough to have just one copy. He'll have copies kept hidden away all over the place.'

Moscroft continued.

'But that's our problem. Even if we could prove Dugdale was involved somehow with the murders of the train robbers and of Tanner, the case would never get to court. Dugdale would simply wave the Iraq dossier in the air and the government would see to it that no charges were brought. It's perfect.'

'So what are you saying? Do you mean there's no point in going on with our investigation?'

'No,' replied Moscroft, 'I don't mean that. We go on, of course, but only with the investigation into Jimmy Damon. Dugdale will have to wait.'

'Or will he?' replied Deadman, getting to his feet. 'Just suppose I could find evidence linking Dugdale to the murders and the attempt on me, as well getting hold of the truth about the Iraq dossier...'

'You'd have a full house.' Moscroft grinned. 'The trouble is, how would we expose them and show them to the world?'

'The press, of course,' replied Deadman. 'Let's face it, the British press likes nothing better than dishing the dirt on high profile people and they don't come much higher than the government. The dossier would almost certainly bring down the government, which would take away Dugdale's trump card. If we give it away to the press he'll have nothing on the government, and if we can pin something on him at the same time we could nail two birds with one stone.'

'Of course,' said Moscroft triumphantly. 'Which leaves just one question; how are we going to get the dossier and the evidence from Dugdale?'

There was silence for a few moments before a big grin spread across Deadman's face.

'Moscroft my old chum, I think I know how to get the dossier.' He stood up and walked around the room. 'Dugdale has just bought the television station, Channel 6, hasn't he?'

'Yes,' replied Moscroft, 'we know that. How is that going to help us?'

'I'm sure I read somewhere that Dugdale is holding a reception at his HQ to mark the takeover.'

'And I suppose you'll be getting an invitation, will you?'

Deadman rolled his eyes at Moscroft's sarcasm.

'Who needs a fucking invite? There'll be so many people knocking about no one's gonna notice me barging in. It'll be one great big party, happy hour and all that. Once I'm inside I'll nip off and take it from there. There's got to be a way up to his penthouse. I mean, the man doesn't have wings does he?'

Moscroft was all ears.

'Okay. So he has a lift. How are you going to get to it. And then what will you do? Call the police?'

'Come on Moscroft. There'll be so many people milling around nobody's going notice one of the guests going to have a piss or something will they. It's always the way. The only people looking out for that sort of thing will be the security.'

'Of which there are bound to be loads…'

'Yeah, of course, but even they can't watch everything every minute.'

'Okay. Assuming you make it to Dugdale's penthouse. What then? Assuming he's got a safe, which I expect he has, do you really think he'd be stupid enough to have a copy there?'

'Why not? You said yourself Dugdale was bound to have more than one copy of the information relating to the dodgy dossier, and why not keep a copy in the office safe? One copy is all we need.'

Deadman walked slowly around the room, stroking his chin. It was a sure sign that something was brewing inside his head.

'Yeah, I can see it now. No problem. A safe, the documents and who knows what else. I mean, there may even be something relating to Damon.'

'Damon?' said Moscroft, 'Christ, I'd almost forgotten about him. Well, yes, I suppose so. There may be something inside the safe, assuming there'll be one.'

'Come on Moscroft, there's bound to be a safe. Don't they all have one?'

'Well you haven't got one,' said Moscroft, sarcastically.

'That's because I've got fuck all to hide.' Deadman continued to stroke his chin. 'No, there has to be a way. If I find the stuff in the safe the next problem will be how to get it away.'

'That's assuming you can open the safe in the first place.'

Deadman looked round at Moscroft, pretending to

be hurt.

'Come on. Do you really think I don't know how to crack a safe?'

'Okay then,' said Moscroft. 'Let's do it. But we'll need to plan for a quick getaway. As soon as Dugdale finds out someone's nicked the documents from his safe it's odds on he'll know where to come looking. And don't forget, MI5 will be on the case quicker than you can say 007.'

'Which is why we need new digs. They'll be keeping tabs on us now I reckon, especially if Trelawney has anything to do with it. He seemed a bit pissed off.' Deadman grinned. 'Still, that'll fucking teach him not to be so pompous. I mean, his head was so far up his own arse he'd have to shove his toothbrush up it to clean his teeth.'

Moscroft laughed. 'Okay. Leave it to me. We'll need a new place to stay and, I believe, a change of car. I may as well dig out the false passports. You never know when they'll be needed.'

'Good thinking,' said Deadman. 'I don't want to be stuck here with MI5 on my tail just because I'd left the fake passport at home. Good idea.'

Monday nights were usually boring. Nothing on the telly unless you wanted to test your brain power by watching University Challenge or catch a Premiership football match on Sky. Otherwise, there wasn't much on. This Monday night was different however.

It was just getting dark when Deadman peered carefully through the window of his temporary home in Conduit Mews. A black Ford Transit had sat a few yards along from his front door for the past few evenings. Deadman sighed to himself and shook his head.

These MI5 guys never change. How bloody predictable.

He let go of the curtain and shook his head once more, smiling at the thought of MI5 agents sitting hunched up in the back of the van, probably scoffing hard cheese sandwiches and drinking cold coffee. Nothing ever changed. It was the unglamorous side of the espionage business, although acting as watchdogs in a London mews hardly constituted espionage work. It was dark when Deadman stepped out onto the cobbled mews outside before making off along Eastbourne Terrace. He turned left into Bishop's Bridge Road, conscious that he was being followed. There was no point in turning round and giving the game away, and in any case the MI5 boys were hardly likely to be following him in a van with MI5 painted on the side. It was just instinct that told him somebody was on his tail. Deadman wasn't worried, however. He and Moscroft had got it all worked out. He skipped across Gloucester Terrace before walking up to the front door of his own home in Gloucester Gardens. He hadn't been back there since returning from hospital following the explosion that had wrecked his Alfa Romeo. But Deadman wasn't going to stay for very long, and if MI5 were going to sit and watch him they were in for a very long wait.

Instead of taking the stairs to his top floor flat Deadman skipped past old Bill's flat on the ground floor, and down the dark passage that led out the rear of the building to the communal garden. Gently opening the door he dropped down into the garden and made his way out to the garages which were accessed via the northern side of Gloucester Terrace. He walked quickly along the road and was soon greeted by the flashing of headlights from a parked Ford Focus on the opposite side of the road. Looking right and left Deadman hurried across the road and swung himself into the front seat of the car.

'Phew. All this cloak and dagger stuff.' He smiled.

'It's easy really isn't it?'

'Either that or those MI5 chaps are complete morons.' Jack Moscroft grinned. 'I mean, how long are they going to sit there outside your place before they realise there's a back entrance? Morons, that's what they are. Anyway, let's get out of here, just in case they're a cleverer class of moron.'

Moscroft put the Focus into gear and it pulled away, joining the busy London traffic which buzzed along the busy streets of west London. Deadman surveyed the interior of the car.

'Don't say anything,' said Moscroft. 'It's a piece of crap but it was the best I could find. Anyway, I don't anticipate having it for very long.'

Just over an hour later the Ford Focus was gliding down the A2 once more into Kent. Soon afterwards the A2 gave way to the M2, by which time it was well and truly dark. Deadman wound the window down for a moment.

'You know, we don't know it but we breathe some really shitty air in London. I mean, get a sniff of that. It's country air, otherwise known as fresh air.'

'Well there's not much we can do about it,' replied Moscroft, 'except enjoy it while we can, and that's just what I intend doing.'

Deadman knew Moscroft was up to something. The grin across his face told him all he needed to know.

'Okay, are you going to tell me where we're going?'

'You'll find out when we get there,' replied Moscroft, wearing an inscrutable look on his face.

Suddenly, Moscroft nudged the car to the left, and leaving the motorway behind started along a dark country lane. The moon was up now and Deadman could just about pick out the unmistakable silhouettes of Kentish hops, hanging from wires stretched between poles.

'You know, my old Dad used to go hop picking when he was younger. In fact, Kent was overrun by cockneys during the summer months when they'd all come down and earn a few quid hop picking. He reckoned it was bloody hard work but it was a great way to get out of the city and have a holiday.'

Moscroft grunted. 'Yes, I mean I hardly think it likely that back in the thirties and forties you'd see a line of cockneys doing a knees up along the Costa del Sol.'

'What, and I supposed you used to go off with the rest of the middle classes to Nice or Biarritz or somewhere like that?'

'Well, not quite,' replied Moscroft, wishing he'd never started the argument. 'It was Torquay actually.'

'Torquay?' Deadman laughed and shook his head. 'Bloody Torquay.'

'Well it was better than grubbing around picking flippin' hops!'

Deadman sat in silence for a few moments before muttering 'Bollocks.'

The two friends sat in silence for a few minutes more as the car cruised slowly along a narrow road. Deadman suddenly realised where he was.

'Here, isn't this where Slater lives?'

Moscroft smiled. 'Well done. I wondered how long it would take you to notice.'

'So where are we staying? There's nothing here at Seasalter except for a holiday park and those beach huts. You don't think I'm gonna stay in that little shack that Slater calls home do you? You've got another think coming.'

Moscroft grinned. 'No, of course not. I've got something far more salubrious. I hope you've brought your bucket and spade.'

Suddenly, a terrible thought surged through Deadman's body.

No, it couldn't be. He hasn't really booked one of those has he?

The Ford Focus swung itself off the road and pulled up in a small car park facing an office. A long wooden barrier barred the way like a road block, and above it a huge sign proudly announced 'The Sunny View Holiday Park.'

'You must be fucking joking!' Deadman looked on in horror as his worst fear was realised. 'You haven't booked one of those mobile homes have you?'

Moscroft turned off the ignition and sighed.

'Look Matt, it's only for a few days I guess until we sort this thing out. Look at it this way; it's part hideout, part holiday home. The sea air will do you good.'

'Ah, fuck the sea air. Look at this place. It's like a bloody prisoner of war camp.' He gestured towards the fence. 'Look, all they need is barbed wire. They've got searchlights. I'm surprised they haven't got machine guns in the towers. This is like fucking Stalagluft III. I bet they have dogs patrolling the grounds after dark.'

Despite Deadman's pleadings Moscroft was bent on checking into the camp site. It made good sense. There were no telephone wires to the mobile homes, no nosey neighbours. It was the last place MI5 would think of looking. Deadman resigned himself to his fate.

'Bollocks.'

Meanwhile, Moscroft had jumped out of the car and had checked in at the office which had stayed open longer than usual to greet them.

'The name's Slasher, Julius Slasher,' said Moscroft, introducing himself to the bleary-eyed proprietor who did his best to look as though he was happy to see him. The man grunted as he consulted his computer, and puffed on a cigarette that hung limply from his bottom lip.

'Slasher, eh?'

A few seconds past before he grunted again.

'Slasher. Yeah. I've got it.' He looked up and gestured towards Deadman who had suddenly appeared in the doorway. 'And who's he?'

Before Deadman could answer Moscroft said, 'oh, this is my friend, Mr Buttock, Mr John Buttock.'

Deadman said nothing but turned away, trying not to laugh. The proprietor looked towards the door for a few moments and then back at Moscroft. 'Buttock? Are you having a laugh?'

'No, really. It's Buttock,' replied Moscroft, struggling to keep a straight face, 'with two tees.'

Ten minutes later, and with the formalities over, Deadman and Moscroft were hunkered down inside their new, albeit temporary, home.

'I called the reception chap from a public phone box, so there's no question of anyone tracing the call. We ought to be entirely safe here while we plan our next move.'

Deadman sighed. 'Famous last words.'

'Oh, come on Matt. Nobody knows we're here. MI5 are probably still there, sitting outside your place in Bishop's Bridge Road. Nobody knows where we are. Trust me. We can lie low and plan our visit to Dugdale's headquarters on Wednesday night.'

Deadman sighed again. 'Well, if you're sure. But I'm still not happy staying here. Look at it.' He pulled back the curtain and was immediately met by a beam of light from a security lamp. He dropped the curtain, moved away from the window and laughed.

'It's like one of those bloody war films. You know, The Great Escape or something like that. The ferrets will be along any minute with the dogs, looking for tunnels.'

'Well,' said Moscroft, 'I'm off to the bar for a beer. I could do with a drink.'

Deadman got up and followed him.

'Yeah, me too.'

As the two friends walked to the club house Deadman started darting between each of the mobile homes that stood rank upon rank, as if trying to dodge German searchlights. Moscroft shook his head in dismay.

'You silly bastard.'

17

London's Canary Wharf was a massive, shiny, glass and steel memorial to late twentieth century architects and planners. For decades thousands of dockers, crane drivers, labourers and general administration workers had handled the capital's daily massive load of imports and exports that had either arrived from the around the world or was being sent out into it. The workers had long since vanished, however. Now, suited office workers walked the neat, wide avenues that ran like veins through the over-developed area that was now home to scores of banks and other financial institutions, and to most of the main British newspapers, London's Fleet Street having long since upped sticks and moved east. The entire area had changed beyond recognition, as had other areas along the Thames. Gone were most of the facilities that serviced the fleets of commercial ships that once plied the river, and whilst many of the old warehouses remained overlooking the water's edge they had long since been converted into luxury apartments. It was enough to make any old East End docker turn in his grave.

The headquarters of Dugdale Media wasn't the tallest of buildings in Canary Wharf but it was tall enough. It sat alongside other similar shaped monoliths that stretched up towards the sky like giant stalactites. It was just getting dark when an old blue Ford Focus drew up just round the corner from the front entrance.

'I don't know where you got this car from but I'll be glad when we get back to the Mondeo.'

'Look, we could hardly use our own car now, could we?' Moscroft looked a bit sheepish. 'Anyway, it was the best I could do in the circumstances.'

'What circumstances?' asked Deadman.

'Okay, it was the last car left outside the

supermarket.'

Deadman laughed. 'Well, it's a piece of shit but it doesn't matter now. As long as it gets us out of here it'll have to do.'

Moscroft said nothing.

The huge glass and steel building that was Dugdale's headquarters was being illuminated by half a dozen powerful searchlights that reminded him of the old introduction to 20th Century Fox films, with the beams of light bouncing off and dancing upon the shiny glass sides of the building. It was spectacular stuff. But Moscroft and Deadman hadn't come to admire the spectacle, nor had they come to join the scores of celebrities, the great and the good, and the rich and the powerful, that had been summoned by Lord John Dugdale to celebrate his becoming the new owner of Channel 6, one of Britain's largest television stations. No, on the contrary, Matt Deadman was there as an uninvited guest, hoping to gatecrash the party and get access to Dugdale's inner sanctum in the hope that his safe might yield up a clue, a document, anything that might help him to solve a fifty-year-old mystery.

Moscroft switched off the ignition and turned to Deadman.

'What if Dugdale doesn't have an office or apartment here? I mean, we don't even know for sure if he has.'

If Moscroft was betraying a touch of nerves he was only echoing Deadman's own thoughts. After all, they hadn't been able to carry out any kind of recce. Sure, they knew the building was likely to house a boardroom or something like that but they couldn't be sure Dugdale actually had an apartment here. And even if he did there was no guarantee that there'd be a safe, although it was odds on that there would be. It was all a great gamble.

'Well,' said Deadman, philosophically, if Dugdale

doesn't have a safe or even an office I'll either be thrown out on my arse pretty quickly or I'll need you to bail me out when the cops arrest me for trespassing.'

Deadman turned to his friend. For once he was being serious.

'Look, Jack, what other choice do we have. You and I know Dugdale is mixed up in this Damon business somehow and we're getting nowhere fast. This business with the Iraq dossier makes the Damon case look like a simple missing persons case. I mean, if we can get the evidence to prove Slater's story we'll have the biggest scandal in recent years sitting in our laps. Think about it.'

Moscroft sighed. 'I have thought about it, Matt, and that's what worries me. You realise the amount of shit that's going to hit the fan if we can pull this one off? Dugdale, MI5, the government. And that's only to begin with. And think of the other repercussions. I mean, the US president only has to sneeze and the financial institutions around the world seem to catch a cold. The slightest whiff of a scandal seems to somehow affect the markets. God only knows what will happen if Slater's story is true and if we can prove it. Jeez.'

'Well we can't help that can we? Let's face it, we'll have enough good guys thanking us and Slater afterwards if we can pull it off.'

'Well I hope to God you're right.'

It was Deadman's turn to let out a long-drawn sigh.

'Do you think I haven't gone over this myself? The consequences and all that? But what are the options? Do we just let these sort of people get away with it? No. These bastards have screwed us over for far too long now and it's time for the reckoning. Fuck 'em. If Dugdale's guilty he'll go down and no fucking dossier is gonna save him because I'm gonna find it and hand it over to the press. They'll have a bloody field day stringing these bastards up. It'll serve him and whole rotten government right.'

Moscroft was quite taken aback by Deadman's sudden outburst, but he knew his friend was right. He laughed.

'That's some speech. It might not be in the same league as Henry the Fifth's on the eve of Agincourt but it's stirred my loins alright. Go on then. Do your stuff. And good luck. I'll be waiting around the corner here. Give me a shout if you need extricating in a hurry.'

Deadman turned and offered his hand to Moscroft.

'Wish me luck then.'

Moscroft said nothing but gave Deadman's hand a firm shake. And with that Deadman swung himself out of the car and walked towards the queue of people waiting to enter the headquarters of Dugdale Media. He straightened the bow tie of his smart dinner suit and adjusted his cuff-links. He was about to enter the lion's den.

As Deadman walked towards the entrance he noticed a line of very smart cars parked in the DDM private car park. As usual there were the usual expensive Jaguars, Mercedes and BMWs, but one car in particular caught Deadman's eye. Sitting there in the car park was a black Mercedes with the registration plate, GOSS 1P. It was the same car that had been seen by Joe, the Philippine gardener, pulling away from the scene just after Deadman's Alfa Romeo had been blown up. But it wasn't only this car that caught Deadman's eye, it was also the one parked next to it, a luxurious black Bentley Mulsanne with the number plate D326. It was a curious number, almost unique. It was certainly unusual enough for Deadman to have noticed it a few weeks earlier. But where? Deadman stopped for a moment and scratched his head. Where on earth had he seen the number plate? And then it came to him. Of course; the church in Herne at Lenny Bragg's funeral. It had been the car that the tall stranger had arrived in, the man who had walked up alone to Bragg's grave to pay his respects. Deadman hadn't caught sight of the man's face at the time but now he began to wonder. Had it been Dugdale? But why would one of the world's most powerful media tycoons have gone to Bragg's funeral? It didn't make sense. Or did it? Suddenly, things began to fall into place and when his phone suddenly began vibrating his suspicions seemed to have been confirmed.

Deadman hurried on but shook his head in dismay when he saw the queue of people waiting outside Dugdale media. It was the usual mix of hangers-on, micro celebrities, tanned 'wannabees', footballers and their WAGs, politicians, television personalities and upper-class sycophants who needed to bask in the reflected glory of Lord John Dugdale. The men wore various styles of dinner suits whilst the women were adorned in the usual array of dresses designed to shock and titillate the waiting pressmen whose cameras popped and flashed as each celebrity flashed his or her well-practiced smile at them.

Deadman sighed.

I don't know. These people would come to the opening of an envelope if they thought there was something in it for them.

As the guests filed slowly inside Deadman saw the security men on the door were checking their invitations with scanners.

Okay. Now we have a problem. No invite.

Deadman eased his way into the queue and noticed a stunning blonde, whose backless, see-through dress, perfectly formed long legs and six-inch stilettos were designed with only one thing in mind; to draw the attention of the press boys. After all, publicity like this was cheap and easy but massively effective. Deadman had to think quickly, but went for it all the same.

'Aren't you one of the Sky Sports' girls? Haven't I seen you presenting one of their shows?'

Deadman knew full well that she wasn't, but it was a cheap and easy way to grab the attention of this would-be starlet, who was obviously and easily flattered by his bullshit.

'Well, no, actually I'm not,' she giggled, 'but it's very nice of you to think so.'

'Well, all I can say is that Sky is missing out. You'd put those other girls to shame.'

The girl giggled some more. 'Do you really think so?' Oo. Just think. I'll tell my agent. He might be able to do something for me.'

Deadman was trying hard not to laugh. The girl was not exactly a dumb blonde but she was pretty well the next best thing. Tanned, stunningly beautiful and completely brainless. But the ruse was working. The girl decided to introduce herself.

'My name's Mandy, Mandy Fidget. I'm a model.'

'Deadman, Matt Deadman. I'm not a model.'

Mandy giggled again. 'My agent's trying to get me one of the talent shows, you know, on the telly, or onto one of the reality shows. He thinks I'd be a hit.'

Looking down at Mandy's low cut and very revealing dress Deadman could see why, not that there was the slightest chance of it ever happening. Girls like Mandy were ten a penny and she hadn't a hope of cutting it in the big time. Still, a girl had to try, and if it helped Deadman get inside Dugdale's party then he was more than prepared to give her the big build up. Flattery, as they say, will get you anywhere, and Deadman hoped it would get him inside the building.

'I have a few contacts myself in the business. You know,

I went to the same school as Mick Jagger.'

'Mick Jagger? Ooh...fancy?'

Mandy warmed even more to the tall, dark and handsome man who was buttering her up for no other reason than to get inside. Sure, Mick Jagger had gone to Dartford Grammar School, but Deadman himself had gone to Dartford West which, although just down the road, was a good deal different. The grammar school was for bright kids whereas some of those whom Deadman knew at Dartford West were inside borstal before they'd even officially left school. Still, the comment had the desired effect and although the truth, and the fact that Jagger was old enough to be Deadman's father, was completely lost on poor Mandy the mere mention of the name Mick Jagger drew her even closer to him. She took Deadman's arm.

'I'll have to keep hold of you tonight won't I?'

It was the best offer Deadman had had for a while but much as he would have liked to have explored Mandy a little deeper he was going to have to pass on this one, not that he was going to let on just yet.

'I'll drink to that when we get in,' said Deadman, as he and his new friend neared the security men.

His heart began to beat a little faster now, not because he had a stunning blonde on his arm but because the burly security men on the door were now just a few feet away and were showing no signs of easing up on the scanning of invites. There was no way he was going to get in without one. But, just as things were becoming rather serious, his Mister Micawber philosophy seemed to be about to pay dividends once more. Something suddenly turned up, and it turned up, of course, in the shape of Mandy's dress, or rather what was in it.

As Deadman and Mandy finally reached security one of the photographers suddenly shouted Mandy's name, and waved. He was obviously a plant from Mandy's agency but it had the desired effect. As Mandy stepped forward to thrust out her ample chest towards the photographer, others, seeing the stunning vista, suddenly surged forward. Her chance had come. And so had Deadman's.

As Mandy stepped forward to pose for the photographers she thrust her cumbersome invitation into Deadman's hand. In an instant she was lost in blaze of bright camera flashes that blinded everyone close around her. As quick as one of the camera flashes that caught Mandy's dazzling brilliance Deadman stepped forward and handed the invitation to one of the security men who, half blinded and careless, scanned the invite and waved him through into the building. He passed beyond a second barrier, straightened his bow-tie and helped himself to a glass of champagne that was offered by a waiter, standing with a silver tray at the entrance to the main reception area. Part one of the mission was accomplished.

He turned towards the entrance once more to see Mandy arguing with the security men and pointing towards the reception. One of the men took her by the arm and led her away, struggling. Deadman turned to the waiter once more.

'I don't know. These girls will try anything to get publicity. I don't know what the world's come to.'

The waiter smiled. 'No, sir. Me neither.'

The large, expansive reception area of Dugdale's media's headquarters was a picture of modern corporate hospitality; tables creaked beneath the weight of hundreds of glasses of red and white wine, mineral water, various juices and, of course, champagne that was quaffed eagerly by the freeloaders who continued to file in. A bevy of beautiful hostesses saw to their needs, mixing and talking and generally being bland but welcoming. A sumptuous buffet was spread over a number of other tables, whilst waiters, resplendent in smart, elegant uniforms moved unobtrusively amongst the assembled guests offering small but very expensive bites which were gobbled up as eagerly as the champagne had been guzzled down.

Deadman had been to more functions like this than he cared to remember but no matter how many times he'd been he never really warmed to them. The arrogance of the guests towards the staff who served them always grated, treating them like dirt without so much as a 'thank you'. The freeloaders who turn up for anything provided there was a free lunch on offer, the superficial snobs, down on their luck, who could mix and mingle with their peers, pretending to be this and that, exchanging boring stories of their imaginary travels, or simply name-dropping, out to impress and to maintain an assumed but ultimately false position of higher rank in society. To Matt Deadman it was all superficial bullshit.

Thirty minutes passed with Deadman engaging in painful dialogue with one or two of the guests, posing as an entrepreneur. It had worked with the brainless Mandy Fidget; why not try it with these other braying types. There was no sign of Dugdale himself but when members of DDM began shuffling into position around a small makeshift stage it soon became obvious that he was about to put in an appearance.

Lord John Dugdale was no recluse, no Howard Hughes, but he did limit his personal appearances to a bare minimum. Hence the interest and the demand for invitations once it became known he was to hold a reception to mark his takeover of Channel 6. On the stroke of eight-thirty, and with the guests well and truly set for a good night, a man wearing a dinner suit walked onto the stage and gave the microphone a good thump to call everyone to attention.

'Good evening, ladies and gentlemen, and members of the press. Welcome to the headquarters of Dugdale Media, and may I say what a pleasure it is to see so many of you here tonight on this very special occasion. I am, of course, talking about Dugdale Media's having acquired Channel 6 Television. My name is Neil Johnson, personal secretary to Lord Dugdale. It is my privilege not only to welcome you all here tonight but also to introduce the man who has made all of this possible, a man who stands head and shoulders above all others in the media industry in Britain, and, arguably, the world.'

This last comment brought polite applause from the audience. By now a number of giant television screens flickered into life and there, staring out from them, was the face of Lord John Dugdale. A shiver ran back and forth down Deadman's spine. Sure, he'd seen pictures of him before, but they'd been blurred, hastily taken photographs, most of which were snapped by paparazzi. To see a large, quality image of the man who possibly held the answers to so many mysteries staring out of the screens made even Deadman swallow. And then, as Johnson left the stage, a tall man appeared from stage left and stepped forward to the microphone.

The effect was magical. A hush descended upon the audience as if some sort of God-like figure had stepped out of the shadows. Tall, slim and tanned, and wearing an obviously expensive dark blue dinner suit, Dugdale looked every inch a captain of industry. Even Deadman was impressed. There passed a few seconds, the audience, pregnant with expectation, holding its breath as they waited for Dugdale to speak. Then, finally, came the voice of the great man.

'Ladies and gentlemen....'

Deadman listened intently for about a minute or so

whilst Dugdale went on about how proud he was to have acquired Channel 6 as well as going through the usual polite acknowledgements. As he did so, Deadman couldn't help noticing something swelling up inside, a sort of hatred, and his pulse began to beat faster and faster. This was not on account of the fact that he was about to go and burgle the mogul's office but rather that he was staring at the man who a few weeks before had tried to kill him, and was almost certainly mixed up in the deaths of others. But there was nothing he could do right now, not with a host of burly security men dotted around the reception area. No, he would have to wait for the right moment. Right now he had to concern himself with slipping away from the party and trying to gain access to Dugdale's private apartment which should, if his hunch was correct, be the penthouse flat of this huge office tower.

Deadman had already located the lifts earlier in the evening. All he needed now was the right moment to slip away, and he didn't have to wait too long for it. As the audience continued to listen Deadman noticed Dugdale was making a joke at the expense of one of his staff away to the left, affording him the chance to slip behind a huge glass partition, beside which ran a corridor leading to the lifts. As quick as a flash he slipped away unnoticed towards the lifts. But first he had one other important job to do.

On the opposite side of the lifts was the DDM security office. The security men themselves were busy in reception listening to Dugdale. Deadman slipped quietly inside the office and immediately spotted a draw which housed computer discs with the previous day's filming on them. He took out the disc which covered the previous evening, slipped it into a disc drive and ran the film. Fortunately, no date appeared on screen, only the time. He was able to set the programme running, so that any security guard watching the screens later on would see a film showing the previous evening's activity instead of a live feed. The last thing Deadman needed was some eagle-eyed boy scout watching as he went about his business. The job completed, he slipped unnoticed out of the office and walked to one of the lifts. Fortunately, one of them was already open and waiting on the ground floor. It was a stroke of luck. Deadman needed the pinging of an opening door along with the usual 'doors opening' message like he needed a hole in the head. He skipped inside but was disappointed not to find any button marked 'Penthouse.' It wasn't a major setback, however. After all, it was highly unlikely that any big shot like Dugdale would allow a lift to get anywhere near his own apartment. Nevertheless, it left Deadman with a bit of a problem. Where the hell was the penthouse? There was nothing for it but to take the lift to the top floor and take it from there.

A few moments later the lift doors swished to a close behind him.

Oh well, here goes.

And with that Deadman pressed the button marked '46', and in an instant the lift was on its way, speeding smoothly through the forty-five floors before coming to a sudden halt on the forty-sixth floor. A ping and a voice announced the lift's arrival. Deadman stepped cautiously out and found himself in a smart corridor, lined with deep red carpet from wall to wall. This was obviously not a floor for the normal office plebs who grubbed and scratched out a living on Dugdale's behalf. This was something different. Sure enough, Deadman realised why. Just around the corner there was a second lift, with just a single door, flanked by ornate potted plants. There was no call button, nor any way of calling the lift, other than a small panel with nine digits on it. It was just what Deadman had hoped to find. It was

Dugdale's private lift. The problem now was how to crack the four-digit code that had to be pressed in order to activate the lift?

Things had certainly come on a great deal since Deadman first became involved in the world of private investigation. Gadgets that seemed to be reserved only for fictional heroes such as James Bond had now become a reality and were available from all good retailers. He reached into his pocket and produced one of his own.

Well, here goes nothing. Fingers crossed.

The gadget in question was a simple infra-red fingerprint reader, like a small torch, which was designed to pick out fingerprints or marks that suggested something had been either pressed or held, marks that could not be seen by the naked eye. Deadman hit the switch and the small torch-like gadget sent a beam of invisible light against the key pad.

Bingo.

In an instant, four of the numbers, one, three, six, and nine, lit up in blue. These were obviously the keys that had to be pressed in order to operate the lift. The next problem was how to figure out the sequence?

Thank god for Moscroft and his mathematical brain.

Maths was never Deadman's strongpoint but Moscroft had worked out that the number of possible sequences for four digits, from one to nine, was twenty-four. All Deadman had to do was go through various sequences until the code was broken. It might take twenty-four attempts but he might be lucky and hit the jackpot at the first attempt. In any case, there was no point hanging around. He reached inside his jacket and produced a small piece of paper on which Moscroft had written the possible sequences. Deadman began with one, three, six, and nine, hoping he might be lucky first time. There was nothing. He tried another sequence. Nothing. A third sequence was tried but still nothing happened.

Fuck this for a laugh. Any minute now the bloody cleaners are going to be here and that'll be it.

Deadman's hands were beginning to sweat now, and small beads of sweat ran down his forehead. He tried a fifth sequence; nothing. Suddenly, there was the sound of the lift engaging its gear. Somebody was coming up.

For Christ's sake, come on. What's the fucking code?

The sound of the lift approaching grew closer and closer as Deadman tried a sixth combination. One, nine, six, three. A click followed and suddenly the lift doors opened.

Hallelujah! Thank gawd for that. Thanks Moscroft, you get ten out of ten for that.

Deadman entered the code a second time on the panel inside the lift, and just as the doors closed he heard the sound of the other lift doors opening. He'd made it, but by the skin of his teeth. He hoped to God nobody noticed Dugdale's private lift in operation. A few seconds later and the doors opened once more. Deadman stepped out to find himself inside the sumptuously furnished penthouse apartment of Lord John Dugdale.

A brief glance around the apartment was enough to suggest that Dugdale was very much 'old school', with dark wood furniture and desk, oil paintings on the walls and elegant ornaments dotted here and there on cabinets and desks. The only concession to the modern age was a huge state of the art television screen that hung upon one of the walls, as well as a very smart computer system that sat on a desk in one corner of the room. Three sides of the room were decorated with rich, dark red wallpaper whilst the fourth side of the room consisted of a giant wall of glass which looked out over the Thames and South-East London. Night had well and truly descended now, and the illuminated streets below looked like so many thousands of stars.

Deadman thought it looked quite beautiful but remembered he hadn't come to admire the view. He had a job to do.

The first thing Deadman had to do was locate the safe, if indeed there was one. There had to be, otherwise the whole evening's risky venture had all been for nothing. He peered around the room.

Right then, where are you?

He had seen countless films where the safe had been hidden behind a painting. Dugdale was obviously a traditionalist, so what more obvious place to hid a safe than behind one of the paintings hanging in the room. Hanging on a wall behind Dugdale's desk was a fine oil painting of a fox hunt. Deadman stood there for a few seconds admiring it, and wondering whether the fox would get away. He smiled at the irony. Will Dugdale or Damon get away with it? Not if he could help it. He walked up to the painting and carefully pulled it forward. It seemed too obvious.

Surely Dugdale hasn't hidden his safe behind the painting?

But there it was, a safe, about two feet by one, and there, sitting to one side, was a panel with nine numbers on it. Deadman's hunch was right after all; Dugdale had a digital safe. He sighed with relief.

No need for any long, drawn out safe-cracking.

Deadman took out his little infra-red torch again and shone it at the panel but froze when he saw the result. Only three numbers turned blue.

Bollocks! Now what? Only three numbers.

What Deadman didn't realise was that there were even fewer combinations as there were only three digits being used for the code. The trouble was his mind had gone completely blank. Moscroft had written down the different combinations of four digits but it hadn't occurred to him that

Dugdale might use one digit twice or more.

Suddenly, and as quickly as everything seemed to be stalling, everything seemed to fall into place. Of course; it was obvious. Deadman smiled. If his hunch was right he would enter four digits even without having to use his magic gismo. He put the infra-red torch back in his pocket and took a deep breath.

Well, here goes then.

He leaned forward and entered eight, eight, six, three. Then, just as he hoped, there was the reassuring sound of a click from within the safe. Deadman turned the handle and the door opened. A feeling of pure elation rose through his body. Hunches only ever seemed to pay off for others, but now his turn had come, and how.

At first, it seemed as though Deadman had risked all for a bundle of junk. Inside the safe were a few bank documents, a bundle of twenty-pound notes, and a couple of company files, none of which interested him in the slightest. Surely there must be something else, something worth taking the risk for? And then, sitting at the back of the safe were the things he had come for. He had expected to find one thing but hoped to find another also. He was right on both counts.

He took from the safe two cardboard files and placed them on Dugdale's desk. He then turned and placed the other items back in the safe. Then, with his hands trembling slightly, he opened the first of the files. It was the one that contained the truth about the Iraq dossier, the document that effectively sent Britain to war in 2003. It was Dugdale's trump card. Deadman's job was to ensure it was never played. But what really took his breath away were the contents of the second file. Inside was a large manila envelope. He pulled it open and reached inside. He pulled out a passport, some old newspaper clippings and a couple of tattered black and white photographs. Deadman smiled and shook his head.

Well, well, well. I was right. The shit's really gonna hit the fan when this lot comes out.

He was so consumed by what he was reading he failed to notice the door of the office opening. He was looking at the passport when a voice suddenly came out of nowhere.

'Good evening, Mr Deadman. Or should I call you Lazarus? I must say you look rather well for a man who was supposed to be dead. Now to what do I owe the pleasure?'

Deadman was caught cold. He looked up and found himself staring down the barrel of a pistol. Holding it was none other than Lord John Dugdale. Deadman calmly put the passport down and turned to look Dugdale in the eye.

'I think the pleasure is all mine. I've been waiting a long time to meet you, Lord Dugdale...or should that be Jimmy Damon?'

18

'Jimmy Damon.' The words hung in the air like a peel of thunder. Dugdale himself looked shaken but quickly composed himself. He smiled.

'That's very clever of you, Mr Deadman. But what makes you think I'm this Jimmy Damon fellow?'

'Oh, nothing really. It never occurred to me until this evening. Okay, there were a load of small clues which, on their own, meant very little. But put them all together, and, bingo!'

Dugdale laughed. 'Please go on.'

'Well,' said Deadman, 'first there was the stranger at Lenny Bragg's funeral. I remember the car, D326. I saw this parked outside your office just now. It's your car isn't it? It was you I saw at Bragg's funeral, wasn't it? And as for the number plate, D326, I received a call this evening. D326 was the number of the locomotive robbed during the Great Train Robbery. And then, of course, there was the code to your safe, eight, eight, six, three; the 8th of August 1963, the day of the robbery, and even the code to the lift, one, nine, six, three, the year. It all fell into place this evening.'

'That's all very well,' replied Dugdale, 'but it proves nothing other than I've got an interest in the Great Train Robbery, as I'm sure many people have. They're absolutely fascinated. But you've got no proof that I'm this Jimmy Damon.'

'But that's where you're wrong. You know, you really ought to put your old documents somewhere a bit safer.'

Deadman picked up the passport and opened it.

'James Damon. It's your old passport, isn't it?

Dugdale said nothing.

'And then there's this photograph. I saw a similar one

at Stan Tanner's place before you had him killed. This photograph shows you, Bragg and Higgins together, the Three Musketeers, plus Tanner.'

'Hm,' said Dugdale, walking slowly forward, 'that's quite a bit of detective work, isn't it?' He walked to a cabinet, put down the gun and poured himself a scotch. 'Can I get you anything?'

'I'm okay thanks,' replied Deadman, shaking his head.

Dugdale picked up the gun again, walked slowly towards the desk and picked up the passport. He sighed.

'James Damon. Now that's a name I haven't heard for many a year. Well, I suppose there's no use denying it any longer. Congratulations Mr Deadman, you've done well. Go to the top of the class. I could do with someone like you working for me. You're a very resourceful man, elusive too, and, apparently, indestructible.'

'Forget it,' snapped Deadman, 'I've got a job to do and I intend finishing it.'

'And what would exactly would that job be, may I ask?'

'To bring you to justice for the robbery all those years ago.'

Dugdale looked surprised. 'For God's sake, it was fifty years ago. Do you really think anybody cares about it anymore?

Deadman shook his head. 'I don't care about that. That's a matter for the police. And I'm sure there's someone out there who can nick you for something relating to the Iraq dossier.'

'Oh, that.' Dugdale smiled. 'Yes, I must say that's been very handy over the last few years. Very handy indeed.'

'You smug bastard,' snapped Deadman. 'I could almost forgive you for the train robbery. After all, nobody really suffered, other than the poor bloke who got whacked over the head. But to sell out your country and send our blokes to their deaths just for a peerage? That's pretty low.'

'Well, Mr Deadman, one has to stoop to some pretty low depths to get where I am today.'

'And just how did you get where you are today?'

Dugdale laughed. 'I'm afraid it's a long and very boring story.'

'Try me. I'm a good listener. I'm all ears, and I love a good bedtime story.'

'Should I begin with, once upon a time, then?' asked Dugdale, sarcastically. 'Well then, where to begin?' Dugdale took a sip of scotch and sat down in one of the leather armchairs. He waved the gun at Deadman. 'You'd better take a seat, oh, and please keep your hands where I can see them.

'I think I'll have that drink after all,' said Deadman, walking slowly to the drinks cabinet. He helped himself to a brandy and walked back before sitting down in one of the other armchairs. Dugdale's pistol followed him every step.

'So, where to begin?' said Dugdale, sighing. 'Where to begin? I don't suppose there's any point in starting with the robbery. You'll know all about that. Well, for various reasons which I won't go into, I decided it would be safer to leave the old country and go to Australia. Lenny Bragg came with me but never made it beyond Gibraltar. He couldn't stand puking his guts up every day. Sea sickness, you know.'

'So that's why he came to end up in Spain?' asked Deadman.

'Yes. He met Carmen and stayed. Oh, I believe you two have met. Yes, it was good of her to call me the minute you'd left her house in Spain. It was Carmen who alerted me to your investigation.' Dugdale took another sip of scotch. 'Now, where was I? Oh yes, Gibraltar. Well, anyway, I continued on to Australia and worked for a while on the

Snowy Mountain Scheme. I must say the government's 'Ten Pound Pom' scheme came in very handy at the time. Very handy indeed. Nobody cared who you were or what you could do. So long as you turned up each day and did your work you got paid and that was it. It was all very convenient. Needless to say, it was rather tiresome having to work knowing I had today's equivalent of almost two million pounds safely stashed away in a Swiss bank account.' Dugdale went suddenly quiet and spoke to himself softly. 'Hm, I paid rather a good deal of commission for that service, far too much.' He shook himself out of his little aside and carried on with his story. 'So, there I was, accumulating a good deal of money, legitimately mind,' Dugdale made a point of emphasising this, 'and was soon in a position to start a new career for myself by buying a local newspaper.'

'Yes,' said Deadman, 'I think that's where I picked you up. We all know the story from there, the way you bought one paper after another and built up your media empire.'

'And I'm bloody well proud of it too. Listen, I turned those newspapers around through hard work and invention. Okay, I may have been a little, shall we say, frugal with the truth about where the funds came from with which I bought the first paper, but from then on it was solid hard graft. You can't take that away from me.'

Deadman stayed silent.

'Nobody knew who I was. I managed to obtain a new passport in the name of John Dugdale and the rest, as they say, is history.

'So who exactly is or was John Dugdale?' asked Deadman.

'John Dugdale? Oh, him. Well, it's me of course, or at least it is now. The real John Dugdale was a fellow 'Ten Pound Pom' who came over on the same ship as me. There was nothing for him in England, no relatives. He was after a new life in Australia.' Dugdale allowed a smile to come over his face. 'It was a shame he met with his accident.'

'His accident?' asked Deadman. 'Accidents seem to hang around you like flies around a rotting corpse.'

'Yes. I must say the finger of Providence has certainly been upon me over the years. Still, here I am, a captain of industry and now a peer in the House of Lords.' He took another sip of scotch and smiled. 'It's ironic, don't you think, that given the establishment's reaction to my comrades who robbed the mail train, the thirty year sentences, that I'm now very much part of that same establishment.'

'Not for much longer,' snapped Deadman.

'Oh come now, Mr Deadman, 'do you really think anyone is going to believe you when you take your little story to the authorities, authorities over which, might I add, I exercise a little, shall we say, influence? No, I don't think so.'

'I'd hardly call it a little story. I mean, there's the Great Train Robbery for a start, followed by your involvement in the deaths of Field, Edwards, Wilson, Higgins and Tanner, not to mention the attempt at killing me. Oh, and by the way, thanks for blowing up my Alfa. I was fond of that car.'

Dugdale smiled. 'Oh yes. That was an unfortunate business. We were led to believe you'd been fried in your car. Pity really. Oh well, you can't win them all.'

'Try telling that to Steve Bates, the poor bastard who did get fried.'

'Steve Bates? Was that his name? Oh.'

'So what was the deal with the others? Why kill your old mates, the ones involved in the robbery?'

'Mates? They were never friends of mine except for Higgins and Tanner. We didn't know any of the gang, save for Edwards. Bragg, Higgins and I were brought in by Edwards and the first we ever saw of Reynolds, Goody and the rest of the gang was when we turned up at the farmhouse just before the robbery.'

Dugdale got up and poured some more scotch into his empty tumbler. He sat down again and began to recount his version of events of August 1963, of the robbery and the immediate aftermath. As he gave his account he seemed to forget the situation in which he found himself but drifted back instead to those heady days fifty years before when the gang pulled off its audacious robbery. There was the robbery itself, the getaway afterwards, and the business with Daly's money and his subsequent acquittal which was the reason for him leaving for Australia. When he
finished his story he fell silent and seemed to drift off again, reflecting on the events, seemingly oblivious to the fact that Deadman was in the room with him.

'That explains the mysterious business with the money found in the telephone box.'

Deadman broke the silence and brought Dugdale back to the present.

'The phone box? Oh, yes. It was a neat trick, and was one that would have worked had it not been for Daly's unfortunate acquittal.' He spoke softly to himself again. 'Yes, that was somewhat irritating.'

He snapped out of it once more.

'As for Field and the others, well, it was a simple case of them or me. When I heard through my newspaper contacts that each of them was about to reveal my identity in exchange for rather large payments I simply had to put a stop to it. Most of the gang had seen their cash taken by so-called 'friends' who charged somewhat exorbitant prices for their services. There's no honour amongst thieves, Mr Deadman, I can assure you of that.'

'Obviously.' Deadman nodded in agreement.

'The deaths were all carefully planned and executed, of

course. In fact, each one was so well carried out the police had no idea they were anything other than unfortunate accidents. And let's face it, was anybody really interested in investigating the deaths of former train robbers and villains? No, I don't think so. Eliminating Danny Higgins was perhaps the most unfortunate business, but then Danny never did quite have the backbone for the business, always worrying about this and that. Still, it was either him or me. As for Mr Tanner, well, you've seen for yourself just how easy it was to glean information from him. It was too much of a risk to have him drinking away in his south London squat. One careless word and that would have been it. So, Mr Tanner had to go.'

Dugdale sighed. 'Poor Stan. He never did really cut it with the three of us, always wanted to be like us, but never quite fitted the bill.'

'Which left just Bragg as the only one to remain loyal?'

'Yes,' said Dugdale, taking a sip of scotch. 'Lenny took my secret to the grave, but he did at least feel the need to confess to being one of the gang. I suppose it was his way of cleansing his soul.'

'Or merely taking the chance to cock one last snook at the establishment.'

'Yes, perhaps. But he remained loyal, which was one of the reasons I felt the need to attend his funeral.'

Deadman listened with a mixture of serious interest, disgust and curiosity. Sure, he was appalled at Dugdale's carefree attitude towards the killings, but was equally entranced by his story. Here was a Great Train Robber, whom nobody had ever heard of, but had got away with over two million pounds in today's money. And not only that, he had forged a new identity for himself and had returned to Britain as one of the most powerful media moguls in the world. It was a remarkable story, even without the postscript involving the dossier on Iraq that had sent Britain to war.

Deadman finished his drink and put the glass tumbler on the table in front of him. 'It's one hell of a story. I think even Hollywood would have trouble getting people to believe it.'

'Yes,' replied Dugdale, 'it is indeed. It's a great pity that nobody will ever get to hear it.'

So far, the evening seemed to have been passed amid an air of almost friendly conviviality, as though Dugdale and Deadman were friends exchanging stories after years apart. But the atmosphere suddenly changed. Dugdale got to his feet, still pointing his gun at Deadman, who realised the evening's pleasantries were coming swiftly to an end.

'You know I can't let you leave this building alive. I'm afraid I've got far more to lose than your good self.'

Dugdale pressed a buzzer on his desk and when a voice crackled back over the intercom Dugdale said simply, 'You may come in now gentlemen.'

The media mogul stepped back from the desk. A few seconds later a door opened and two well-built and obviously very fit and toned security men walked into the room. Deadman could see in an instant they were serious guys. Both had ear pieces plugged into wireless radios, they wore expensive dark blue suits and the slight bulge in their left breasts suggested the presence of firearms.

'Would you escort Mr Deadman from the building please, and see to it that I never hear from him again?' Dugdale nodded towards Deadman. 'You understand what I mean?'

'Yes sir, we understand. Leave it to us.'

And with that one of the men walked straight up to Deadman and grabbed him, whilst the second man came and delivered a powerful punch right into his midriff.

Deadman never saw it coming. He dropped to his knees, coughing, but was yanked to his feet and dragged away towards the lift.

'Oh, and you'd better use the service lift on the forty-sixth floor. Take him out the back. We don't want the evening's frivolities interrupted for any reason do we?' Dugdale grinned.

Deadman was hauled towards the same lift that he'd used earlier that same evening.

'Goodbye, Mr Deadman. It was interesting...reminiscing with you.'

19

Deadman was still recovering from the blow to his stomach as the lift dropped one level to the forty-sixth floor. There was the usual ping and swish as the doors parted. The two burly security men then dragged Deadman from the lift and walked him down the corridor to the service lift. One of the men pressed the call button and the familiar sound of gears being engaged followed. Being a service lift there was no need for the usual high-speed installation and one of the security men cursed at the time it was taking to arrive. Deadman, on the other hand, welcomed the delay as it gave him time to recover, and to think. A minute passed before the lift finally arrived and when the doors opened Deadman was bundled in followed by his two minders. The button was pushed and the lift set off once more, dropping slowly towards ground level.

Deadman watched as the digital panel indicated the passing of each floor; 40...39...38...37...One of the security men cursed again.

'Come on, for fuck's sake, this is taking forever.'

'That's why we never use it,' said the second man. 'But as we're taking out the trash we've got to use it.'

The two men glanced towards Deadman and laughed.

The lift continued to descend; 29...28...27...

Deadman had to think fast.

19...18...17...

One of the security men sighed once more. 'Come on...come on.'

10...9...8...

'Thank Christ for that. Here we go...'

3...2...1...0

The lift finally reached the ground floor. There was a

ping, a swish and the doors slowly slid apart.

'Thanks for the ride, guys. I appreciate it.' And with that, Matt Deadman stepped out of the lift, adjusted his cufflinks and bow-tie and stepped out into the corridor. Behind him, lying crumpled, bleeding and unconscious on the floor inside the lift were Dugdale's two security men.

Just as the lift had approached the ground floor it had suddenly shuddered, throwing the first goon off balance. Deadman saw his chance. As quick as a flash he hurled himself forward and drove his shoulder into the man's back, sending him crashing face first against the lift's door. Before the second security man could react Deadman brought up his foot and drove it deep into the man's crotch. The man doubled over, howling in pain. Deadman grabbed him by the hair and lifted his head up, delivering a solid punch into the man's face at the same time. There was the usual sound of bone splintering as the man's nose dissolved in a mush of blood, skin and bone. The force of the punch sent him reeling backwards, insensible, against the wall of the lift. Deadman then turned to the first man who was shaking his head and trying to regain his senses. Before he could do so Deadman slammed him against the door again and drove a good solid punch deep into his midriff, driving the wind from the man's lungs. He grabbed him and turned to the second man. Then, picking him up also, he brought the two men's heads together in a sickening crunch. Both men fell unconscious to the floor. There was just room enough for Deadman to deliver a good kick into the face of each man as they lay helpless on the floor. Just to make sure.

That ought to keep them quiet for a while.

Deadman bent down and relieved the two men of their pistols, emptied the contents of one of the magazines and threw the bullets back into the lift. The doors of the lift then opened and Deadman stepped out into the corridor. A few seconds later the doors closed again. Deadman took out a small penknife from his pocket, forced the control panel open and yanked the wires free, jamming the lift where it was and leaving the security men stranded, and still unconscious, on the ground floor. He then walked away, throwing the pistol into a nearby waste bin whilst stuffing the other gun into the waistband of his trousers.

Now for Dugdale.

In his penthouse apartment on the forty-seventh floor Lord John Dugdale was flicking through some papers on his desk. He added his signature to a couple of sheets, tapped them together and placed them back in a brown cardboard folder. He took a sip of scotch from his glass tumbler and glanced towards the assortment of papers and documents that were lying on the desk in front of him. He sighed to himself and shook his head. There was enough evidence here to put him behind bars, bring down the government and generally cause mayhem throughout Britain and, probably, the world. He picked up his old passport bearing the name 'James Damon' and flicked through its pages.

'I'd forgotten all about you,' he said to himself quietly, as his mind wandered back once again to August 1963. 'And as for you,' he said, reaching for the document which contained the truth about Iraq dossier, 'you're going back into the safe where you belong.'

As he gathered the documents together he heard the sound of the lift humming its way up to his apartment. There was a ping, a swish, and the doors opened behind him. Dugdale continued to gather the documents together.

'Come in, gentlemen. That was quick work. I do

hope Mr. Deadman didn't give you any trouble.'

'Oh, I wouldn't say that.'

Dugdale froze. A burning sensation suddenly went searing through his body and his heart seemed to want to burst out of his chest. He turned slowly around to find himself face to face with Deadman who was holding one of the pistols which Dugdale had expected to be used to kill his troublesome guest. Instead, it was he who now found himself staring, literally, down the barrel.

'I think you could say the boot was now well and truly on the other foot. Wouldn't you say?' Deadman waved the pistol at Dugdale. 'Now, get your fucking hands up.'

Dugdale sighed but did it anyway. 'Oh, come, come, Mr Deadman, you've been watching too many gangster films.'

'Well you ought to know. I mean, you're the biggest fucking gangster in town, aren't you? Now, get 'em up!'

Dugdale sighed again but did what he was told. He slowly raised his hands, keeping his eyes fixed firmly on his would-be captor.

'Now, get away from the desk.' Deadman waved the pistol again and Dugdale stepped back.

'I'll take these if I may. There are some people who will be very interested in these.' Deadman scooped up the small pile of documents, including the passport, the old photographs and, of course, the document relating to the Iraq dossier. He placed them all in a large manila envelope and stepped away from the desk.

'Right then. What am I going to do with you?'

'Don't be a fool Deadman. Do you really think the police are going to bring charges? Think about it, man. You've got MI5 on your tail already. They'll never allow these documents to see the light of day. They've too much to lose.'

'Well, they should have thought about that before the government went to war. I've heard all about the Iraq dossier and what a crock of shite it is. The public deserves to know what sort of people are running this country.' Deadman paused and stared at Dugdale. 'And as for you....well, I'll leave that to the police. Without your trump card they'll be free to bring charges.'

'Face it, Deadman. These documents will never see the light of day. When the government realises you're going to hand over the truth about the Iraq dossier they'll issue a D-Notice. Now, I assume you know what a D-Notice is?'

'I know what a D-Notice is,' snapped Deadman, 'and I don't think this comes within its remit. This isn't sensitive information that could compromise national security or anything like that. The press will grab this story with both hands. And in any case, the world is going to take great pleasure in knowing who you really are. I mean, you rub shoulders with the great and the good, don't you? It'll be like having shit smeared all over them.' Deadman laughed. 'The press will have a field day with you. They'll hang you out to dry good and proper.'

Dugdale wasn't really in a position to argue. He suspected it was unlikely the government would be able to issue a D-Notice. After all, they were only issued when the interests of national security were at risk, and there had already been a public inquiry into the dossier anyway. The worst that he could be accused of, should the truth be revealed, was that he had been bought off with a peerage. Okay, so it was pretty low, but it wasn't a crime. In fact, it would look worse for the government, which would be guilty of buying Dugdale's silence, in effect, by bribery. But what would really crucify Dugdale was the revelation that he was, in fact, Jimmy Damon, one of the great train robbers. It may well have been fifty years since the robbery but the case was never officially closed. The other gang members had each received sentences of up to thirty years and there was no reason why Dugdale would not receive the same if brought to justice.

Dugdale realised he'd been backed into a corner and there was no way out.

'Look,' he said, adopting a more conciliatory attitude. 'Be sensible. I'm sure we can come to some sort of arrangement.'

'Oh,' replied Deadman, in his best sarcastic tone. 'You mean the arrangement whereby you pay me off in return for my silence and then one night I get a visit from MI5 or some more of your watchdogs? Come on, Dugdale, do you think I was born yesterday? Stick your money up your arse. I'm being well paid for bringing you in anyway.'

The problem was, as Deadman knew only too well, that he couldn't bring him in, at least not just yet. All the while Dugdale possessed the truth about the Iraq dossier – and he probably kept more than one copy of course – the police would be powerless to act. Dugdale would simply play his trump card if threatened. No, Deadman had to reveal the truth first of all to the public and the only way to do this was to go to the press. Once the truth was revealed Dugdale's trump card would no longer be any good. He could then reveal Dugdale's true identity and bring him to justice.

But for now, Deadman had to get away from Canary Wharf with the evidence and he needed to make sure he gave himself a head's start. He couldn't take Dugdale with him. That would be too dangerous. No, he needed to keep him somewhere secure, at least for a few hours, until he and Moscroft got out of town. None of the rooms were lockable, at least not from the outside. Deadman looked round the apartment, looking for somewhere to keep Dugdale safely tucked away for a few hours. And then he saw it. A smile broke over his face.

'Right, Dugdale. Over here.'

And with that Deadman led his prisoner towards the huge glass windows and doors that led out onto a balcony. Dugdale was suddenly seized with panic and hung back, forcing Deadman to grab him and push him forward. In his panic the mask of respectability and social standing slipped from Dugdale's face as his working class roots re-emerged once more.

'For fuck's sake, you can't throw me over the edge! You're fucking mad!'

Deadman was taken aback.

'Wow. That sounds like Jimmy Damon speaking. Hello Jimmy, nice to meet you.'

Deadman was enjoying lording it over the man who had twice tried to have him killed. He grabbed his prisoner and dragged him onto the balcony.

'Don't worry. I'm not gonna chuck you over.'

Deadman raised the pistol to Dugdale's head.

'Mind you, I'd really fucking love to use this on you. All the blood on your hands….'

Dugdale could see Deadman's finger twitching on the trigger. He went white as a sheet and flinched. Deadman lowered the pistol.

'You're lucky I'm not like you. I'll let the authorities deal with you. And in any case, by the time the press have finished humiliating you, you'll wish I'd had pulled the trigger.'

Deadman then backed away and slid the glass doors shut. He locked them from inside, leaving Dugdale completely helpless and stranded on the balcony outside.

'I'll fucking freeze out here, you stupid bastard.'

'Never mind,' said Deadman, laughing, and

shouting through the glass. 'The cleaners will be in the morning. They'll let you out.'

'You're dead, Deadman. I'll fucking see to it. You'll see. You don't know who you're messing with.'

'Oh, fuck off. I've heard it all before. Now belt up, save your breath and wait for the cleaners.'

Deadman gathered up the envelope with the documents inside and waited calmly for the lift to arrive as if he were waiting in a department store. Then, with a swish of the doors, he was gone.

Dugdale, meanwhile, was left outside on the balcony, hammering on the thick glass and shouting as loud as he could. But it was all in vain. Stranded outside on a balcony, forty-seven floors up, nobody was ever going to hear his screams.

The party was still in full swing when Deadman's lift arrived on the ground floor, not that he ever had any intention of hanging around. He slipped unobtrusively through the crowd, past the security men on the door and through the front entrance. A minute later he had slipped around the corner of the building to where Moscroft waited in the car. He swung himself into the front seat.

'Let's go. Let's get out of here.'

'Did you get it?' asked Moscroft.

'Did I get it?' replied Deadman. 'You bet your arse. And a lot more besides.'

'Well you can tell me about it later. Right now we've got to get out of here and change cars.'

'What again?'

'Look, Matt, this place is crawling with CCTV cameras. They'll follow us every step of the way. Anyway, don't worry. I've got it sorted.'

Moscroft steered the Ford Focus towards the northern end of the Blackwall Tunnel before heading off along the A13. A few minutes more and he was driving along the Barking Road where a glow of bright light in the distance indicated some sort of event.

Deadman groaned. 'Don't tell me West Ham are playing at home tonight?'

'Not for much longer.' Moscroft glanced at his watch. 'It's perfect. There'll be so many people milling around in a minute or two we'll be completely lost.'

Hundreds of fans were already pouring out of the ground by the time Moscroft pulled up opposite the main entrance to the ground, parking illegally on a yellow line in Green Street. He turned to Deadman.

'Don't worry. Remember, I borrowed this car anyway. The police are welcome to it.'

'You hardly borrowed it. You nicked it' said Deadman, laughing.

Moscroft said nothing but got out of the car. Deadman followed and was immediately jostled by some fans.

'Looks like the Hammers lost again.'

'Come on, Matt. Let's get in here for a minute.' And with that Moscroft led his friend into The Boleyn pub, which stood on the corner. 'We'll hang around for a few minutes until the final whistle…' He looked at his watch again. '…which ought to be any minute now.'

Sure enough, the sight of thousands of disgruntled West Ham fans pouring onto the streets signalled the end of the game. Scores of fans poured into the pub to drown their sorrows and complain, leaving Deadman and Moscroft to slip out through another exit, joining the thousands of fans streaming along the Barking Road. After a couple of minutes Moscroft pulled his friend across the road and down St

Martins Avenue, a row of typical East End terraced houses. Halfway down the road Moscroft stopped and produced a key.

'Okay. Get in.'

Deadman just stood there.

'What? In that?'

'Look, just get in.'

Deadman was all for changing cars but he had hoped that Moscroft had at least been able to 'borrow' something decent. First the Ford Focus, now this. Moscroft had got hold of an old green Rover 214.

'Look,' said Moscroft, 'nobody's going to notice this old banger are they? Think about it; if I'd had nicked a Ferrari or a Porsche we'd stick out like a proverbial sore thumb. Now, get in.'

'When this business is over I'm gonna claim the reward from Trubshaw and splash out on a decent car.'

'Well, maybe you ought to have done a deal with Dugdale. You know, your silence in return for a flash car.'

Deadman went silent for a few seconds. He looked across at Moscroft, grinned, and the two men started laughing.

'Nah. I think I'll pass on that one. Come on, let's get back to the prison camp.'

And with that Moscroft steered the Rover out towards the North Circular and down the A13, bound for the Dartford Crossing. About an hour after Deadman and Moscroft had left DDM's headquarters in Canary Wharf they were well south of the river once more, driving through the night into Kent and their temporary home. Part one of the plan was complete. The problem now was how to get the information to the press before Dugdale used his contacts to block off all avenues.

20

'Yes, this is it. It's just how I remember it.'

Harold Slater flicked through the file containing the truth about the government's dossier on Iraq and what a work of fiction it had been.

'Yes, look at it. It's worthy of Jules Verne or any good writer of science fiction. How the country ever bought into this bullshit is beyond me.'

Moscroft and Deadman were back in their temporary home at the Sunny View Holiday Park in Seasalter. It was almost two in the morning when they'd stopped off at Slater's nearby home to collect him. Now, all three men sat at the table in the mobile home going through the damning evidence.

'The truth is,' said Moscroft, 'the country never bought into it. Nobody in their right mind believed for a minute that Iraq had weapons of mass destruction, but when the Yanks said jump, Bland asked how high? It was as simple as that.'

Deadman sighed. 'Yeah. We've been dancing to their tune for far too long. It's about time the old country stood up for itself and made its own decisions without being told what to do by the Americans.'

'So what are we going to do with all this?' asked Slater. 'I mean, the last time I tried to get this into the public domain I got sidelined by the paper, whilst Dugdale himself went off and came back with a peerage. What chance have we got this time?' He picked up the passport belonging to Jimmy Damon and flicked through the old photographs that lay scattered on the table. 'And as for this stuff; blimey, if this ever got out the shit wouldn't just hit the fan it would bury it.'

Deadman laughed. 'Well, that's the whole point. But we can't do a thing to expose Dugdale's real identity unless we make the dossier public, and getting to the press before Dugdale shuts down all avenues is gonna prove very difficult.'

The three men sat in silence for a few moments until Slater suddenly got up and walked slowly around the table.

'I think I might know a way.' He sat down again. 'Look, when the Iraq war was being mulled over you'll remember Peter Burrows, the MP. You must remember. They used to call him 'Pete the Heat' because he was forever putting pressure on the government to come clean over the dossier.'

Moscroft shook his head. 'Yes, but isn't he a sort of crank or something? He'll jump on any sort of bandwagon if he thinks he'll get a free ride.'

'No,' replied Slater. 'That's where you're wrong. Sure, he's a bit of a loose cannon at times but if he thinks a cause if worth pursuing he'll give it a hundred per cent. Let's face it, he's an independent MP so he's got nothing to lose, and if he can lay this whole rotten business before the public he'll be a hero.'

'Well I was rather hoping to be a hero myself,' laughed Deadman. 'So how are we going to reach him?'

'Have you got a mobile phone?' asked Slater. I have his number. He was always good for a story. A good contact. You know what I mean.'

Slater had never installed a telephone in his own home for fear of being traced. He'd seen far too many people who had rubbed Dugdale up the wrong way meet with some sort of accident or another. Nor did he have a mobile. Better to be completely cut off than risk being traced. Deadman reached into his inside pocket and handed him his phone.

'Here. Use this. It's a pay-as-you-go phone. Only I have the number.'

Slater looked at the display. 'I'll go outside and call from there. The reception's poor inside this place.' And with that he stepped outside and closed the door behind him.

'What do you think?' asked Moscroft. 'Can we trust this Burrows chap?'

Deadman shrugged his shoulders and sighed. 'Well, we haven't got much else to go on at the moment. Not that I can think of. And we're running out of time. Dugdale's people will have found him by now.' Deadman laughed. 'He'll be going fucking mental.'

'Yes,' replied Moscroft, 'and he'll also be setting wheels in motion. Take it from me, when he cools down he'll be on the phone to MI5 quicker than you can say 'cover up'. The streets around the press and television stations will be crawling with men in dark suits and earpieces. Maybe 'Pete the Heat' is our only chance. He certainly sounds like the sort of bloke who would relish the opportunity of embarrassing the government.'

'I don't think embarrass is the right word,' said Deadman, getting to his feet. 'Bring the government down more like it.'

The door suddenly creaked open and Slater stepped back in, shaking himself.

'Blimey, it's getting cold out there. Right. Burrows is our man. He'll see us. I didn't tell him the whole story but let him know I had the biggest story that was likely to ever land in his lap.'

'And where are we gonna meet him? Where does he live?' asked Deadman.

Slater hesitated. 'He said it's too dangerous to meet at his place. He's suggested we go directly to his office and meet him there at seven-thirty.'

'But he's a member of parliament. You don't mean the House of Commons do you?' Moscroft was incredulous. 'That'll be like entering the lion's den.'

'No, I've just come from the lion's den,' said Deadman. 'The Commons is a different matter altogether.'

'Yes, but we'd be crazy going there,' snapped Moscroft. 'We'll be caught like rats in a barrel if it all goes wrong. And don't forget, it gives Dugdale a good few hours to warn MI5 or whoever set us up.'

'Look, nothing will go wrong.' Slater was pacing up and down now. 'Once Burrows sees these documents he'll be able to take them directly to the people who matter, like the Opposition, for example.'

'So why don't we go directly to them?' Moscroft laughed. 'They'll be laughing all the way to the ballot box if they could see this lot.'

'The trouble is, I don't know them,' replied Slater. The current leader of the opposition, John Hankey, only took the post after I left Fleet Street. I've never had any contact with him or any of his people. No, Burrows is our best bet. Trust me.'

Moscroft and Deadman said nothing but sat back in their chairs. Deadman broke the silence.

'Well, what do you think Jack?'

'What do I think? I think we're bloody mad. Taking this lot to the House of Commons is crazy. We should act now. Why wait until 7.30?' He sighed. 'But…

'But what?'

'But, if it's our only way to get the documents into the public domain we'd better do it. I'd just feel a hell of a lot safer if we were doing in sooner rather than later. Otherwise, Dugdale and MI5 between them will have sealed off all outlets.'

Deadman sighed. 'It's a pity we can't make copies of

these documents. Trouble is everywhere will be shut at this time of the morning. And we can't hang about for the shops to open.' He looked at his watch. 'It's almost three o'clock now. We can grab a couple of hours' sleep. By the time we get into central London it'll be about seven. It'll be staring to get light. We'll leave at five.'

Their adrenalin was flowing fast now and any thoughts of sleep had been quickly banished by the prospect of bringing the case to a satisfactory conclusion. But it had now been twenty-four hours since either Deadman or Moscroft had had any sleep and both men knew they it wouldn't do either of them any good if they were out on their feet when they returned to London, once they went up against the dark forces of MI5 and Dugdale Media.

'It's ironic, isn't it?' said Deadman.

Moscroft yawned. 'Ironic? What is?'

'Well, think about it. MI5 is going into battle against us, purely and simply to ensure that the truth about the Iraq dossier never sees the light of day. They know what would happen to them and their paymasters should the truth ever come out. So, they have to keep the secret safe and prevent idiots like us from ever revealing it. That's the irony, they're keeping Dugdale's trump card safe. He's playing us off against each other, using MI5 to ensure the secret remains safe. And yet MI5 has no idea of Dugdale's real identity, not that they could do anything anyway, not while he knows the truth about the dossier. They're preserving his trump card. He lives a lie and they guard a lie. It's all about two lies isn't it?' Deadman shook his head. 'We have to let the public know the truth, take away the trump card. As soon as we've done that we can reveal Dugdale's real identity. His empire will then crumble like a pack of cards, if you'll excuse the pun.'

Deadman smiled and seemed quite pleased with

himself and his little joke.

'Okay then, Let's do it. Let's go.' Moscroft stood up, stretched and shook himself. 'Into the valley of death and all that.'

It was difficult to relax, knowing what lay ahead of them, but both Moscroft and Deadman managed an hour or so of uncomfortable sleep before the alarm on Moscroft's phone burst into life, bringing them shuddering back into the real world. Deadman stood up, yawned and stretched. He looked towards Slater. 'I'd better have my phone back, Harold.'

'Oh, yeah, sorry Matt. Here. Thanks.' Slater handed the phone back and turned away leaving Deadman to take a quick glance at the display.

Meanwhile, Moscroft gathered the documents together and placed them all back in the manila envelope. He looked around. 'That's all of them. Let's go.'

Slater and Moscroft stepped out into the cold early morning air. It was still dark and their breath hung upon the air. Deadman followed but turned suddenly.

'Give me five minutes, will you? A call of nature.'

Moscroft rolled his eyes and shook his head. 'Come on, Harold. Get in the car. This might take a while.'

Ten minutes later Deadman emerged from the caravan with a grin on his face. 'Sorry chaps. These things can't wait. Right. Let's get on with it then. London, here we come.'

21

It was almost seven in the morning when the green Rover 214 came trundling up the Old Kent Road towards the Elephant and Castle. Darkness had given way to a chilly, grey, spring morning. The roads themselves were still wet, the street cleaners having had a busy morning washing down the capital's arteries. Dustcarts were still busy here and there gathering the previous day's rubbish, their bright orange lights flicking and twirling, whilst the first wave of commuters was beginning to emerge from the city's network of underground stations. The events of the next few hours would determine whether it would be just another day in London or whether it would be one of those extraordinary days that would, in years to come, prompt people to say, 'I remember where I was when...'

Matt Deadman guided the green Rover easily over Waterloo Bridge before swinging left into The Strand. Cafes and restaurants were already busy serving full breakfasts to workmen whose day's work was usually over before most of the capital's workforce had even arrived in the city. Here and there early birds walked along the street holding large paper cups in front of them.

'Are these people carrying coffee cups or are they some sort of GPS? Look at them.' Deadman shook his head.

'Yes. Strange that, isn't it,' replied Moscroft. 'I must say I've never really noticed it before, but, yes, look, everyone's doing it.'

Slater was amazed that, at such a potentially momentous moment the two men in the front seat of the Rover were discussing this strange phenomenon. But he too was suddenly struck by the sheer number of people who were walking along The Strand with coffee cups held out in front of them.

'Maybe it's a London fashion. I don't come to town all that often.' Slater sighed. 'Why don't they drink at home?'

'Search me,' said Moscroft. 'Apparently everyone leads too busy a life to stop for tea or coffee.'

'Maybe the city's been taken over during the night by aliens from the planet Costa.' Deadman laughed to himself.

When the Rover reached Trafalgar Square Deadman guided it through Admiralty Arch and into The Mall. Moscroft straightened up in his seat but said nothing. However, as the car approached Buckingham Palace he finally piped up.

'Going to see Her Majesty are we?'

Deadman said nothing but turned the car right up Constitution Hill towards Duke of Wellington Place and Hyde Park Corner. At first Moscroft thought Deadman might have been taking the scenic route to the Houses of Parliament but now he realised his friend was taking them in the opposite direction. The car cruised north up Park Lane.

'Okay, Matt. Are you going to tell us where you're going then?'

'A little detour,' replied Deadman. 'I just have to pop into my old place for five minutes to grab some papers Trubshaw gave me.' He looked across at Moscroft and winked. 'All part of the evidence and all that.'

Moscroft couldn't believe what he was hearing but tried to keep calm as he protested. 'Home? You do realise they'll probably be waiting for us? If you go home now you won't even have a chance to get the papers, let alone present them to Burrows.'

'Trust me, Jack. Just go with it. Yes, they'll probably be there but I need to pop in for five minutes. It's a chance

I'll have to take.'

Moscroft sat back in his seat. He knew his friend well enough now to realise that something was afoot and that Deadman wouldn't be returning to his home in Gloucester Gardens without good reason. Method in the madness and all that.

The Rover continued around Marble Arch, up the Edgware Road and left into Praed Street. The car negotiated the early morning traffic around Paddington Station and a few minutes later pulled up between a smart BMW motorbike and a Ford Focus that were parked in front of the imposing façade of Gloucester Gardens.

'Wait here. I won't be a minute.'

The Rover's engine was still ticking over as Deadman jumped out of the car. He walked briskly to the front door and disappeared inside. Moscroft noticed he'd taken the manila envelope with him. He also noticed that Slater, who was looking out of the rear window, was growing increasingly nervous.

'Don't worry, Harold. Matt knows what he's doing. If there had been a trap MI5 would have sprung it by now.'

Suddenly, Deadman reappeared, this time clutching a fine brown leather brief case. He swung himself into the driver's seat and handed it to Moscroft.

'Very nice,' said Moscroft, 'Texier?'

'Yeah,' replied Deadman. 'I thought it'd look more impressive if we turned up with a decent case instead of an envelope.'

Moscroft shook his head. 'You do know we're only going to a meeting, not a job interview?'

Deadman looked across at him and grinned as he put the Rover into first gear and swung the car out into Bishop's Bridge Road.

'Well, you know me. One must keep up

appearances.'

As the Rover turned into the main road a black Jaguar that had also been parked in Gloucester Gardens started its engine and pulled away. The green Rover turned right into Eastbourne Terrace. The black Jaguar did the same, a few cars' lengths back. Deadman reached Edgware Road and turned right, taking the Rover south. Moscroft looked at his watch.

'You'd better hurry, Matt. It'll be seven-thirty soon.'

'Oh, there's no rush. Not just yet.'

The car reached Marble Arch. Deadman took it carefully around the square but once again confused his friend by taking it, not down Park Lane, but back around the square once more.

'Okay,' said Moscroft, sighing in frustration. 'Is this another sightseeing tour or something? I mean, we've had Buckingham Palace. Now we've got Marble Arch.'

'No,' replied Deadman calmly, 'it's not a sightseeing tour. I just had to be sure that a certain black Jaguar was actually following us.'

Slater looked round. 'I can't see anything.'

'Well, you would say that, wouldn't you? But take it from me, we're being followed.'

Deadman swung the car into Park Lane and slowly began to increase his speed. The Jaguar kept pace with him a few cars' lengths behind.

Moscroft glanced in the wing mirror. 'Got him.'

The Rover retraced the route back towards Buckingham Palace, turning left into The Mall. As it passed Marlborough Road a second Jaguar fired up its engine and emerged from the shadows of St James's Palace before turning left into The Mall.

'Okay. Our mate's got a friend.' Deadman nodded towards the rear-view mirror.

'I do hope they realise we've got an appointment to keep,' said Moscroft, calmly.

'Well, Jack, old chap, I don't think they want us keep it. Look.'

Moscroft peered out of the front window. Coming long Horse Guards Road towards The Mall was a third Jaguar.

'Do you think MI5 does fleet car hire?' Deadman smiled but continued along The Mall. Then, just it approached the junction with Horse Guards Road he shouted, 'Hang on!' and swung the car violently around, and with a screech sped off back towards Buckingham Palace with the three Jaguars in hot pursuit along The Mall.

Slater gripped his seat tightly as the Rover sped past the palace, turning left into Birdcage Walk.

'I do hope this old banger's got something left in her.' Moscroft laughed.

Deadman gripped the steering wheel. 'Don't worry. Not far now.'

The four cars sped along Birdcage Walk, bouncing violently over the speed humps. As Deadman's Rover approached Great George Street he thought he could see another car, parked illegally by the side of the road ahead of him. It could only mean yet another MI5 car. He wasn't going to take any chances. The three Jaguars were close behind him as he swung the Rover right into Storeys Gate and right again into Old Queen Street.

'Christ, Matt, you do realise it said no entry. You've just gone down a one-way street the wrong way.'

'So sue me.'

The three Jags followed suit, straight down the narrow street. It widened towards the end although parked cars on either side allowed only one vehicle to pass, which was why it was a one-way street. The Rover sped along it but suddenly came screeching to a halt as a dustcart appeared in front of them, coming out of Queen Anne's Gate.

'Fuck it!'

The Jaguars closed on them. There was no way out.

Deadman glanced over his shoulder at the oncoming Jags and back at the dustcart, whose driver was sounding his horn and waving and leaning out of his window, cursing.

'Hang on!' shouted Deadman as he put the Rover into first gear. There was a burst of smoke from the rear wheels as the car lurched forward, squeezing into a space alongside the dustcart between two parked cars. The dustcart lumbered slowly forward, the crew cursing and swearing as the Rover squeezed past. Then, as quick as the Rover had passed the dustcart, it stopped dead. Deadman turned off the engine.

'Are you mad?' shouted Moscroft.

Deadman ignored him but grabbed the Texier case and shouted at the others to get out of the car. They needed no prompting. Moscroft and Slater dived out of the car and joined Deadman who was making off down Cockspur Steps, a narrow passageway that led back into Birdcage Walk. He tossed the keys into a nearby bush.

'That'll keep 'em off us for a while'

Meanwhile, the three Jaguars had come to a halt in Old Queen Street. They couldn't move forward as their path was blocked by the dustcart, which in turn was stuck fast, caught between the Jags and the abandoned Rover.

Deadman, Moscroft and Slater stood breathless in Birdcage Walk, whilst commuters continued going about their business, oblivious to what had just happened in Old Queen Street. Suddenly, Deadman leapt into the middle of the road to wave down a passing taxi. The driver looked puzzled but stopped anyway. Business was business. He wound down the window.

'Where to guv?'

'The Houses of Parliament.'

'Blimey, guv. You can walk there in five minutes!'

'We've had a hard morning,' explained Deadman.

And with that, the three men jumped into the back of the taxi which squealed off towards Parliament.

'Well, that was a close call,' said Moscroft, wiping his brow. 'I thought we were done for then.'

'So did I,' replied Deadman. 'Anyway, we'll be there in a minute.' He looked at his watch. 'Only five minutes late. I'm sure Pete the Heat will wait. What do you think, Harold?'

'Hm…what?...Sorry. What did you say?'

Slater seemed preoccupied and nervous, something that Moscroft had noted earlier that morning.

'Are you okay Harold? You seem a bit jumpy.'

'Oh, nothing. It's just that I'm not used to all this cloak and dagger stuff.' He smiled. 'Yes, I'm sure Burrows will wait for us.'

The taxi arrived in front of the public entrance to the Houses of Parliament. The days when visitors could walk freely up to the entrance were long since gone. Nowadays, concrete road blocks, iron barriers and bomb-proof cages were all in evidence. It was more like Fort Knox.

Deadman stepped out and handed the driver a fiver. 'Cheers, mate.' He looked around and thought he saw a plain-clothes security man touch his ear. Elsewhere, armed uniformed police were well in attendance. The three men approached and were asked to produce some ID. They explained they had an appointment with Burrows and were waved through to the security checkpoints. After passing the metal detectors and body searches they were waved through and were greeted by a member of staff who escorted them the short distance to the Great Hall.

'Wait here, please. A member of Mr Burrows' staff will be with you in a moment.'

'Well, that was a lot easier than I expected,' said Moscroft.

Deadman glanced around. 'Yeah. A bit too easy if you ask me.'

Moscroft looked around. The grey walls of the Great Hall had seen more than their fare share of history. Numerous monarchs and public figures had lain in state in the hall. It had also been the scene of the trial of King Charles 1 as well as Guy Fawkes.

'If walls could talk,' he said quietly to himself.

'What was that?' asked Deadman.

'Oh, nothing.'

Presently, a young man in a dark suit approached. Deadman thought he was a little young to be in politics.

'Mr Slater?' he asked, staring at the three men.

'That's me.' Slater turned and offered his hand.

'Come this way please gentlemen.'

And with that the man led Slater, Deadman and Moscroft up some steps and along a corridor. The walls were adorned with frescos depicting great events from Britain's glorious past. There were paintings of famous prime ministers, of kings and queens, and of famous battles. The group disappeared down a small staircase and along a smaller corridor. Television monitors, broadcasting BBC and Sky news hung at regular intervals along it. Other screens, indicating the current state of debates, stared blankly back at the group as they passed. Finally, the young man stopped and opened a door.

He stood back and waved his hand. 'In here, please gentlemen.'

Slater entered first, followed by Moscroft. Deadman was the last to enter, and as he did so he froze and turned to Slater.

'You bastard!'

Deadman made straight for Slater and landed a good punch squarely on the chin. The former reporter went down like a sack of potatoes. Deadman stood snarling over the prostrate Slater, his fists clenched. 'I knew you'd stitch us up, you bastard.'

Moscroft was still standing there, dumbstruck by what was happening, when two men suddenly appeared and pinned Deadman's arms behind his back.

'It's nice to meet you again, Deadman,' said the man sitting at the head of a large oak table in the middle of the room.

'Would someone please tell me what's going on?' asked Moscroft.

The man in the navy blue blazer, grey trousers and Brigade of Guards tie got up from his the chair.

'Jack Moscroft, I assume? Allow me to introduce myself. The name's Trelawney, Marcus Trelawney, MI5.'

Moscroft said nothing and showed no outward signs of anxiety. Deep inside, however, the pieces were beginning to fall quickly into place. There was no sign of Burrows, no chance to hand over the documents. It was a setup. Either Slater or Burrows had double-crossed them, although Deadman clearly seemed to think it was Slater who had sold them out.

'So, you're Trelawney, eh? Still fetching and carrying are you? Still being the skivvy for your masters?'

'Do be quiet, Mr Moscroft, there's a good chap.' Trelawney was trying hard not to rise to the bait. 'Just sit down. I told your friend here he was out of his depth. Now you're about to find out just how far out of your depth you really are. Now, sit down please.'

Moscroft and Deadman sat down. They had little choice. Here they were, trapped in a room deep inside parliament just as Moscroft had feared. Two men, both armed, stood guard over them, whilst Trelawney sat down again, a smirk breaking across his face. Slater was back on his feet now, clutching his injured jaw. He said nothing but sat down at the table.

'Well, this is nice,' said Deadman, sarcastically. 'Do we get breakfast? I'm a little peckish.'

'I think you'll be getting more than breakfast. Just wait a moment.'

The room remained deathly quiet, with Trelawney, sitting alongside an empty chair at one end of the table, Slater to one side and Deadman and Moscroft on the other. The two plain clothes security men stood with their hands clasped together in front of them, on either side of the door. Deadman had been in the game long enough to know that something big was about to happen.

'Is this the bit where we finally get to meet the bad guy?'

Trelawney said nothing, but slid back his cuff and glanced at his watch.

A few more minutes passed.

Then, suddenly, the crackling of a hand-held walkie-talkie could be heard coming from outside in the corridor, followed by the sounds of doors opening. There was the thumping of several pairs of feet as they made their way along the corridor. Deadman looked at Moscroft and raised his eyebrows.

For what we are about to receive…

One of the security men in the room suddenly touched his earpiece. He stood back and opened the door. The other man stood back also. Then, suddenly, two men in dark suits swept into the room and walked to Trelawney's end of the table. Trelawney got to his feet, bowed, almost solemnly, and stood to one side, leaving the two men to sit down in the two seats.

Deadman and Moscroft sat rigid in their seats.

'Well, gentlemen, I need not introduce myself,' said the first man.

He was right. Deadman and Moscroft glanced at each other, their hearts beating a little faster now.

The man who spoke was the Right Honourable Anthony Bland, MP, the Prime Minister of Great Britain and Northern Ireland. The man sitting alongside him was none other than Lord John Dugdale.

22

'Well now, gentlemen. It appears that you're in possession of something that really doesn't belong to you.'

Anthony Bland was just about as dynamic as his name suggested. Lean, suspicious and with a receding hairline, sunken narrow eyes and a pronounced jaw, his features had given him the look of a hawk. His actions and policies, on the other hand, were more in keeping with his name. Nevertheless, through weak opposition, toadyism, and general good fortune he had been in power now for almost three terms, coming to power in 2001, and while Britain was never going to be a dynamic force in world affairs the country was, at least, safe in his very careful and unimaginative hands.

Bland's greatest trial had come following the Iraq War when he was accused of 'sexing up' the dossier which claimed Iraq possessed weapons of mass destruction, claims that were discredited after the war when, following extensive searches by United Nations inspectors, no such weapons were found. Bland went to great lengths to cover his tracks during the hue and cry that followed the end of the war and the removal of the Iraqi regime. However, things changed one day when the proprietor of the *Daily Chronicle*, John Dugdale, walked into Downing Street with evidence that proved the dossier was a complete work of fiction. The trade off was, of course, a peerage for Dugdale in exchange for his silence and an uneasy truce that had remained ever since, a truce that put Dugdale beyond the reach of the law. What Bland didn't know was that Dugdale was, in reality, none other than Jimmy Damon, the missing Great Train Robber. Thus, if the truth about the dossier was Bland's great secret, Dugdale's true identity was his. Both men were, in effect, living a lie.

Dugdale remained silent as Bland continued.

'You may think you're doing your country a service but I can assure you that you are not. On the contrary, if the details contained in the document in your briefcase were laid before the public we'd have anarchy. I don't think you're aware of the consequences, not only for Britain but for the world generally.'

'Oh, I'm not sure about that,' replied Deadman. 'I think we're all well aware of the consequences for you, and quite frankly I couldn't give a damn about the rest of the world.'

'Well that's where you're wrong, of course. Any discredit heaped upon the present government would inevitably reflect badly on Britain and its standing in the world. You may think, in the tiny, sheltered world in which you live, Mr Deadman that you can simply lay the information before the public and expect justice. Well, I'm here to tell you you're sadly mistaken.'

Deadman leaned forward and stared at Bland across the table.

'Well, if you're so sure why don't we let the public decide? After all, I think they're the best judges. Let them decide the difference between right and wrong.'

Bland sat back, shook his head and laughed.

'Mr Deadman, the public at large couldn't tell the difference between black and white.'

'But are you prepared to take that chance? You may think you know it all, sitting in your ivory towers, in a world where the poor fucking tax payer picks up the bill for your lavish lifestyles, and where the poor bastards out there on the front line have to pay for your mistakes with their lives. But I can tell you, you're out of touch baby. Out of touch. And I mean to make you pay.'

Bland smiled and shook his head. 'We appear to be at loggerheads, don't we? Well, in such cases as this I have the casting vote, and my vote says you hand over your briefcase now please.' He extended his hand.

Deadman said nothing. He looked at Moscroft and then Slater. There was nowhere to go. Two of the most powerful men in Britain sat in front of him, whilst two of their henchmen, armed and presumably dangerous, stood at the door. He sighed and sat back in his chair.

'It doesn't look as though I've got much choice then does it? Well, before I hand this over you might like to know who you're sitting next to.'

Dugdale suddenly shifted in his chair.

'Should I tell him or are you going to?'

Bland looked at Dugdale who had gone white. 'What's he talking about?'

'Oh, I wouldn't pay much attention to him.' Dugdale opened his mouth for the first time. 'You know his sort; always trying something out of sheer desperation.'

'Okay then,' replied Deadman. 'What if I told you your friend Dugdale's real name is Jimmy Damon?'

Bland looked at Deadman and then at Dugdale. He shook his head. 'I'm afraid you've got me there, Mr Deadman. The name means nothing.'

'Jimmy Damon? Oh come on now. The Great Train Robbery of 1963? Damon was one of the three men that got away with it.'

Deadman suddenly realised how stupid this must have sounded. Nobody other than Grappler and some of his officers knew about Damon, Bragg and Higgins, and most of these officers were dead now. Fifty years had passed and the story of the robbery had long since passed into legend. The robbers had all been caught, tried and convicted, even the elusive Ronnie Biggs.

Bland dismissed the claim and laughed. 'You'll be telling me next that Lord Dugdale was responsible for the assassination of President Kennedy. Now, come along, hand over the case. Or do I have to ask my men to take it?'

Deadman realised he was getting nowhere. The revelation about Dugdale's true identity had fallen on deaf ears. He had nothing else left up his sleeve.

'Come on Mr Deadman,' said Bland. 'I'm a busy man. You have no other cards to play.'

'Ah, but that's where you're wrong,' replied Deadman, looking at his watch. 'I've a pair of jokers…any minute now…'

Dugdale suddenly erupted. 'For fuck's sake, give us the bloody case!'

Bland was quite taken aback by Dugdale's sudden outburst. He shook his head, sighed and told one of his men to take the case. One of the security men stepped forward, produced a gun and took the briefcase from Deadman, who moved aside.

'Woh, easy there cowboy. No need for the gun.'

Dugdale snatched the case and unfastened it. He rummaged through it, tearing out the wads of paper, throwing them onto the table.

'It's not here! There's nothing but blank paper!'

Bland stood up and grabbed the case. 'What? Let me see.'

It was true. There was nothing in the case but sheets of blank paper. Bland threw the briefcase aside and took the pistol from the security man.

'Okay. This has gone far enough. Now, Mr Deadman, for the last time. What have you done with the documents? And if you think I won't use this please think again. You should know we have the ways and means of having you disappear off this planet for good. And your friend here too. Now, for the last time, where is it?'

Bland was fast losing his cool.

Deadman smiled. 'Well, let's see. I had it this morning…

Bland shook his head and waved the pistol. 'Really, Mr Deadman, you're trying my patience.'

'Just fucking kill him!' Dugdale was fast losing control. 'If you won't. I will!'

'Sit down, Dugdale. If we kill him we'll never know where it is.'

Deadman laughed. 'Yes, and that's my second joker.' He glanced up at the clock. It was just on eight o'clock. 'Any minute now and I think you'll find the joker wins.'

Bland and Dugdale looked at each other.

'He's bluffing,' screamed Dugdale. 'Kill him, kill him!'

Bland levelled the pistol at Deadman. His finger twitched on the trigger.

Deadman took a deep breath.

Suddenly, there was a commotion outside in the corridor. Walkie-talkies crackled into life and there was a frantic knocking on the door. The second security man opened it and one of the prime minister's aides, breathless and panicking, popped his head into the room.

'Sir, I think you'd better come quickly!'

23

There was a flurry of frantic activity in the corridor outside the room where Deadman and Moscroft had been held. Prime Minister Bland jumped to his feet and rushed from the room, followed soon after by Dugdale. Trelawney and the two armed guards were left standing there, looking like spare parts, while a drama was evidently unfolding outside the room in the corridors of power.

'Well,' asked Deadman, now beginning to enjoy himself, 'aren't you gonna run along and join your mates?'

Trelawney looked confused. He had no idea what was going on but guessed it was something serious. He waited a few moments before suddenly heading for the door, hissing a curt, 'bollocks to this,' as he passed the two guards who promptly followed him.

Deadman and Moscroft turned to Slater, still nursing his jaw.

'There never was any meeting with Borrows, was there?' asked Moscroft.

Slater said nothing at first but when Deadman got to his feet he started to confess his sins.

'Okay, okay. No, there was no Burrows, no meeting. It was all a setup.'

Deadman walked slowly towards the cowering Slater, who continued to talk.

'Look, you don't understand. I've got nothing. No money, nothing, and I'm living in a shithole, waiting for one of Dugdale's men to come knocking on the door. You don't know what it's like.' He calmed down. 'Look, Dugdale knew who I was and that I had the inside story on the Iraq dossier. If I hadn't gone to ground I'd be dead meat by now.'

'We know all of this,' said Moscroft wearily. 'Get to the

point.'

Slater went on. 'The point is, when you two showed up with the documents about the dossier and Dugdale's true identity I thought I'd be able to make some money by tipping him off. You know how it works.'

'So you decided to sell us out?' Moscroft shook his head in disgust.

Slater said nothing. By now, a few minutes had passed since Bland, Dugdale, Trelawney and the guards had left the room, and Moscroft suddenly realised he and Deadman were on their own again, unguarded.

'What are we waiting here for?' he asked.

Deadman was looking at a painting of an execution at Newgate Prison that was hanging on the wall. He stretched and yawned.

'It's a shame they can't bring back public executions, especially for bent politicians. The crowds would be enormous.' He turned to his old friend. 'What are we waiting for? Well, nothing really. I think my joker has just been played and I can safely say I've won.' He smiled. 'The shit has well and truly hit the fan, as they say.'

Deadman and Moscroft walked out into the corridor, now the scene of frenzied activity, as government officials, aides and junior staff ran up and down, clutching phones or folders, frantically trying to deal with a situation that was growing worse by the minute.

'Hey, what about me then?' asked Slater, still sitting in the room.

'You? Oh, you can go fuck yourself,' replied Deadman. He turned to Moscroft. 'I think my mate Mervyn will be paying him a visit sooner or later. He'll think of a charge. Now, come on. Let's go and see what the fuss is all about.'

Moscroft knew by the tone of Deadman's voice and by the smirk on his face that he knew damn well what the fuss was all about. As the two men strolled along the corridor the television screens were breaking the news. It appeared that detailed evidence had emerged proving that Bland's government had doctored the dossier on Iraq and that there was no real legitimate reason for Britain going to war. The dossier had been a complete work of fiction. Opposition leaders were hastily tumbling out of their homes to give statements to the waiting press, whilst the usual array of pundits were being wheeled out to give their verdicts on the astonishing revelations. It spelt the end for Bland and his government. After all, no government would be able to survive such a scandal.

Information was coming in thick and fast, and even the darling of Sky News, Bev Curley, was having difficulty in keeping up with the unfolding drama. She was on screen, desperately shifting through leaves of paper as they were planted on her desk.

'Well, er…it appears that as we're trying to get to the bottom of this story about Prime Minister Bland and the Iraq dossier, we have…er…well, it looks as though we've got a second story which may or may not be connected with it.' She looked around. There was obviously nothing on her autocue. There hadn't been time to write anything. She was on her own now, doing her best to keep astride the fast moving drama.

'This is all quite amazing. We've also received proof that…and I find this very difficult to believe…that one of the government's most staunch supporters, the media tycoon Lord John Dugdale, is, in reality Jimmy Damon.' Bev looked around, totally confused. She was starting to ad lib now. 'Well, I have to say I have no idea who Jimmy Damon is, but the evidence that has apparently been handed in to Sky News and, I understand, the BBC and other news networks, is to the effect that Damon was one of three men responsible for the Great Train Robbery in 1963 who subsequently evaded arrest and lived on to enjoy their share of the money.'

Bev was almost breathless as she read out the story.

'I must say, this is all quite incredible and almost unbelievable, but the evidence is apparently irrefutable. And to think that Lord Dugdale is a close friend of so many public figures, including minor royals. It's amazing. The fallout from this story is going to be shattering for so many people.' And in an aside, Bev looked directly at the camera and almost in comic fashion said something that would probably go down in broadcasting history.

'I have to say, but these fantastic stories are like buses. You wait for ages for one to come along, then two come along at once.'

She picked up a sheet of paper and fanned herself.

'Phew. Well, Where do we go from here?' She touched her earpiece. 'Okay, I think we can go to Downing Street where there have been dramatic developments…'

Moscroft looked at Deadman as the two men stared up at the screen. He smiled and nodded.

'You crafty bastard. How did you manage that one then?'

SEASALTER, SIX HOURS EARLIER.

Harold Slater had just given Matt Deadman his phone back. The meeting with the MP, Peter Burrows, was now arranged. But when Deadman glanced at the call history his heart skipped a beat. He looked at the last number and saw that Slater hadn't phoned Burrows at all. Deadman had no idea what Burrows' number was, but he did know the number of Dugdale Media, and it was this number that was staring him in the face.

The bastard. Slater intends to sell us out. Well, I'm afraid he's got another think coming.

Later that evening Deadman, Moscroft and Slater were about to get into their old Rover when Deadman excused himself and went back into the caravan to use the bathroom.

'Give me five minutes, will you? A call of nature.'

By the time Moscroft and Slater were inside the car Deadman was already on the phone.

'Hi Angie, it's me…'

'For Christ's sake, do you know what the bloody time is?'

'Yeah, sorry Angie, but I need another favour, and it's a bloody big one.'

Deadman explained to his ex-wife what was happening, or at least what was about to happen. He told Angie how he'd got wind of Slater's plot to double-cross him and Moscroft and to sell out to Dugdale. Knowing that he and Moscroft would almost certainly be walking into a trap at the House of Commons Deadman needed a safe and secure way of keeping the documents and ensuring that the press and television boys got hold of them.

Angie Deadman listened intently. It was around five in the morning when her phone had rung and she had great difficulty rousing herself an taking it all in, but when she heard what had happened the previous night at Dugdale Media headquarters and how her ex-husband had secured the documents relating to both the Iraq dossier and to Dugdale's real identity, she was soon wide awake.

'Look, Matt. You know I deal with these kind of documents every day.'

'Not like these you don't,' replied Deadman.

'Oh, shut up for a minute will you? Let me

think...Okay, I think I know a way to get the documents to the news people.'

Matt Deadman was all ears as he listened to Angie's proposal. She suggested that he bring the documents to London and meet her in his flat in Gloucester Gardens. She'd come over on her BMW motorbike. Nobody would know who she was if she entered wearing her motorcycle helmet, dressed like just another biker. She'd take the documents from her ex-husband and would smuggle them into Sky and the BBC disguised as a motorcycle courier. After all, who would notice yet another courier entering the respective buildings? Couriers came and went all the time. Angie also explained she had formed some useful contacts at both Sky and the BBC as a result of her work in the Ministry of Defence archives. It was a perfect plan. Deadman rejoined Moscroft and Slater in the Rover and set off for London.

And so, even as Bland and Dugdale were grilling Moscroft and Deadman inside parliament, the actual documents were being delivered to two unsuspecting news broadcasters, Sky and the BBC. The story was dynamite, and although editors still had to verify some of the details the story was good enough to broadcast as soon as possible. Deadman's joker was well and truly played.

Back inside the House of Commons pandemonium had well and truly broken out.

'I think we can safely say our job's done here,' said Deadman, turning to Moscroft.

'I think you're right. Let's get out of here. I reckon it'll be okay to get back to Gloucester Gardens. The villains will have been brought to book very soon.'

'And about time too,' said Deadman. 'Come on, let's go. I feel a good breakfast coming on.'

24

Matt Deadman was sitting in the living room of his flat in Gloucester Gardens. With the downfall of both Bland and Dugdale there was no need to lie low anymore. Ever since the scandal had broke two days earlier MI5 had retreated, whilst a host of fickle celebrities, politicians and, indeed, any public figure that had previously been associated with Dugdale, now shunned him and tried to deny ever knowing him.

Deadman called out to Moscroft who was making tea in the kitchen. The two had been going over the case and discussing Dugdale's possible whereabouts.

'Jack, come and take a look at this.'

Moscroft joined his friend in the living room and sat down. The television was on and Bev Curley was back on screen, anchoring the coverage of yet another huge story that was just breaking. The Skycopter, as Sky TV's helicopter was affectionately known, was following Anthony Bland's limousine along The Mall. A few minutes earlier he had left Downing Street, declining to make any comment to the hordes of pressmen and women who were crowded onto the pavement outside Number 10.

'We fully expect an announcement from Number 10 at any minute,' said Curley, 'and we expect it will be to announce that Prime Minister Bland has resigned. He will be seeing Her Majesty the Queen in a few minutes and will ask her to accept his resignation.' The camera switched back to the studio and Curley's beaming face. 'I wouldn't want to be in his shoes over the coming weeks…'

Of Lord John Dugdale, or Jimmy Damon, as the press were now delighting in calling him, there was neither news nor any sighting. He had gone to ground.

'Well,' said Moscroft, it's not as if he doesn't know how to disappear, is it? He managed it for fifty years. I don't suppose a couple of days will trouble him.'

'You say that,' replied Deadman, 'but he's still got a business empire to run.'

'Or rather save.'

Moscroft was quick to point out that shares in Dugdale Media had plunged to an all-time low and were essentially worthless. Ever since the revelation that Dugdale was, in fact, Jimmy Damon, and that Damon had been one of the gang that robbed the mail train back in 1963, there had been a huge media frenzy. In fact, Dugdale's story had almost been on a par with the exposure of the truth behind the Iraq dossier. It was as though there were no other news stories anywhere in the world. Bland was now gone, however, or soon would be, and he would no doubt be left to face an enquiry into the dossier, and possibly even face prosecution. But of Dugdale there was still no word, nor any sign. He had vanished.

'Anyway, whatever has happened to Dugdale or wherever he's gone he's finished now,' said Moscroft, reflecting on the case.

'I guess so,' replied Deadman, 'but I'm not gonna allow Dugdale to get away with it just like that. I'm not gonna let him slip away a second time. And in any case, I'd hate to disappoint Trubshaw. He's counting on me to settle this business once and for all.' Deadman grinned. 'Then, of course, there's the little matter of my reward, the legacy from Grappler. I'm not gonna let that slip through my grubby little hands.'

Moscroft was still at Deadman's flat when the phone rang later that same evening. It was Mervin Rabble, his friend from Scotland Yard. He answered the phone and handed it to Deadman.

'Matt, I've got some news that may interest you...

'I'm all ears,' replied Deadman, taking a mouthful of tea from his mug.

'We've picked up your mate Jimmy Damon, or at least he's been spotted.'

Deadman quickly put down the mug and grabbed a pen. 'Okay, let's have it.'

'Well,' said Rabble, 'a car bearing the registration plate D362 has been picked up travelling north up the A5. We had him on CCTV for a while but he turned off and we've lost him again. We've alerted the local Bobbies and they'll be keeping an eye open for him. I'm afraid that's the best I can do for now.'

'Cheers Merve. That's all I need for now.'

Deadman put down the phone and turned to Moscroft.

' Dugdale's been sighted, and I think I know where he's heading.'

'Okay, Matt, I'll be....'

Before Moscroft could finish his sentence Deadman had already grabbed his jacket and was tearing down the stairs.

'Hold on a minute, Matt!' shouted Moscroft, running after his friend. 'You're not going to get very far without these!' He caught up with Deadman on the lower landing and held out his hand. 'The keys to the car...'

'Thanks, Jack,' said Deadman, catching his breath. 'Are you coming?'

'I think this one's between you and Dugdale.' Moscroft put his hand on Deadman's shoulder. 'You'd better hurry.'

The A5 was less than a mile from Deadman's home and within a few minutes he was heading north in

Moscroft's Ford Mondeo. Maida Vale, Kilburn and Cricklewood were all quickly passed before Deadman swung his car out onto the M1. It would be quicker than taking the A5 the whole way. He fumbled at the GPS as he typed in the sequence of letters which he hoped would take him to Dugdale. It was getting dark now, and rain was starting to fall. Car headlights blurred and fragmented as the windscreen wipers thunked back and forth. After about twenty miles Deadman left the M1 and turned onto the A5.

The roads were narrower now, and there were few street lamps. The rain grew heavier, and each oncoming car seemed to shoot a ray of bright light into Deadman's face, making driving difficult and unpleasant. Still, at least he had the comfort of knowing his was on Dugdale's tail, or at least he hoped he was. He hadn't told Moscroft where he was going but he had a pretty good idea where the fugitive tycoon was heading, not through any hard evidence, but through instinct, and he was getting closer and closer by the minute. The Mondeo slipped through Dunstable, a veritable ghost town as it neared midnight, before heading off down another poorly lit country road. Deadman took the road for about six miles before turning left onto the Tring road, an even narrower and darker country lane. The rain was
beginning to lash down now and Deadman squinted through the windscreen, trying to catch a glimpse of his quarry or at best simply stay on the road. Every now and then bursts of lightning lit up the countryside.

'Bollocks, that's all I need,' muttered Deadman to himself.

Any minute now. The turning should be somewhere up here on the right.

The wipers squeaked and thudded across the windscreen as the rain continued to pour down, whilst the roar of thunder heralded another flash of lightning. Then, finally, he was there. He swung the car right, down another country lane, before bringing it to a halt. He sat motionless, staring out of the window, the only sound being the beating of the rain upon the car.

So that's it, eh? Where it all began.

To Network Rail, the company responsible for maintaining the bridge, it was Bridge Number LEC1/127. But to the rest of the world it was known simply as Bridego Bridge, the scene of the Great Train Robbery.

Deadman continued to sit in his car and imagine the events that happened here in August 1963. There was no rain back then, just a balmy early morning. He turned on the ignition again and drove slowly forward, passing beneath the bridge and coming to a halt once more at the place where the two Land Rovers and the army truck were parked on that momentous evening. He turned off the engine. Deadman imagined the line of men forming a human chain from the road up the grassy bank to the train itself, which sat motionless, and powerless to stop the gang unloading the sacks of money. The rain continued to beat upon the roof of his car, and another roll of thunder brought him back to the present.

Of Dugdale, however, there was no sight, but his car, D362, was parked on the right, just where the gang's vehicles had been parked. Deadman reached over into the back seat of the car, grabbed his Barbour jacket and got out, squinting into the rain and blinking as the thunder rumbled and the lightning flashed overhead. He pulled up the collars of his jacket and started to climb the bank to the railway line itself. He slipped on the muddy grass, whilst branches from the overhanging trees that had grown up since 1963 smacked him in the face as he pushed his way up. He stepped over a low stone wall and finally found himself standing beside the line itself. The rain washed his face as he peered into the darkness looking up and down the line. Then he saw him.

It was Dugdale.

It was pitch black, and the rain showed no signs of easing up, but there was no mistaking the tall figure of Lord John Dugdale, picked out in the darkness by yet another flash of lightning. He stood motionless by the side of the railway line, completely oblivious to Deadman's presence and seemingly unaware of the bolts of lightning that were bursting overhead. The thunder roared. Dugdale remained unmoved. He wore no coat, just a suit, and was soaked to the skin. Suddenly, he called out. Deadman struggled to hear what he was saying above the beating of the rain and the crash of thunder.

'Danny…Lenny...it's me…Jimmy! This way lads, throw me another sack…'

Dugdale could see his mates, Lenny Bragg and Danny Higgins. He could see Reynolds, Goody, Jimmy White and Charlie Wilson. Yes, he could see them again.

'Come on lads!...let's go…we've got it all…we've got it all!...'

'Jimmy…Jimmy…'

Suddenly, a voice brought Dugdale back from the past.

'Jimmy…Come on Jimmy, let's go.'

Dugdale squinted into the darkness as the rain poured over his face. A flash of lightning revealed Deadman standing a few yards away down the track. The disgraced media tycoon said nothing but held up his hand as if telling Deadman to stop. It seemed to Deadman as though the tycoon hadn't recognised him. Dugdale had lost everything; his power, his sycophantic friends, his media empire, and was about to lose his freedom. He had obviously lost his mind too. Dugdale turned back towards the railway line.

Deadman had no idea whether it was electrified or not but shouted a warning to Dugdale. 'Get away from the line! You'll kill yourself…Dugdale…get back.!

'The name's Damon, Jimmy Damon!' Dugdale turned to face Deadman once more and laughed.

'I've had a good run from you coppers! I've had the money and I've spent the lot. You won't get a penny out of me!' He laughed again. 'It took you over fifty years to get me, fifty years!'

He turned and looked back up the track towards Sears Crossing, where the mail train had originally been brought to a halt during the raid. The light of an approaching train began to loom out of the darkness in the distance. He turned to Deadman again.

'Get down! Here it comes! Get ready!...Here comes the loot!'

Deadman squinted through the darkness. He saw no train.

Dugdale's really lost it.

Dugdale turned again and waved at Deadman.

'Get down!…Get down!…Don't let them see you!…'

Then, suddenly, Deadman saw it. It was a train. And it was coming on fast. He could hear the roar of the engine above the rain and the thunder. Lightning flashed in the sky and there it was, hurtling down the track towards them. But it was no mail train, and this wasn't August 1963.

'Dugdale! Get back! For fuck's sake, get back!'

But it was too late. Dugdale turned towards Deadman, smiled, and then stepped out onto the railway line. There was nothing Deadman could do but throw himself over the low stone wall as the express train flew past with a deafening roar. Ten seconds later Deadman raised himself from behind the wall as the sound of the train died away, its rear light fading away in the distance also. All that was left was the sound of falling rain and the odd rumble of thunder. Otherwise, there was nothing, nor any sign of Dugdale. Nothing. Deadman stood up and walked towards the track. He could see very little in the darkness. He looked down the line. The train had disappeared completely now. He shook his head. It wouldn't until first light that they'd be able to examine the track for signs of Dugdale, or what was left of him.

Or maybe he'd gotten away with it again…?

It was still raining when Deadman returned to Gloucester Gardens. He was still soaked to the skin. Moscroft emerged from one of the bedrooms and rubbed his eyes.

'Crikey, Matt. You look like shit.'

Deadman said nothing but threw the car keys on the table and poured himself a large scotch. He then disappeared into the bathroom, closed the door and turned on the taps. Moscroft heard the sound of rushing water as the bath filled up. It had been a hard, filthy morning and Deadman was too tired to tell his friend what had happened.

Moscroft understood. He shook his head and went back to bed. Best wait until morning.

25

Cornelius Trubshaw tapped a sheaf of paper on his desk before placing it inside an old, dog-eared manila folder.

'That, as they say, is that.'

He got up and walked to one of the steel filing cabinets in his office at Number 4 King's Bench Walk, in London's Temple. He placed the file gently into the cabinet, closed it, and stood there for a few seconds before retuning to his chair. He sighed.

'I think I can safely say the case is now closed. It's taken many years but I'm very grateful to you Mr Deadman for finally bringing it to a satisfactory conclusion.' He took off his thin-rimmed reading glasses and smiled. 'I'm sure Inspector Grappler is up there somewhere, smiling.'

'Yes,' replied Deadman. 'I think he can put away his binoculars now.'

'His what?' asked Trubshaw, puzzled.

'Oh, nothing. I was just thinking about something his daughter said to me.'

Trubshaw said nothing. 'There's only one more thing left.' He opened a draw in his desk, took out an envelope and slid it across to Deadman.

'I think you'll find that Grappler was more than generous with his legacy. Go on, take it. I must say you richly deserve it.'

Deadman reached out and took the envelope. He didn't open it but placed it in his jacket pocket. He smiled to himself. The money would go towards buying another Alfa Romeo to replace the one which Dugdale had blown up. Nothing special, probably a direct replacement.

Trubshaw continued. 'And I'm not the only one that thinks you deserve it. Have you seen this morning's newspapers?' He picked up a copy of *The Daily Telegraph* that lay to one side of his desk. 'They're even calling for you to be knighted for services to your country, for exposing the truth.'

'Well,' replied Deadman, 'I guess they would, wouldn't they? I mean, it's a Tory paper isn't it?'

'That may be,' replied Trubshaw, 'that may be. But stranger things have happened. And as for Dugdale and Bland, well, it's in all the papers. They're talking about it everywhere. Such a scandal.' He shook his head. 'Not since the Profumo Affair…' He fell silent and seemed to drift back to the 1960s until he snapped out of it. 'Well, that's why they think you deserve something.'

Deadman was embarrassed by the talk of him becoming a knight of the realm. He moved the conversation on. 'Have they found Dugdale's body yet?'

'I'm afraid not,' replied Trubshaw.

Deadman sat up in alarm. 'You don't think he got away again do you? I mean, surely they must have found his body by now. He couldn't have got away.'

'Relax, Mr Deadman, relax. It's true that they haven't found his body but they have found Lord Dugdale, or Jimmy Damon, to be precise.'

'They've found him. Where?'

Trubshaw was teasing Deadman. He smiled again. 'Well, at least they found what was left of him. It was scattered in pieces along a length of track south of Bridego Bridge. By all accounts it wasn't a very pretty sight. Blood, bone, tissue. The train hit him with such force that…Well, you know what I mean.'

Deadman sighed and sat back in his chair, deep in thought. 'The poor bastard.'

'Not poor, Mr Deadman. Jimmy Damon was a crook, and a very rich one indeed, He lived off the fruits of his ill-gotten gains for fifty years, taking the lives of several innocent and not so innocent men along the way.

'Yeah,' replied Deadman, 'and I was nearly one of them.'

Trubshaw gave out a sigh of satisfaction. 'Well he's gone now. The case is closed and the mystery solved.'

Both men sat in silence for a few seconds, reflecting on the case. Suddenly Trubshaw burst back into life.

'And now we've got a General Election on our hands, and it's all thanks to you Mr Deadman, all thanks to you!' He stood up. 'Well, I've got work to do! Well, thank you very much indeed, Mr Deadman. It's been a pleasure.'

Trubshaw extended his hand and Deadman shook it. 'I can't say it's been a pleasure, but it's certainly been interesting. Thanks.'

The sun was shining as Deadman stepped out from the old, peaceful sanctuary that was London's Temple, back into Fleet Street and back into the real world. It was a changed world also. Bland's government had fallen and a General Election loomed. Some things never changed, however. The morning traffic was as heavy as ever. Buses crawled along at a snail's pace, taxis squealed and cars sounded their horns. Deadman decided to walk back to Paddington. The long walk would do him good. As he turned towards The Strand he was still deep in thought and he bumped straight into a couple who were walking in the opposite direction.

'Here, watch it mate. Who do you think you are? Jimmy Damon?'

Deadman smiled.

No, not Jimmy Damon. Maybe Sir Matt Deadman though....

He laughed and walked off down the Strand.

HISTORICAL NOTE

Our private investigator, Matt Deadman, is, of course, a fictional character but most of the events in this book did actually happen or are based on real events. Most people in Britain will have heard of the Great Train Robbery that took place in August 1963. Most will have heard of Bruce Reynolds, Buster Edwards – largely owing to the film, 'Buster' – and Ronnie Biggs, arguably the most famous member of the gang and yet, somewhat ironically, a late-comer and a very minor player in the event. Many will also have heard of Jack Mills, the train driver who was coshed during the raid, something that his family always claimed was a major factor in causing his premature death in 1970, although the official cause was Leukaemia. Ask the majority of people in the street and they will tell you that all of the gang were eventually caught and that they received savage sentences of up to thirty years' imprisonment, sentences that caused even mild-mannered law-abiding citizens to question their severity.

But few people realise that three members of the gang were never caught but got clean away with it, and this is what has inspired this book. In Reynolds' own autobiography, *Autobiography of a Thief,* he cites three other gang members but gives them all aliases. However, *In The Great Train Robbery: Crime of the Century: The Definitive Account* by Nick Russell-Pavier and Stewart Richards, the authors for the first time produced the two lists that were given to detectives chasing the gang, lists based on information received from the underworld and other sources. The authors guessed, but could not be certain, of the identity of one member of the gang who avoided arrest. They named their man as Henry or 'Harry' Smith, and although they were tantalisingly close they could not be sure as the files were closed until 2045. However, when Andrew Cook came along in 2013 with his *The Great Train Robbery: The Untold Story from the Closed Investigation Files*, he blew the whole thing open. By using The Freedom of Information Act, Cook managed to get permission to see most of the closed files and there, lying before him in one of the files, was the evidence that proved beyond doubt, that Smith was indeed one of the gang that got away with it. It was a remarkable piece of work and an amazing revelation. Police statements, and one from Smith's own father, all but confirm that he was indeed one of the gang. It is not my intention to lay out the evidence here but the fact that Smith, a man with a criminal record who ran a modest car-hire company in north London, suddenly bought thirty-two houses, a hotel and a drinking club shortly after the raid would suggest that the police had got their facts right. The problem was they had no evidence and so Smith went free, dying in 2008. A police photograph of Smith features on the front cover of the book.

Evidence was a big problem for the police at the time, for not a shred of evidence, not a fingerprint, nothing, was found at the scene of the crime at Bridego Bridge. Nothing. The evidence that convicted the robbers was either found at their hideout at Leatherslade Farm or was through the robbers' own carelessness afterwards, such as paying for items in large amounts of cash, something that raised suspicions back in 1963. It is almost certain that some of the evidence, particularly in the case of Gordon Goody, was planted by the police themselves. Goody acknowledged being one of the gang but the evidence that convicted him – some yellow paint that had been found at the farm – was as flimsy as the pair of his shoes upon which the paint was also found. He had been 'fitted up.'

But where does fact meet fiction? Well, of course, there was never any legacy, nor was any 'Matt Deadman' ever employed to find the three who got away, although bounty hunters and *The Sun* newspaper were indeed instrumental in capturing Ronnie Biggs when he was living in Brazil. But it is said that Chief Inspector Tommy Butler of Scotland Yard, was so obsessed with catching the criminals that he did in fact take binoculars with him on holiday and would scan the beaches in the hope of catching one of the gang. Then there was the strange acquittal of John Daly, Reynolds' brother-in-law. There was no doubt he was one of the gang that attacked the train. His fingerprints were found on the famous Monopoly board that the gang had used during their stay at Leatherslade Farm. And yet the judge decided the prints could have been put there some time before. They were not evidence that Daly had been at the farm itself. He walked away, scot free, despite being one of the gang. When he died in April 2013 he did so never having enjoyed his share of the loot as it had been stolen by other criminals to whom he had entrusted it whilst he was under arrest.

And then there was the strange business of the two sacks of cash amounting to £50,000 that were found in a telephone box in Great Dover Street in December 1963. It is claimed that one of the robbers who had got away deposited the money there in return for freedom from prosecution. This may well have been the case and although the identity of the robber in question remains unclear it is probable that it was one of those who got away. He was simply taking the heat off himself.

Three of the gang members, Brian Field – the man who offered the plan to Reynolds in the first place – Buster Edwards and Charlie Wilson, all died in unhappy circumstances. Field was killed in a road accident in 1979,

Edwards hanged himself in 1994, whilst Charlie Wilson was shot dead by an unknown assassin at his villa in Spain in 1990. It has never been suggested that anything sinister lay behind these deaths. Otherwise, at the time of writing, only four of the gang members remain alive, Robert Welch, Ronnie Biggs, Tommy Wisbey and Gordon Goody, one of the main players in the act.

All of the locations mentioned in this book are real and are based either on the places connected with the Great Train Robbery or on my own experiences as a youngster, growing up in South London in the late 1950s and early 1960s. Sadly, some of them, such as my old home in Silcote Road, have disappeared, our entire street being pulled down in the 1980s to make way for the lake that now sits in Burgess Park. The houses in Kalmington Road shared the same fate. Cobourg Road School still stands, however, as does the house in Kelvington Road (my old gran's house!) where Jimmy Damon buried the loot. The Thomas A Beckett pub is still there at the corner of the Old Kent Road and Albany Road. The boxers have long since gone but the ghosts of famous boxers like Henry Cooper and even Joe Frazier, who trained there on one occasion, still haunt the place. Otherwise, the locations featured in this book are real.

The controversy surrounding the so-called 'Iraq Dossier' will probably continue on and off for years. It is generally accepted now that the dossier – the contents of which took Britain into war against Iraq in 2003 – was 'sexed up' and was a work largely of fiction. A subsequent 'off-the-record' conversation between weapons expert David Kelly, who apparently knew the dossier was wildly inaccurate, and a BBC journalist, Andrew Gilligan, led to the former being called to give evidence before a parliamentary Select Committee. Two days later Kelly was tragically found dead in a field, with a verdict of suicide given at the inquest held afterwards, a verdict which continues to be the subject of various conspiracy theories. The controversy surrounding the 'dodgy dossier' at least enabled me to introduce Lord John Dugdale as a media tycoon with a prized 'get out of jail' card, that card being the truth about the Iraq Dossier.

Printed in Great Britain
by Amazon

36704262R00156